BLUEGRASS STATE OF MIND

BLUEGRASS SERIES #1

KATHLEEN BROOKS

LAURENS PUBLISHING

Forever Devoted - coming January 2018

To the memory of my Grandmother and Aunt,
who taught me so much,
including how to shop for great shoes.

For my husband, daughter, parents,
family, and friends who have shown me
love and support every day.

PROLOGUE

HER BARE FEET pounded down the concrete stairs. Her panty hose were ripped from snagging the cold metal strips on the edge of each stair. Her feet stung with every step she took. She heard the door above her open. She pushed herself faster. She couldn't let him catch her.

She jumped the last stair on the sixth floor, the impact of the jump reverberating up her body. She felt as though she had stopped breathing two floors ago. Her lungs burned as she forced her legs to move faster. Her hand was sliding along the railing to brace herself as she raced down the stairs at breakneck speed.

She heard him yell her name. She turned around to see he was now just one floor away. The look cost her dearly as she missed a step and had to slow down to steady herself.

Her heart beat in turn with each slap of her foot. Faster. Louder. She just had to make it to the garage. He would kill her if she didn't. He called her name again as if she were a disobedient child. He was taunting her, triggering her fear. Her heart felt as if it would explode as she ran faster and faster down the stairs.

She didn't feel the cuts causing her feet to bleed. She didn't feel the pain running up her legs. All she knew was she had a couple more flights to go. She tried to suck in a breath of air but could only manage a small gasp. He was closer now. She could feel him right behind her.

The door to the garage was so close. She could see it now. She had to reach it. He closed in on her. She could hear him breathing. She willed her legs to move faster. He reached out his arm to grab her....

CHAPTER 1

MCKENNA LOOKED AROUND and saw nothing but black, four-plank fences and green grass for as far as she could see. Daffodils were playing peek-a-boo with the bright morning sun. She looked down at the GPS in her cherry red BMW M6. Only five more miles until her destination. Bringing her eyes back up to the narrow country road, Kenna gasped and hit her brakes as hard as she could.

The stabilization in her car kicked in and kept it from fishtailing off the road. She fought for control of the car as her brakes locked. A massive horse was standing in the middle of the road, calmly watching her scrambling for control over her car. She rested her head against the steering wheel and let out a shaky breath when she stopped the car in the opposite lane. Hearing tires squealing, she lifted her head and saw an old pick-up truck heading straight for her, fishtailing out of control. Kenna shifted into reverse and floored it. The truck skidded by her, narrowly missing her car. The truck came to a sudden stop in the grass ditch off the side of the road.

Kenna watched a jeans-clad woman wearing a black, long-sleeve shirt and bright pink scarf belt jumped out of the truck. The woman with beautiful, shiny, shoulder-length brown hair was the polar opposite of what McKenna expected to see. Instead of being concerned about her truck, the woman slowly approached the horse with her hand out. Kenna saw her mouth moving as she talked to him. Ever so slowly, she placed her hand on his head and gave him a smile. Sliding her hand down, she grasped the halter and scratched his nose.

Kenna opened her door and got out on shaky legs. She could hear the woman talking on the cell phone as she walked toward the scene. "Yeah, Bets, I'm out here on Route 178, and it looks like one of your stallions is loose. Another woman and I almost hit him. Yes, we're okay. No, I have him now. You better have one of the boys bring a trailer. Okay. Bye."

"Hi. Are you okay?" Kenna asked after the woman put away the cell phone.

"Yes. Thanks. Looks like you made it out okay. I'm Paige Davies. Do you mind helping me for a sec?"

"McKenna Mason. What do you need?"

"Here, hold this." Paige walked the massive stallion over to her and indicated where she was to hold him. "I need to see if my truck is able to run or if I need to call a tow. Thanks!"

Kenna took a hold of the halter and stared at the horse. She hadn't been around a horse in decades. She held on for dear life, even though the horse seemed content to just stand off to the side of the road and watch the world go by.

Paige's truck roared to life. She drove it out of the ditch and parked next to Kenna's sports car. What a sight: a brand new sports car next to a rusted, blue, pickup that had to be fifteen years old. Paige gracefully jumped down from the cab and walked over to her.

"Thanks. Now we have room for the little guy to be picked up. I wonder how he got out?"

"I'm just glad we didn't hit him."

"This is part of Ashton Farm, and unfortunately they've been having a lot of problems recently."

"Ashton, as in Will Ashton?" Kenna couldn't believe it. She hadn't even pulled into town and she had just found the person she was looking for.

"Yes. The family owns and runs it. You know Will?"

"I used to. I haven't seen him in seventeen years."

"Are you here to visit them?"

"Yes and no. I'm here to interview with Tom Burns for the assistant district attorney job, but hoped to run into Will."

"That's great." Paige was so excited for her that Kenna couldn't help but smile as Paige stepped forward and scratched the forehead of the large horse.

"Actually, I'm glad I ran into someone from the town. Can you tell me a good place to stay? I couldn't find any hotels online."

"That's because there aren't any. You'll want to go see Miss Lily Rae Rose. She has a bed and breakfast. Just continue straight and make a left at the first and only stop light you come to. She's in the big white Victorian. And, if you're looking for a good place to eat, Miss Lily has two sisters, Miss Daisy Mae Rose and Miss Violet Fae Rose, who run the Blossom Cafe. Great place to eat some chocolate after a close call like this!" Paige laughed and Kenna couldn't help but like her. This was a woman after her own heart!

"Thanks a lot. I'm guessing you're from Keeneston. What do you do there?"

"I have a store on Main Street named Southern Charms. I have all local made products. Everything from statues, paintings, jewelry, clothes, painted wine glasses, to cookbooks."

"Sounds amazing. I'll have to stop by."

"We should have lunch together. I can be the official welcoming party!" They both turned to the sounds of a diesel engine and saw a massive truck with a horse trailer come around the corner from the direction Paige had come. "Ah, good. Now we can get this boy home."

Kenna stood back as three men jumped down from the truck and with an apple helped convince the horse to get in the trailer.

"Thanks for the help with him. I look forward to our lunch. It was great meeting you and welcome to Keeneston," Paige said as she and Kenna walked to their cars.

Kenna's legs had finally stopped shaking when she slid into her car. Pulling out after Paige, she headed into town, wondering what her new home would be like.

"JUST SHOOT ME NOW," Kenna thought as she squeezed her eyes closed. She slowly opened them, hoping against all odds the scene before her had changed, but to her utter despair, it was the same scene she had just driven upon. Kenna had pulled her sports car to the side of the road and stared at the town before her with a critical eye. She was sitting on the edge of Main Street and could see the other end of what she guessed to be downtown just two three blocks away. The town was straight out of Mayberry, she thought. She couldn't help but start whistling the theme song to the Andy Griffith Show as she looked around her new hometown: perfect trees lining both sides of Main Street, American flags waving from every light post, and the people wandering down the sidewalk seemed to know each other since they were tipping their hats and smiling to each person they passed by.

Kenna had spent the last eleven years in the Big City. So when she took a deep breath that lacked pollution and listened to the honking of cars that were strangely not honks of anger, but honks of greeting as they passed someone they knew, she felt out of her element. Not for the first time, Kenna wondered how she ended up here. Just a month ago, she was at the hottest nightclub in New York City with her best friend Danielle, celebrating her twenty-ninth birthday with all her friends from Greendale, Thompson and Hitchem, the largest law firm in New York City. Kenna sighed wistfully as she thought about the six figure salary, the hot clubs and a condo in the Upper East Side of Manhattan that she had left behind in a hurry.

With her eyes closed and her mind firmly set in what might have been, Kenna thought about how she had dined with professional athletes and actors at the best restaurants on the company dime since they were clients. Standing only five foot four, but blessed with what she called womanly curves, Kenna had not only wined and dined famous people, but had dated and been pursued by some as well. Kenna's auburn hair, milky skin and dark green eyes that hid an intelligence and sharp wit had made her sought after inside and outside of the courtroom.

Kenna continued her trip down memory lane by giving herself a moment to gloat. She had just made junior partner, one of the youngest associates to have ever done so and the only woman to ever do so.

She cringed as she remembered the night it all changed. The night she fled from her six figure salary and left her amazing condo. She had fled from New York City with her ex-boyfriend hot in pursuit of her. Kenna fought a shiver as she remembered Chad trying to find her to prevent her from leaving not only the city but most likely her beautiful condo ever again. It was in the early morning hours of the city that never sleeps that Kenna found herself running for her life and looking for a place to hide. She had sat in her car and thought about what always made her feel better - chocolate. She had suffered a chocolate craving to end all other chocolate cravings that night after the panicked run for her life.

Now sitting in her car in Keeneston, she remembered the shivers of fear that had wracked her body and the feel of the cold bite of the February wind. And all she wanted was chocolate. That's when the idea hit her, the perfect place to hide and the perfect place to indulge in the mother of all stress induced chocolate cravings. She had turned her car towards the interstate and headed to Hershey, Pennsylvania.

Kenna's lips twitched with amusement at outsmarting her ex. She had been right. Since he had no idea where she was, she was left alone. And in turn, Kenna was surrounded by chocolate for a month. The second night she spent in Hershey, Kenna knew it was time to develop a plan for the rest of her life, or at least for the next phase of her life. Even though she was tempted to apply for the taster's job opening at the Hershey plant, she decided she couldn't waste the law degree her parents' death had paid for. They died when a drunken truck driver jackknifed his semi-truck on a patch of ice, leaving no place for her parents' car to go. The trust they established for Kenna was more than enough to pay for her attendance at law school, and she even had a good part of it left to be able to live off of if she wanted. However, after her parents' death, Kenna had lost the carefree ways that the life of privilege provided and had gone to law school to learn how to put away drunk drivers for the pain they caused innocent families.

Kenna sat on her bed in the extend-a-stay hotel with the smell of chocolate in the air and started looking for a job. She started with Alabama and worked her way through the states alphabetically, looking for places that were hiring. She kept an eye out for cities that were small but not isolated, cities that Chad the Bastard wouldn't think of looking for her. But most importantly, cities that were looking for prosecutors. One week later Kenna pumped her fists in the air and jumped up and down on the bed when she saw the opening for a prosecutor seventeen states later. Not too big, not too small... just right.

It was a good thing she had found the opening when she did, Kenna thought to herself. She couldn't put on any more weight after spending a month in Chocolate Heaven. She pushed the thoughts of the past back in her mind and opened her eyes again. Mayberry was still there. When she was in Hershey the week before, waiting to hear back about an interview, a memory floated up to the surface from some hidden depth of her mind. That memory was Will Ashton. "What the hell," Kenna thought. It's not like she had any place else to go and no idea what the future held besides a job application for an assistant district attorney position. Kenna knew her subconscious had led her here to Will Ashton and to Keeneston, Kentucky.

Kenna pulled herself out of her thoughts as she drove up the road, surrounded by Bradford pear trees, and made her way towards the bed and breakfast Paige had recommended. "It's picture perfect," Kenna said to herself as she got out of the car and looked up at the three- story, white brick Victorian.

The green front door opened and a little woman with a helmet of white hair stepped out. "Can I help you, dearie?" she asked Kenna with a soft, Southern tilt to her voice.

"Are you Miss Lily?" Kenna asked as she started up the steps to the wraparound porch.

"Yes, surely I am," Miss Lily answered, her hands clasped in front of her and with a dishtowel casually draped over her shoulder.

"Paige Davies said you had a room to rent for a couple of nights?"

"Yes, I do have a room for you, dearie. Come on in." Miss Lily turned and walked into the house, presuming Kenna would follow right behind.

Kenna turned back to her car, grabbed some of her bags out of the trunk, and hurried into the bed and breakfast just behind Miss Lily. The house was huge with a grand entranceway whose focal point was a wide sweeping staircase. There were large, square shaped rooms off to her right and left.

"Over here are the private quarters," Miss Lily said, pointing to the right. "This first room here on the left is the sitting room for our guests. There are books and such in there, and we have a fire at night in the old fireplace. The room behind the staircase is the dining room."

"I love it."

"Well then, I'll put you on the second floor. If you go up these stairs here, there will be another sitting room. Your room is off to the left," Miss Lily said, handing her a key.

"Thank you, Miss Lily. I'm McKenna Mason. It's nice to meet you, and thank you for making me feel so welcome in your lovely house."

"Not a problem, dearie. I'll give you a moment to settle in and lunch will be served in an hour," Miss Lily said as she turned to head into what Kenna guessed to be the kitchen.

Kenna grabbed her bags and headed up a staircase obviously made for a different time, a time when ladies wore ball gowns so large they needed the six-foot wide stairs to sweep down while making a grand entrance for a ball.

The sitting room on the second floor was as large as the entrance way and full of overstuffed furniture and a braided rug on the floor. It was the perfect place to curl up and read a book. Two large windows overlooked the front yard and the street. Kenna turned to her left and opened the door to the Man O' War room. She had seen a lot of Man O' War names and couldn't figure why a large and deadly jelly fish was so prominent in Kentucky. Oh well, another Southern mystery she thought as she tugged her bags into the room.

In the center of the room stood a huge, king- sized, four- poster bed so high up, it had little steps to climb up to get into bed. A TV was on top of an old oak dresser that ran the length of the opposite wall. A window seat looked out to the side yard and down towards Main Street. A private bathroom with an iron claw tub finished off the room. It was amazing. Just sitting in the room with the white lace curtains billowing softly with a spring breeze coming in the open window was enough to make her feel safe for the first time since she had left New York City.

Kenna unpacked some of her clothes, put them into the drawers, and went to wash up. It was almost time for lunch and amazing smells were coming up from the kitchen. Her mouth started to water as she thought back to the last meal she had at McDonald's the night before in West Virginia. She finished putting the clothes away and opened the door to head downstairs. The door across the hall from her opened and two impeccably dressed people stepped out. They were dressed casually, well, as casually as you can be dressed in designer clothes, Kenna noted.

"Oh, we have another guest!" sang the woman. She was a couple inches taller than Kenna and in her early forties. Her makeup was perfect in that understated way only movie stars could manage. Her blond hair was pulled into a perfect pony tail tied off with a white ribbon. Kenna realized that if one wasn't used to shopping the expensive department stores like she was, one would never know the woman was wealthy, well, except for the eight carat diamond weighing down her ring finger. Compared to this bubbly woman, Kenna felt much older than her twenty-nine years after the pressure and stress of the last month. Kenna pasted on a smile and turned to face the perky couple.

"So we do, honey," her husband said to her. He matched her perfectly. Kenna placed him at fifty years old and dressed in designer jeans and a white button up shirt. His salt and pepper hair was perfectly trimmed. He let his right hand rest lightly at the small of his wife's back.

"Are you here for the sales as well?" Mrs. Perky asked Kenna.

"Sales? I didn't see any department stores in Keeneston. I could do a little shopping." A happy feeling washed over her and Kenna's smile turned into a real one. The kind of feeling that only spending money on the perfect pair of sexy shoes or finding that little black dress that hid ten pounds and increased your bust at least one cup size could do for you.

"Oh! Oh, ha, a joke. Good one, little lady." Mr. Perky laughed. Kenna darted a glance back and forth between the couple, and apparently Mrs. Perky picked up on her creased brow and look of utter confusion at the apparent joke she had made.

"Julius, she's not joking. Dear, I'm so sorry. We thought any visitors would be here for the Keeneland horse sales."

So, Mr. Perky was Julius. Apparently they had come from out of town, out of state by Kenna's guess, for horse sales. That was good news for her since she had found out Will still has a horse farm.

"I am so sorry. Since June and I are so horse crazy, I just assumed you were too. I'm Julius Kranski and this is my wife, June." Julius turned and took his hand off his wife's back to shake Kenna's.

June clasped Kenna's hand and lightly held onto it when she introduced herself to Kenna. "So nice to meet you!"

"Nice to meet you both. I'm McKenna Mason, but you can just call me Kenna. It's nice to meet some other people from out of town. Where are you from?" she asked as she looked back at June.

"We have a horse farm in Ocala, Florida," June said as she smiled and gently squeezed Kenna's hand again.

She's a toucher, Kenna thought as June continued, "I hope we can be friends. I always love coming to Miss Lily's for the sales. We always meet the most wonderful people." June continued to talk as they made their way to the dining room for lunch, explaining all about the sales and about the horses they were hoping to buy. Kenna looked around the dining room and noted that it was casually set with a buffet of olive nut and pimento cheese sandwiches. Fresh fruit was in a bowl and a large salad was set in the middle of the round.

"Come in, come in. Have a seat just anywhere at the table y'all. I'll be out in a jiffy with the sweet tea," Miss Lily said as she quickly zipped into the kitchen. Kenna's eyes widened slightly. Miss Lily was remarkably fast for someone in her early seventies. She reappeared with a pitcher of sweet tea, and her white apron was blown back from her flowered dress as her orthopedic shoes sailed across the polished hardwood floors. The room was bright with sun streaming in through the open windows.

Kenna picked up her sweet tea, tentatively gave it a sip, and found that she was pleasantly surprised by the taste. Julius and June began to talk about one of the horses they were hoping to sell and which barns they should go to first when they went to the Keeneland sales after lunch as Kenna listened with half an ear and nibbled at the pimento cheese sandwich. Not bad, she thought and then took a bigger bite.

"So, are these horse sales a big deal? I mean, do lots of people go to them?" Kenna asked while she tried the olive nut sandwich. She was definitely going to have to learn how to make these sandwiches and had a feeling Miss Lily would teach her in a heartbeat if she asked.

"They sure are, hon," Julius told her. "The Keeneland sales bring in tens of millions of dollars every year. There are smaller sales in Florida and some good sized sales in Saratoga, New York. But if you want the next big thing or the best selection, you go to Keeneland."

"It's also the best place to see the who's who of racing," June chimed in. "For example, some Middle Eastern royalty own racing stables. There's a Sheik from some small oil country who's trying to build the next big stable right here in Keeneston. He's not the only royalty. Queen Elizabeth has been known to have a horse or two stabled in the area."

Kenna thought that this was as good a time as any to ask about one of the reasons she had come to Keeneston , "When I was a kid, one of my Nana's friend's family had a horse farm here. This morning I found out the Ashtons are still here. Do you know them?"

"The Ashtons!" June practically squealed. She clapped her hands lightly together and beamed at Kenna, "Of course we know them. Everyone knows them. After all, they have Spires Landing at stud on their farm here in Keeneston."

Kenna breathed a sigh of relief and felt a little of the weight lift off her shoulders. Maybe June would know how to get in touch with Will. That would be easier than trying to find the entrance to the farm. She would feel strange just knocking on the door. "So, you think they'll be at the sales?"

"Of course, although I don't know if Betsy and William will be there. But I'm sure someone from the family will be," June said.

Will had gotten married. Kenna knew it was wishful thinking or stupidity on her part to think that after all these years he wouldn't be married. After all, he was a couple years older than she, probably around thirty-two by now. She had heard that he had graduated from the University of Kentucky and played in the NFL for a couple of years, so it was definitely stupid to think him still unmarried. Childhood crush aside, she needed help and he was the one she was depending on to give it to her.

"If you want to go to the sales this afternoon, we'd be happy to take you. Wouldn't we, sugar?" June said, interrupting Kenna's thoughts.

"Of course we would. You just come along with us if you'd like," Julius responded.

Kenna looked at her phone calendar and saw that her appointment with the Keeneston District Attorney's office was scheduled for two days from now, so time was not a concern. It was best to go track down Will now and beg him to put in a good word with her potential boss. Or see if he knew of any other jobs in town if she didn't get the D.A. job. "That would be great. Thanks, June, Julius."

After finishing lunch, Kenna went to freshen up before heading out to the sales. She stared at her hair in the mirror and attempted to fluff it, but then it just ended up looking tangled as opposed to that Hollywood, windswept 'just had great sex' look. She looked at her clothes hanging in the closet and decided to compensate for not having the 'just had great sex' hair with a skin- tight, green cable sweater. She slipped her small feet into her black two- inch heel boots to boost her shortened height up to what she thought of as a normal height. With that, she was ready to go. Wiping sweaty hands on her jeans, she headed downstairs, trying to prepare herself for what would equate to begging and pleading for help finding a job, something she never, never, never did, especially from an old crush she thought as she rolled her eyes, who would probably not even remember her name.

Kenna found the Kranskis on the wraparound porch and walked with them down the stone path lined with daffodils. She slid into the back seat of their white Mercedes sedan.

She looked out the window as they headed toward the "big city" of Lexington. She guessed being from New York City, anything under a couple million people seemed small, but she could understand if you're from the surrounding towns of fewer than twenty-five thousand people, that Lexington with its population of three hundred thousand would be a "big city". As she stared out the window, she felt some comfort come over her as she watched the rolling hills of the farmland dotted with corn, tobacco, soy bean, cows, horses and beautiful manor houses pass by. So open and so green... she had never seen so much green.

Fifteen minutes later they approached Keeneland and turned with a steady stream of traffic into the race track. Kenna observed the beautiful landscaping and how open it seemed. They drove through fields of green grass, all trimmed and lined with huge old trees, up to a clubhouse. A valet came out and took the keys from Julius and went to park the car. Julius and June started a constant stream of chatter between themselves and then deftly went through the clubhouse to the paddock area. Pictures of past Derby winners and stakes winners lined the stone walls from the times they had raced at Keeneland.

The majesty of the pictures, the feel of the stone building, the sounds of the horses' hooves, and smelling the scents of cut grass, hay, oats and leather, she could just feel the history of the place and start to understand why horse racing has been such a popular sport for hundreds of years.

They stepped out of a stone walkway and into the paddock where horses were being led around with a number stuck to their hips. Hundreds of people were milling about, looking at each horse or just talking to one another. Some people were wearing Armani suits while some were in worn cowboy boots and faded jeans. She caught the sight of one man in a simple button- up shirt, faded jeans with some tears in it, and boots that looked like they had stepped in nothing but horse crap. Yet he pulled out a state of the art Smartphone and had the keys for an luxury car carelessly dangling out of his pocket. She smiled at the strange scene. Who these people were, what they wore, and the type of car they drove was of no importance. Luxury car driving cowboys chatted with beat- up truck owners over which horse to bid on.

Taking in another deep breath, Kenna closed her eyes and let the sounds and scents flow over her. Having always been a history buff, she could just see the men and women walking around in 1936 when Keeneland first opened. While she had been daydreaming, the Kranskis had made their way across the paddock and were heading for a string of barns.

"We're heading over to the Spring Creek Barn to check out a yearling. You see that blue and white flag over the third barn down? That's the Ashton Barn. Just make your way down there and ask for your friend. Whenever you're done, just come find us." And with that, June gave Kenna a finger wave and started to walk toward another barn. Find them? How, could she find them in this massive place?

She took a deep breath and turned toward the blue and white flag. As she walked towards it, she passed by a couple of barns proudly displaying certain colors she took to be the farm colors, much like a family crest. She slowed as she approached the Ashton Barn and saw that many people walking horses around were all wearing blue and white polo shirts. It must be a way to identify farm personnel. Some were taking horses up to the paddock while others were putting them in stalls. Still others took them out of stalls and walked them to groups of people who seemed to be examining them. Kenna assumed that they were potential buyers. She looked around and didn't see anyone she guessed to be Will. Of course, the last time she had seen him she was twelve and he wasn't quite sixteen. However, she didn't think she would ever forget those dark, chocolate brown eyes. She looked around, scanning the faces around the barn.

She sighed as she realized she needed help finding him and turned to the closest man in the blue and white uniform, "Excuse me, I'm looking for Mr. Ashton. Is he here today?" she asked the short young man leading a horse from the barn.

"Si. He over there," the blue and white clad man said in broken but understandable English. He pointed to a little hallway in the middle of the barn. It was lined with more horse stalls, and as she approached, she saw a man rubbing the nose of one of the horses. He was tall, at least six feet one inch, and his brown hair had a slight amount of gray in it near his temple. He still looked good though, even if he was a little prematurely gray.

She walked up behind him and stood for a moment staring at his back, trying to figure out how to say, "Hi, I know you haven't seen me in seventeen years, but I was hoping you could help me start a new life here in Kentucky by helping me get a job and maybe find a place to live."

Before she could make her presence known, Will turned to her and asked, "You here to look at Miss Thing, hon?"

Kenna's mouth opened, but nothing came out. She stood momentarily locked in place taking him in. The graying hair, the brown twinkling eyes, the huge smile that showed one dimple on his left cheek, the wrinkles around his eyes, and the hands gave away his age. It wasn't Will. She let out the breath she hadn't realized she was holding, "I'm sorry. I was told Mr. Ashton was in here," Kenna said with a distracted smile on her face. She was fighting off the strange feeling that she knew this man, but couldn't place him.

"Well, then you found him. William Ashton. Nice to meet you, ma'am." Mr. Ashton stepped forward with his hand outstretched. Kenna stared for a second and then reached her hand out to grasp his. He gently, yet firmly shook her hand and gave her an approving nod when she returned the firm handshake.

CHAPTER 2

"I'm sorry for the confusion, but the William Ashton I need is a little younger. It was a gamble he'd be here anyway. I hadn't talked to him since we were kids and I probably got some information mixed up. I'm sorry to have bothered you." Kenna started to turn away and scan the crowd once again when she heard Mr. Ashton chuckling.

"Don't go telling my wife about me being too old for you now. I love her, but bless her heart, once she gets hold of something she never lets it go. Besides, you don't have the wrong place. I'm guessing you're about my son's age. Will is running around here someplace. Is that who you're looking for? Will Ashton?"

At the mention of his son, Kenna took in a deep breath of air. She then slowly let it out and fell back onto her courtroom demeanor as to not show her nerves. "Yes, sir. I'm looking for Will Ashton, more particularly, the Will Ashton whose grandmother Alda used to live in Upstate New York," Kenna stated clearly, as if making point of clarification to a judge. She was so close to finding who she was looking for, she couldn't take another failure in the search for Will. Her nerves were becoming frayed, but she was determined to come across as the confident lawyer she was in court. People took her more seriously that way and tended to tell her what she wanted to know if she was businesslike.

"Then you found the right one. That would've been my mama. You knew her?" Mr. Ashton's face lit up as he asked about his mother.

"She was roommates with my grandmother Victoria Mason at the Liverpool Retirement Community."

"Ah, you're Vicki's granddaughter. McKenna, isn't it?

"That's right. It seems Alda told you as much about me as my nana told me about Will." Kenna smiled, remembering her nana and her antics with her roommate.

"That's right. We heard all about you until your nana passed away when you were, what, thirteen, fourteen?"

"Fourteen," she answered. Mr. Ashton saw her eyes misting over and before Kenna knew it, he enveloped her in a fatherly bear hug. Surprised, she stiffened, but then melted into him as he started to pat her back. She suddenly felt as though she were fourteen years old again. Since her parents had died, no one had hugged her like this and she missed it greatly.

"Before she passed away, Alda told us that your parents were killed in an accident. Bless your heart. You've had it rough, haven't you?"

His question was more rhetorical so she just nodded and buried her head deeper into his shirt. He smelled like horses and hay with a slight whiff of cologne - he smelled fatherly. She took a deep breath and reluctantly pulled away once she had collected herself. Kenna looked up and found Mr. Ashton's kind eyes looking down at her as he patted her head like she was a good little girl.

"I'm pretty sure Will is in the barn. He'll be back in just a second." He stopped scanning the barn area and turned to Kenna. "What brings you to our neck of the woods?" he asked with a great amount of interest.

She wanted to answer that fear and running for her life brought her here. Instead she worked up a fake smile and answered, "Actually, I'm interviewing for the assistant D.A. job with Thomas Burns. I might become a Southerner after all these years of cold winters in the North."

"That would be great. I'll tell Tom he should hire you when I see him for our weekly golf game tomorrow morning," William said. "After all, you're practically family."

Kenna's smile widened into one of genuine warmth as she looked at Mr. Ashton. Well, that was fortunate. Guess some old boys' clubs could work for her instead of against her, she thought.

Mr. Ashton's eyes lit as he focused on something over her shoulder. "Will! Over here! I got a surprise for you. You'll never guess who's here," Mr. Ashton yelled while waving his arm in the air.

Kenna took a deep breath as she heard strong, booted footfalls coming nearer. She turned around slowly with a wobbly smile on her lips, prepared for the embarrassment of not being remembered. Suddenly the deep breath she was taking got stuck, and her green eyes widened at the sight of the grown up version of Will Ashton. He was gorgeous: strong, masculine, and with an air of good humor about him. He had a boyish smile on his face, showing off one dimpled cheek. His dark brown hair matched his eyes that vibrated with energy. Gone was the scarecrow of a boy she knew as a fifteen-year-old teenager, replaced with a thirty-two year old man's body. He was easily six feet two inches and muscled, very muscled from the way his thighs looked as they filled out a pair of worn jeans. His wide shoulders looked squeezed into his white, button-up shirt. His square jaw was starting to show a slight amount of stubble from a long day. But he still looked like he had enough energy to play a football game.

Will strode up to Kenna, stopped right in front of her, and smiled with genuine happiness. "Hi."

"Hello, Will." She lifted her head to look him in the eyes. When she did, their eyes met and she felt her smile falter. She just knew he had no idea who she was. Why would he? She had just turned twelve the last time he had seen her. She was shaped like a boy and had a mass of untamed red hair. Over the past seventeen years, her hair had turned more auburn with strong red highlights. And she was definitely not shaped like a boy. She was both top and bottom heavy, with a well-defined waist she had obtained through running multiple hours a week. She wasn't a stick thin model, but she always felt that her size ten jeans fit perfectly and showed off those curves rather well.

Just when she was gathering the courage to embarrassingly introduce herself, his father cut in. "Will, I need to steal you for just a moment before you get caught up with your old friend here if you don't mind. Nice to see you again, dear. Remember, you're family. Stop on by anytime," Mr. Ashton said with a slight smirk. She thought she caught sight of a quick flash of mischief across his face. But when she looked again it was gone.

"Sure, Dad. Excuse me for just a moment," Will said before turning and walking off a few feet with his dad.

Kenna took the time to collect herself. Little Will had turned into a gorgeous man. He probably had so many women in his life that there would be no way he remembered her.

Will finished the conversation with his dad and walked back to Kenna. "Sorry about that. I guess I also better apologize that I don't seem to know you as well as you seem to know me, although you do remind me of someone I knew when I was just a teenager," he said with a cocky smile that showed he wasn't embarrassed in the least about not being sure if he knew who she was.

"Well, I guess you're close to knowing who I am. We haven't seen each other in seventeen years. And we only saw each other for one week up in New York."

"McKenna Mason," his smile grew to a full grin. "My, my you have grown up well." His smile faded and he turned serious, "I sure am sorry about your grandmother and your parents."

"Thank you," she said with a slight bob of her head in acknowledgement of the sympathies.

His grin came back and his eyes went straight to hers, "That sure was one fun week though. I remember your grandmother catching me kissing you in the garden." Seventeen years later and the thought still brought a blush to Will's face. "I thought it was bad enough she interrupted my first kiss, but then she went and told my granny. And before you knew, I was being dragged into her apartment with one grandma on each ear giving me a lecture on the birds and the bees." Will faked a shudder, "A sex lecture from two senior citizens... It was worth it to get that kiss from you."

Remembering the incident made Kenna laugh hard. It was the first real laugh in a month and she found it hard to stop. After all these years, she still remembered the look on Will's face when he had left his granny's kitchen. His head hung low and his feet shuffled as both his granny and Kenna's nana had followed him out the door still lecturing him. Kenna felt a tear of joy start to roll down her cheek, "You wouldn't be laughing if you had been given that lecture. I didn't have sex for years after that. Every time I tried to get lucky, the picture of our grandmothers popped into my head. It was like they were lecturing me again," Will laughed. It caused Kenna to laugh even harder.

"Sure, sure, laugh it up," Will teased. He didn't give her a break though. "Do you know what they told me? Of course not, because they said it was the man's role to control the situation. You were completely innocent in their eyes. And if I remember correctly, you weren't all that innocent," he said as he winked at her.

Kenna slowed her laughter enough to answer him, "That's right. It wasn't like I dared you to kiss me... Okay, so I did dare you. But you were enough of a gentleman not to tell Nana."

"I remember that week so well. It truly was one of the best of my life."

It was Kenna's turn to blush at the compliment. "It was for me too."

"Our grandmothers were something else. I still can't believe you took down a whole room of seniors in bingo that first night. I thought you were going to be lynched with support hose."

"Yeah, I guess I shouldn't have gotten on the table and told them they got whipped by a kid. Probably not the smartest move on my part," Kenna said, remembering being twelve and thinking she knew everything.

"That was the night I had gotten there. There you were, up on the table yelling bingo and jumping around for winning sixty bucks. I knew right then I wanted to kiss you but was much too shy," Will admitted.

"That, and our grandmothers always got us into trouble. We couldn't have any privacy. You remember how they snuck us into the cafeteria that night for a celebratory ice cream? And we got busted by security since no one was allowed in there after seven?" Kenna asked.

"Then your grandmother said, 'Officer, our dear grandchildren came in here not knowing the rules. We just came to bring them back to bed. All the while, she was hiding a pint of ice cream behind her back." Both Will and Kenna broke out into a new round of laughter. Yup, their grandmothers were hell on wheels, wheels being the rascals they occasionally drove.

Will placed his hand over Kenna's and looked down at her. Kenna's laughter died in her throat as she looked at Will. She saw him looking at her lips and had to admit, all the talk about their first meeting and their first kiss sure got her in the mood to do just that.

Will cleared his throat and shook his head just a bit as if coming out of a trance. "So, what brings you to Keeneston?"

Kenna bit the side of her lower lip before she caught herself. "Well, I'm actually here to apply for a job. I'm applying for the assistant district attorney opening. I know how the legal world can be a men's club, so I was hoping you could help me get my foot in the door. I also needed to find a place to stay, but I think I got that worked out".

"Yes, I know about the old guard's clubs around here. Dad plays golf with the D.A. and I'm sure he'll put in a good word. It's hard for outsiders to work their way into a job like that. But I know Mr. Burns pretty well. I'll tell him my granny approved of you, and that should make you a shoo-in."

"Thanks."

"I know you said you worked something out, but I can help you find a place to stay if you want. There's plenty of room out at the farm."

Her eyes widened slightly in surprise. "I'm staying with Miss Lily, and my room is perfect. Thank you for the generous offer though."

"Miss Lily will look out for you real well. I'm glad you're there. I was worried you were staying by yourself at some hotel." His kindness made her heart melt a little. It was possible to find those kinds of manners in New York, but she was beginning to notice that it was bred into men down here.

"Actually, the other guests staying there gave me a ride today, Julius and June Kranski. Do you know them?" she asked.

"Of course. Nice people. They come up every year for the sales and then back for Derby every now and then."

"I was supposed to meet up with them again, but I have no idea how to even find them. This place is so crowded," she said as she started to scan the people walking around the various barn areas.

"Come on, I'll help you find them. It's actually pretty easy to find people, you just start asking," he said with a grin. He reached down and took her hand and walked her out of the barn toward the paddock area where the horses were parading around. Every couple of yards Will would stop and ask someone if they knew where Julius was. It seemed Will knew everyone there. It also seemed Julius and June knew everyone there since all the people asked pointed in the same direction. In no time at all, they found Julius and June looking at a horse about to go into the sales arena.

"Will, darling, how are you doing?" June asked as she gave him a peck on the cheek.

"June, Julius. It's good to see you again," Will said as he shook Julius' hand.

"I see McKenna found you. Are you ready to go back to Miss Lily's, dear?" June asked as she turned to Kenna.

"Anytime you are, June. If there's something else you need to do, like buy a horse, I can wait," Kenna said with a smile. They had been so kind to her and she didn't want to hurry them. She had a meeting with the Green Book, a four-inch thick book that held Kentucky's criminal law and procedures. She needed to read it before her meeting with Mr. Burns. She needed to prove to Mr. Burns that she was very capable of picking up Kentucky law.

"Well, we were hoping to buy one more, and he isn't up for probably another hour," Julius told her.

"I can take her home. I'm done for the day," Will said, his hand moving to gently cup her elbow in a subtle show of possessiveness.

"That would be great. Is that okay with you, Kenna?" June asked her.

"Sure, as long as it isn't out of your way," Kenna said.

Will's grip on her elbow tightened as they said their good-bye's and walked back to his barn. "If you don't mind, let me just check on things one last time to make sure everything is in order," he said, heading into the barn.

CHAPTER 3

As WILL WENT to check on things at the barn, Kenna took a breath and felt more of the rock lifting from her shoulders. She was pretty lucky that both Will and his father would put in a good word for her with the job. She knew her previous experience and grades spoke for themselves, but that didn't mean much if the D.A.'s best friend's cousin wanted the job. Sometimes you had to get dirty, just enough to get your foot in the door.

Kenna looked at the bustle of people moving around at the sales. She was over seven hundred miles from New York, but she still felt so nervous that they'd find her. And then what? She had no idea, and that was part of the problem. Taking on a case at trial was one thing, but taking on the unknown with your life at stake was another. She just couldn't quite get rid of the feeling that things weren't as safe as they appeared.

She heard Will approaching and turned around to see that he had a set of car keys in one hand and briefcase in the other.

"Everything okay with the horses?"

"Yeah. I just had to get the files on the horses we were interested in and make sure our night manager had enough people to patrol the barn. We like to make sure the horses are not only well looked after in the terms of care, but also in the terms of safety." Will stood beside her and took one last look at his army of blue polo wearing workers. "Are you ready to head back? If you'd like, we could stop and get dinner together. I know a great home cooking type place just a couple of blocks from Miss Lily's."

Will looked so eager that Kenna couldn't refuse. Besides, now that she had worked herself up when she was scanning the crowd, she thought some company for a while longer would be a good distraction. "That would be lovely," Kenna said as she and Will locked eyes. He smiled at her, showing the dimple in this cheek. Then he gently placed his hand at the small of her back and applied slight pressure to move her in the direction of the car.

'Car' wouldn't be the proper term for the vehicle she approached. It was shiny and new with a huge metal grill. As she looked at the Ford F-250 truck, she was very glad she had decided on pants. She wasn't entirely sure how she could gracefully climb into the truck if she had worn a skirt.

Will's hand dropped from the small of her back and reached around her to open the door. He held out his hand and helped her in the cab just as if she were getting into a carriage in Regency England, a smile tugging on her lips at the thought. She took in the clean interior with lots of knobs and the soft leather seats. Everything appeared larger, especially the man who climbed in with the natural grace of getting in and out of a pickup for his whole life. She certainly didn't have anything like him in her small sports car.

Will started the truck, angled out of the barn area and headed toward Keeneston Road. Will turned and asked her, "What is your career plan here? I thought I should warn you that the mayor's nephew, Wayne Givens, is being pushed to take the spot. He's sitting for the bar for the third time next month. Are you signed up to take the bar exam?"

"Yes, I signed up before I came down, with the hopes of getting the job and needing to pass the Kentucky portion. Luckily, I don't have to take both parts again as I already passed the federal section when I took the exam three years ago now. I'll have a lot of studying to do, but first I have to get the job." She turned her head and focused out the window.

"And, if you don't get it?" he asked softly.

"Well, if I don't get it, then I'll start looking at other states. Probably move out West some place." She opened her mouth, wanting to say more, but then closed it. They sat in companionable silence for another couple of minutes until they arrived downtown.

"We're going to the Blossom Cafe," Will said as he pointed to the cafe across the street from the old courthouse. Standing beside the courthouse was an old church, both had historical markers. As Kenna waited for Will to come around to open her door, she saw both were built in the late seventeen hundreds. It looked like the stained glass rose window over the massive wood double doors of the church was original. The four-story courthouse was built with Kentucky limestone and framed by massive white pillars along the street side, main entrance. A single massive chandelier hung directly over the front doors, casting a warm glow over the entrance way. Two statues stood out front, a white marble statue of Lady Justice astride a large horse and a monument to the local heroes listed as POW and MIA from foreign wars. It was entirely different from the imposing Greek Parthenon-like courthouse in New York. The courthouse seemed welcoming instead of intimidating. Flowers and plants surrounded it, compared to the concrete jungle of the big city. She was still staring at the courthouse when Will opened the door and took her hand. His hand was warm and slightly callused from the work on the farm. His grip was gentle, yet full of contained power. Will helped her down from the truck and moved her hand to the crook of his arm as he escorted her across the street to the Blossom Cafe.

Blossom Cafe stood on Main Street in a historical building, three stories high with tall, arching windows painted off white. Beneath each window was a box filled with flowers, potted plants, and small trees with twinkling lights. The whole first floor was open to Main Street by giant plate glass windows. Inside was awash in light. Booths with tablecloths covered in glass and tables with mismatched chairs gave the cafe a clean, down-home feel.

Will opened the front door and ushered Kenna in. An elderly lady looked up from where she was chatting at a table and waved. Will waved back and pointed Kenna to an open booth in the back. As they walked past the packed tables, talk of the patrons quieted and then grew even louder as soon as Kenna and Will sat down. An elderly woman bustled over. Eyes twinkling and note pad at the ready, she stopped in front of the table. Her feet, encased in bright white orthopedic shoes, were practically dancing with excitement. She was small, barely over five feet, but she had the look of strength about her.

"Miss Daisy, you ready to take me up on my offer of a date yet?" Will asked, giving Miss Daisy a wink.

She blushed and smacked his hand with her small note pad. "William Ashton, you devil. If I was only thirty years younger.... But, look at you with your bad manners. Bless your heart. If I didn't know your mama raised you better, I'd think you were a total failure of a gentleman for not introducing me to your lady friend." Miss Daisy looked pointedly at Kenna, and she thought Miss Daisy said the words 'lady friend' a little strangely. Kenna was also pretty sure if Miss Daisy were walking the streets of New York, a mugger would think she was easy pickings only to be thumped by a purse and grabbed by the ear for a lecture.

"McKenna Mason, this young lady is Miss Daisy Mae Rose. One of her sisters is Miss Lily, your landlord," Will smiled at her and then nodded his head toward the back of the cafe, "and her other sister is Miss Violet Fae Rose, but she's usually in the back, riding hard on the cooks."

"That she is. And you dear, you just call me Daisy Mae. So, you're staying with Lily Rae. Well, I'm sure she'll feed you fine, but you just come on down here anytime you want to eat. Most of the time, we supply some of the food to Lily Rae anyway." Miss Daisy turned to Will, "You know Violet Fae will be out to see you as soon as I put in the order. Do you both know what do you want to drink?"

Will looked up at Kenna and signaled her to go ahead with her order, "This raspberry ice tea looks great. I'll have some of that," Kenna said.

"Sweet tea for me. Thanks, Miss Daisy," Will said with a genuine smile for her.

Daisy Mae turned to Kenna, "It was real nice to meet you dear, and I'll be out in just a jiffy with your drinks. Specials are on the board." With a wave, she walked to the back with their drink orders. Kenna noticed her stopping at every table on the way. Some quick glances darted her way while others openly stared.

The bell over the door tinkled, and the gazes of the patrons shifted from her to the person coming into the cafe. Will leaned forward and explained to Kenna that the jolly looking man with the rounded belly was Mr. Wolfe. He was a kind of legend in the town and the main source of the Keeneston grapevine. It amused her to see him greet a majority of the people there. John turned his attention to the table where Will and McKenna sat. He began to wind his way through the tables. He shook hands and nodded his head in greeting all the way to the back.

"Uh-oh, here comes trouble," Will said as he stood up from the table to shake Mr. Wolfe's hand. "John, good to see you again." Will turned to Kenna. "This beautiful lady is McKenna Mason. Kenna, this is John Wolfe."

"I see you wasted no time is welcoming this beautiful young lady to our town. I hope he's treating you well, Miss Mason."

"He sure is, Mr. Wolfe." Kenna said.

"Little lady, you can call me John. I heard a rumor you were in town to interview for the assistant D.A. job. Good luck with that. I saw Tom this afternoon and told him I hoped he'd give you lots of consideration. It wouldn't hurt to have a pretty thing like you to counter his bad looks either!" John guffawed.

Kenna felt her cheeks start to blush but was more amazed he knew why she was there, not to mention his remarks about her being pretty didn't seem to stem from sexism but from gentlemanly manner. "How on earth did you know I was interviewing for the job?

Mr. Burns said the application process was confidential and I haven't told anyone but Will and his father?" Kenna asked.

Will's smile grew and he shook his head in slight bafflement. "We don't know how he does it, but John always finds everything out. He has for as long as I've known him. The prevailing town theory is he bugged the whole city. Either that or he has a magic crystal ball. We can't decide and John has never revealed his sources."

Miss Daisy appeared behind John carrying their drinks, "What's this I hear? John, did you say McKenna is here to apply for the assistant D.A. job?"

Kenna cringed. Miss Daisy had not only asked her question loudly, she did it in such a way that her voice projected through the whole cafe. Kenna saw another white head of hair pop out the back servers' window and figured that was Miss Violet. All conversation had stopped, and the only noise was chair legs scrapping the floor as the patrons angled toward her awaiting an answer.

"You better just come clean with the group," Will said.

His smile was starting to irritate her. He wasn't the least bit surprised or embarrassed that half the town was blatantly staring and patiently waiting for her to answer.

"Um," she cleared her throat and then decided if this was turning into a sudden cross-examination, then she better act like the accomplished attorney she was. She scooted to the end of the booth and stood up. Her hands were sweaty and she felt slightly confused by the attention. She put on her best lawyer face, which consisted of softening her face and attaching a small, polite smile. She clasped her hands in front of her and spoke in her courtroom voice, "Yes, I've come from New York to apply for the assistant D.A. job. Will has been showing me around this lovely town that I hope will soon be home." She gave one more smile and went to sit down.

"Excuse me, Miss, but what does a big shot, city lawyer know about Keeneston? Why did you leave? You weren't busted in one of those sex-for-hire stings that brought down the governor up there were you?" asked a man who looked to be one hundred years old.

Kenna froze. She wasn't completely prepared to tell them why she had left. She couldn't just announce to a group of people that she fled for her life and hoped to hide out here until she could figure out what to do. Stick to the truth, she thought. It makes the lies easier to remember later. She placed her lawyer face back on and even managed a little laugh, "No, no. No sex scandals, I'm sorry. But if you really want, you can walk me home tonight and we can start our own rumors," she joked and then threw in a wink. The place erupted into laughter, but she knew it wouldn't placate them. So she added, "I was just tired of the long hours, the lack of appreciation for my work, and I was firmly stuck in the litigation department. I wanted a change. My nana was great friends with Mrs. Ashton, Will's Grandmother, so I thought this would be a great place to be able to make a home. So far it has exceeded expectations. Are there any more questions?" Kenna looked around, hoping there were no more to come but saw a hand raised toward the front. A group of teenagers wearing letter jackets were all pushing the leader to his feet.

The pimply, but surprisingly tall, muscled young man stood up, "Umm, I was... I mean, we were wondering if you're single or if you're married to some fella'?" His face flushed red and even the tips of his ears appeared to be burning.

Kenna was shocked by the personal question and thought everyone else would be. But as she looked around, clearly everyone was very interested in her answer. "No, I'm not and have never been married," she said in a slightly shell-shocked voice.

She saw another young man stand up, "Are you dating Coach?"

Now she was just confused. Apparently the group was more interested in her personal life than her professional one. She had been expecting questions about her beliefs in capital punishment or stiff jail terms, not if she was romantically involved with someone. "Who is Coach?" she asked the young man.

"He is," the boy pointed to Will.

Will raised his hand, "Guilty. I help coach the Keeneston High School football team when I can."

Kenna's mouth was frozen in an "O" shape and she turned back to the boy, "Well, in that case, no. We're not dating. Actually, today is the first time I've seen him since I was twelve." Some of the younger men in the cafe were smiling and trying to grab her attention. She couldn't believe this. Pretty soon she might be auctioned off for dates.

She almost groaned aloud when she saw yet another hand rise. This one belonged to a middle-aged soccer mom. She was sitting at a table with her husband and two boys dressed in some sort of sports uniform. Kenna gave a slight nod to acknowledge the mother.

The mom put down her hand and stood up, nodding hello's to some people in the crowd, "Where are your people from?" she asked and continued to stand.

Somewhat perplexed at the question, Kenna answered. "Well, I was born in Liverpool, New York. It's just outside Syracuse. My parents met at Syracuse University and we moved to New York City when I was ten." Kenna smiled at the soccer mom to indicate she was done and waiting for Part Two. This was starting to turn into a toughest interview she had ever had. She glanced quickly at Will and smothered her irritation at the fact he was lounging in the booth with a huge Cheshire cat grin on his face. At least one of them found this amusing.

"What do your parents think of you moving so far away? Are they considering moving closer as well?" The soccer mom sat down, indicating the end of her line of questioning.

The fake smile dropped from Kenna's face at the mention of her family. She noted that Will sat up straight and looked to be seconds away from coming to her aid, but she knew she must answer this question.

"Sadly, no. My parents died in an auto accident a couple of years ago. I was an only child, as were my parents. You find me the only member of my family left, the lone Mason. Are there any...."

"Oh, you poor dear!" Miss Violet had apparently had enough of hiding in the back and had come out of the kitchen. Much like her sisters, she was barely five feet tall with the signature white hair. She varied from Miss Daisy in the fact that she looked to be all matronly cushion, which she promptly put to use pulling McKenna into a fierce hug. Kenna found herself bent over with her face buried in pillowed breasts, being slightly rocked. She tried to tell Miss Violet it was okay, but her words got muffled in Miss Violet's ample cleavage.

"Now, now, dear. You have family right here. Doesn't she?" Miss Violet asked the cafe.

There were lots of "Sure does" and "Welcome to Keeneston" going around. Kenna gasped in a deep breath when Miss Violet released her and found a circle of people surrounding her.

"As you probably guessed, I'm Violet Fae, and it's a pleasure to meet anyone who's a friend of old Mrs. Ashton. Will too, I guess." She gestured to the soccer mom who had come over, "And this is Pam Gilbert. She's on the school board here."

Pam, with her dirty blond hair and traditional soccer mom uniform of pressed jeans and a button- up polo shirt sporting her son's team colors, shook Kenna's hand. "I am so sorry I asked about your parents. I just feel terrible. I sure do hope you'll forgive me."

"Of course, it's nice to meet you." Pam stepped back and was replaced by the young man who had blushed beet red when asking her about her relationship status.

She felt Will come stand next to her. Miss Violet and Pam had moved back to Pam's table and continued to talk to each other, so Will took over the introductions. "This young man is our running back on the high school football team. Trey Everett, meet Miss Mason." Trey shook hands with Kenna and then he nervously looked back and forth between Will and Kenna.

"It's nice to meet you, Trey. What year are you? And please, call me Kenna."

Trey's shy expression vanished and was replaced with a grin, "Thanks, ma'am, I mean, Kenna. I'm a junior this year and can't wait to start my senior year of football in the fall. You'll come to a game, right?" Trey asked with eagerness.

"I'd love to," she said with a truthfulness she hadn't felt in a long time. Even though she was pretty sure Ferdinand and Isabella could've used these people for the Spanish Inquisition, they appeared to be well-meaning and were now welcoming her to the town.

A very handsome man about her age approached with the "sex scandal" old man on his arm. The younger man was tall with blonde hair and eyes the color of the sea. He wasn't intimidating in size like Will but was probably five ten and more bookish looking. The "sex scandal" man took Kenna's hand in his old, arthritic hand and patted it. "I know what it's like to lose family dear. I know we set a date for me to walk you home tonight, but maybe we can just have dinner soon instead."

"That's so kind of you. I'm McKenna Mason, but I insist you just call me Kenna."

"I'm Roger Burns and this is my grand-nephew, Paul Russell. I'll call that young buck of a son of mine tonight and tell him to hire you if you promise me a kiss goodnight on our date." He winked at her then as Will and Paul broke out laughing.

"I take it your son is the D.A.? Well, in that case I'll do you one better and start a scandal right now." She leaned over and placed a kiss on his paper thin cheek and then whispered in his ear, "If I get a job, do you think they'll all say I kissed my way to the top?"

Roger chuckled and looked at Will while giving Kenna's hand another light pat, "Son, I hope you don't mind, but I'm going to encourage my Paul here to ask this one out. She reminds me of my sweet Martha, God rest her soul." He squeezed her hand and then slowly started to work his way back to his table.

"I'll gladly take my great uncle's suggestion. May I call you at Miss Lily's sometime this week?" Will's hand found its way back to her waist and as if staking a claim. He pulled her a step closer to his side. "After all, Will, you know as well as I do that no one can outlast Whitney. So you may as well save yourself the time."

Kenna saw Will's jaw clench. Apparently there was a story there. Maybe Will wasn't as free as she thought, even though he appeared to be singling her out. Either way, she didn't like to be treated like she was spoken for, so she smiled at Paul. "I'd love that. Thank you, Paul".

"It was great meeting you, Kenna. I'm glad you've come to Keeneston and look forward to seeing you soon. Good luck with your interview with my uncle," Paul said and then turned to head back sit at his table with his great uncle.

"Come on, you two, sit down and eat. Violet took charge and brought you out tonight's special, on the house, as a welcome to the town for Kenna." Miss Daisy ushered them back into the booth and placed a plate loaded with meatloaf, garlic mashed potatoes, and some steamed carrots in front of Kenna.

"Thank you, Daisy Mae. This is so nice of you both."

Miss Daisy harrumphed and went to fetch more orders.

"I have to apologize for my actions with Paul," Will said after a couple of bites of dinner. "We have been rivals since high school. He was a couple of grades behind me and a star on the soccer team. We often clashed over girls. He's right. I have no claim on you. But that's not saying that I wouldn't like to," Will said as he looked her right in the eyes. He lowered his gaze and went back to eating. Periodically through the meal, patrons would come up to the table and introduce themselves and talk about the law with Kenna or about the town in general. However, most came to talk to Will about his horses or how the football team would look in the fall. After the tension between Will and Paul, it was a nice break to meet so many of the town and avoid thoughts of either man. After all, it wasn't as if she were looking for a boyfriend. She was pretty sure she was cursed in that respect anyway.

When they finished dinner, they got up from the booth, and Kenna noticed Will leaving a twenty on the table even though dinner had been on the house. He placed his hand at the small of her back and navigated her out of the cafe as people waved and said they'd see her later. She had never felt so close to a group of people before.

"How about we walk up to Miss Lily's? It's such a nice night out," he said, helping her slide on a light jacket.

"That would be great." As they crossed Main Street and headed up to Miss Lily's, she turned to Will. His face was in profile as the moonlight shone down to show a slight scar on the bridge of his sharp nose. "How did you get that scar?" Kenna asked, gently running her finger over it.

"I got it during a game. We were playing an away game and were in Green Bay during December. It was freezing outside. Snow was covering the field and this strong wind was blowing. My receivers couldn't get their feet under them and that left me in the pocket longer than normal. One play, while waiting for my receiver to get open, I got hit from behind by a huge lineman. I wasn't prepared for it, so I hit the ground full force with my face leading the way. My helmet slid down a little and cut the bridge of my nose. The good thing was I had just managed to get the ball off, and we ended up winning the game with that touchdown. The other good thing was that it was so cold that I didn't feel much of it. When the doc looked at me after the game, the blood had frozen and there was very little mess."

"I know you played in the NFL in D.C. for a couple of years, but that's all. Did you always intend to go pro?"

"No, I went to the University of Kentucky on a football scholarship. I was red shirted my first year though. They had a great QB and a junior backup so I wasn't really needed. Also, I was still pretty scrawny. I didn't really bulk up until the end of my freshman year. I grew taller, and the strength coach kicked my butt daily. I filled out, and by the time the QB in front of me graduated, I was ready to play. Anyway, I went on to start my junior and senior year. We had this great Air Raid offense that really padded my stats too. Because of my red shirt, I had five years of college. So while it was technically my senior year of football, I had already graduated and was enrolled in the MBA program."

"You got your MBA while playing football? That must've been tough."

"Actually, I only got one of the two years completed then. I had a pretty good senior year and started to get scouted by some pro teams. I thought I'd give it a try since there was some interest, so I entered my name in the draft. I ended up being drafted late in the second round to D.C. Halfway through my first year, I was content riding the bench and watching one of the best NFL QB's picking apart team after team. But late in October we were playing the Falcons. It was a battle of the top teams. They were first in the league and we were second. We were neck and neck through the first half. But then in the third quarter, they started pulling away. They were ten points ahead when our QB injured."

"So, with Number One out, you got your big chance." She smiled and jumped in front of him, pretending to pass a football down the street. "I bet you won the game by throwing the winning touchdown," she laughed.

"Actually, far from it. I caused us to lose. I threw the losing interception. I got cussed out by the coach and slammed by the talking heads. I was totally unprepared to be the starter. I hadn't played a single down before that game but was suddenly expected to lead the team. Lucky for me, Doron, the injured QB, helped me out a lot. He would come in early for practice and spend an hour with me teaching me the system and what to look for."

"So, how long did you stay in the NFL? Were you fired?"

"No, I wasn't fired," Will laughed as they stopped on the front porch of Miss Lily's bed and breakfast. He turned and faced her, "Although I kinda sucked for the next month and we fell in the ranking, we managed to get into the playoffs and by that time the extra practice with the coaches and Doron really paid off. I started throwing more touchdowns and fewer interceptions. We ended up the runner-up in our division that year, which was a big accomplishment for a rookie like me."

"They kept you around, huh?" she said as she playfully nudged him with her shoulder.

"Yeah, they decided I wasn't that bad and paid me a nice bonus to extend my contract with them. Doron and his wife had been trying to get pregnant for over five years, and they didn't think it would ever happen. Then she found out she was pregnant with triplets right before the championship game." Will chuckled, "You should've seen Doron's face when he came into the locker room after finding out. His face was drawn and his eyes kinda crossed. He announced to the whole team that after ten years of playing in the NFL, he was quitting to become a stay-at-home dad. He had even purchased a minivan on the way to practice."

"That certainly sealed your fate then. How long did you play for?"

"I played for seven seasons. All with D.C., which is pretty rare. I loved every moment on the field."

"Why did you stop then?

"I stopped because I got a phone call from my mom saying Dad was in the hospital. She was in tears. She had found him unconscious in the mare barn. He had suffered a heart attack, and luckily she came upon him right after it happened. The stress of running the farm was just too much for him. I decided I'd use my MBA to run the farm. Every summer for three years, I took summer classes and finished my MBA. I focused on agricultural management, but I also learned enough from my first year in the program to be careful with my money. So I didn't really need to play anymore to live comfortably. I quit at the end of the season while I was at the top of my game and took over the farm. I still get together with the guys a couple times a year, so it's not like I've left it totally behind. But I'm having a lot of fun with expanding the farm. This year, we actually have a chance for back-to-back Derby wins."

"Wow! I'm taking it that it's hard to do?"

"Very. Speaking of the farm, you haven't seen it yet. Would you be interested in coming over for dinner one night? I can show you around the place." He eagerly looked at her, waiting for her answer.

"That would be great. I'd love to see the place and some of the horses."

He smiled widely at her answer. From jumping around throwing imaginary footballs, a lock of her auburn hair had escaped from behind her ear and was dangling by her eye. He slowly reached over and brushed his fingers gently across her cheek on the way to tucking the errant strand back behind her ear.

Kenna froze the moment Will's fingers touched her cheek. It was so gentle she thought maybe it hadn't happened, but she saw Will's eyes lock onto her lips and felt her own part in response. His hand fell to her shoulder and pulled her to him. He smelled like the outdoors and freshly cut grass. She saw him bend his head towards hers, and as he angled his head, she closed her eyes.

Suddenly, from behind her closed eyelids, the world became bright. And it wasn't from the kiss she'd been expecting. Kenna opened her eyes and saw Will's face inches from hers. "We're totally busted," he said to her and winked.

Kenna looked around and found that the porch, which just seconds ago had been romantically lit by the moon, was now awash in bright lights. The front door opened and out came Miss Lily with her broom. Ignoring the couple on the porch, she started sweeping, "Don't mind me and finish saying your goodnights. I just saw a leaf I wanted to take care of before the morning. Oh, and William, I expect you to say good-night like a gentleman. There's no hanky panky on my porch until you're officially dating." And with that, she started sweeping the imaginary leaf to the edge of the porch. The bright lights did nothing to hide Kenna's fierce blush of embarrassment. But Will didn't seem similarly affected. Instead, he leaned down again as if to kiss her goodnight on the cheek. She backed up, not wanting to suffer another embarrassment in front of Miss Lily. Thwack! Miss Lily's imaginary leaf had apparently landed on Will's perfect bottom because Miss Lily smacked it again as Will laughed out loud.

"I was just seeing if you were paying attention, Miss Lily." Will laughed, holding up his hands up in surrender.

"Sure you were, young man, now scoot." Miss Lily, standing on the porch in an old yellow bathrobe, used her broom to sweep Will off the porch as he chuckled and waved good-night to Miss Lily and Kenna.

"Now, young lady, I know they play 'em fast and loose in New York. But that isn't how it's done here. Now, come inside before you catch your death," Miss Lily said as she shooed Kenna inside. "And you tell me all about your night out with young William," she added with a wink to Kenna.

CHAPTER 4

IT WAS DARK. The light from the back room was casting eerie shadows off the cubicles and down the hall. The bass of the music was loud. She could feel it vibrating through her body. She walked slowly toward the music and toward the screams.

Her heels made no noise on the thick carpet as she crept forward. Her heart was beating fast. Her palms were sweaty. Her breathing was coming in shallow gasps. She stopped dead when she heard a creak coming from the floor. Taking a breath, she moved closer to the cubicles to keep hidden. Her hands skimmed over the rough industrial fabric as she got closer to the room.

She bent down as she slowly made her way forward, using the cubicles to hide behind. They wouldn't like her being here. There was only one cubicle separating her from the room. Quietly, and on unsure legs, she crept into it. She was so close to the source of the music that the loud bass was shaking her whole body.

Looking around the cubicle, she saw the typical family pictures, desktop, and supplies all behind her. She crawled forward, closer to the room. She sat down with her back against the scratchy fabric and took a deep breath. She was sure it was nothing. She just had to be sure though. She spun around on the balls of her feet. She placed her hands on the cubicle wall and slowly rose up...

Kenna awoke with a gasp. "Oh thank God!" She was still in her soft bed in Miss Lily's. She fell back against the pillows with relief. Looking over at the clock she saw that it was early. Too early, but she might as well get started on her studies. She didn't think she'd be able to go back to sleep anytime soon.

Kenna pushed open the screen door and walked onto the front porch. It was a cool, spring morning so Kenna pulled her Syracuse University Lacrosse sweatshirt on over her white t-shirt. She was glad she had put on her old jeans this morning. She set the heavy stack of Kentucky statutes and criminal and civil procedure books down on the table beside the hanging, white bench swing. The bar exam was just two weeks away, and she wanted to impress the district attorney at her interview tomorrow.

Arranging herself on the cushion, she grabbed the *"Green Book"*, also known as the *Criminal Law of Kentucky*. It held all the relevant penal code statutes and criminal law procedures she'd need to know for the job, and for the bar exam.

She opened the heavy tome and started reading. She had a pen in one hand and highlighter in the other as she alternated between highlighting important issues and writing notes about cases. She had become so engrossed in her studying that she didn't hear Mr. Wolfe's whistling until he was halfway up the steps.

"Good morning, my dear. How are you this lovely spring morning?" he asked, jovial as ever.

"Good morning, Mr. Wolfe. I'm well. Just got up early to study some and prepare for my interview tomorrow," she smiled.

"Well, I'll make sure to let Tom know you're more than prepared for the job when I see him for lunch today," Mr. Wolfe winked. He then added, "You make sure you start calling me John or I'll start thinking you don't like me too much."

"Thanks, John. What brings you by this morning?" John's jovial welcome dispelled the last of the darkness left behind from her nightmare.

But before John could answer, Miss Lily came bustling out the door, wiping her hands on her apron. "John! What a pleasant surprise," she said as she straightened her shirt and wiped imaginary flour off her apron.

"I came by to see if I could talk my way into some of your banana nut pancakes, Lily Rae."

"Of course you can. Come in, come in." Miss Lily, lacking her broom, had to herd John in through the door with the dish towel that had been hanging over her shoulder.

As she ushered John through the door, Miss Lily turned and looked at Kenna. With a slight blush to her cheeks, she hurried in after her guest of honor. Kenna smiled and wondered if there might be something special going on between them. But the thought of how Miss Lily's sisters had cooed over him at the cafe last night came back to her. Kenna laughed. Old John was a player.

Just as Kenna bent back over her book, June came out, looking perfect in another designer outfit. This time it was a black jersey, belted wrap dress that stopped just above the knee. She had on black strap sandals with three inch heels and rhinestones running down the heel. Kenna suffered shoe envy for a moment before looking up at June's perfectly coifed blonde hair and smiling face.

"If I didn't like you so much, there's a very real possibility that I'd knock you down and steal those shoes," Kenna said, eyeing the strapped sandals again.

"I'll give them to you if you want. I almost didn't wear them since they are from Prada's spring line from two years ago," June said with such thought, as if she were still deciding if she should wear them.

"Oh, well, in that case, give them to charity. I couldn't be caught dead in two-year-old Pradas!" Kenna and June laughed.

"That was very shallow of me, wasn't it? Well, do forgive me. The reason I came out was to see if I could get you to join us for breakfast." June waved toward the dining room.

"Sure, sounds great," Kenna said as she marked her place and set the book down on the table. Kenna went to the sideboard and filled her plate with blueberry pancakes, got a glass of mango orange juice, and sat down at the table with June and Julius.

Julius looked up from his copy of the *Wall Street Journal*, "Ah, good morning, McKenna. How is studying going?" he asked.

"Good morning, Julius. It's going well. I have a good understanding of procedure but am trying hard to memorize the penal code," she answered.

"We're going to the sales today if you'd care to join us. We'll be coming back for lunch if you want to make it a short day. It should be somewhat amusing as there will be a little drama surrounding the normal backstabbing, outbidding, and competitiveness that surrounds the sales. You remember Will Ashton, of course. Well, I've heard his wife has come back to town and will most likely show up for the sales." He gave a pointed look to June and went back to his paper.

"What my husband means is that she can't stand to be out of the center of attention. I'm sure she'll cause quite a scene in one matter or another. I don't like to speak ill of anyone, but she is a witch," June whispered as if God would hear her and strike her down.

"Wife?" Kenna asked, her stomach dropping and a painful squeeze taking its place around her heart. She knew she shouldn't care that he was married. She had assumed he was. But last night she got the distinct impression he was single and interested in her. The pig!

Just because his wife wasn't a nice person didn't mean that he could go around taking ladies out to dinner and trying to kiss them under the moonlight. Oh, she was going to those sales today and was going to give him a piece of her mind.

Not knowing the thoughts and feelings flowing through Kenna, June continued, "She dug her perfectly manicured hooks into him when he was playing football in D.C. Her father is in politics and she found herself a big fish all right." June leaned closer and dropped her voice to a whisper again, "But, when he decided to retire and come back to Kentucky, she threw such a fit. Some cameraman from one of those celebrity websites caught her rant as she stood outside some celebrity charity event yelling at Will that she'd never move to some backwater state like Kentucky. She refused to leave their brownstone and move into a 'log cabin'," June said, making the sign of two quotation marks above her head. "As I said, she's a witch. But, now she splits her time between D.C. and Kentucky. She comes for the Derby because of all the fame surrounding it. She'll show up to any event with a red carpet and national broadcast."

"Do they have any kids?" Kenna asked. She was fearful that the man she had once held in such high esteem had abandoned his wife and kids. No matter what, she couldn't ask for help from someone like that.

"No. I don't think she could stand the idea of ruining her figure to have kids although, Will's never made it a secret that he'd like some," June answered.

Kenna sighed and looked over to see Mr. Wolfe staring at her. He gave a slight smile and then stood to help Miss Lily clear the tables as they walked with their heads together into the kitchen. Kenna turned back to June and Julius, "I'm sorry. I wish I could go with you right now. But I just have to get more studying done. You can tell me all about it this evening." Kenna rose up from the table, said her goodbye's, and headed back to the porch. She settled back down in the cushion and opened her book.

An hour later, Kenna looked up from her studying to see some people walking down the sidewalk. They turned and waved, and she waved back. She smiled to herself, thinking the pepper spray and the endless hours of self-defense classes were probably not as useful down here, although, it might come in handy if Miss Violet grabbed her again and suffocated her in her bosom. Kenna laughed at the thought and put her head back into her book.

Upon hearing and feeling her stomach rumbling, Kenna pushed up her sleeve and looked at her watch. Oh gosh, it was almost two o'clock. She marked her page, piled up her books, and carried them back to her room. She grabbed her purse and headed for the cafe.

. . .

MISS VIOLET CAME out of the kitchen carrying Kenna's lunch. "Thank you," Kenna said when her lunch was placed in front of her. When the bell tinkled overhead, she looked up and smiled.

"Hi, Paige!"

"Hello, Kenna. How was your first day in town? I heard you had a date with Will. Looks like you found him all right." She smiled and pulled out a chair at Kenna's table.

"Amazing. I won't even ask how you know."

"That's easy. I ran into John on my way here." Paige smiled and asked for a salad.

"I'm glad I ran into you. I wanted to thank you for all your recommendations. Miss Lily's is way better than any hotel."

When Miss Violet returned with Paige's lunch, she pulled out the extra chair and sat down. Miss Daisy came around the table and took the last chair.

"Now, we dish," Miss Daisy said. "Everyone in the town knows you were in here last night with Will Ashton and that he took you home. And Lily Rae said she had to take the broom to him last night. I didn't take young William as the type who got fresh so fast," Miss Daisy clucked as three sets of eyes turned to Kenna.

She felt her face turn a light shade of pink and had to suppress a giggle. She felt as if she had been part of this town her whole life. The Rose sisters were like fairy godmothers and she was Sleeping Beauty, finally awakening from years of the same old, same old big city grind. The feeling of warmth and family radiated around the table. Kenna, who was normally so quiet and suspicious of anyone but her best friend Danielle, felt like good old-fashioned girl talk.

"You know, normally when I dish on a guy it includes chocolate!" Kenna joked.

Apparently not willing to leave it to chance, Miss Violet jumped up and disappeared into the kitchen screaming, "Don't you say nothin' until I get back!" Less than two minutes later, Violet came back with a huge brownie smothered in homemade chocolate fudge with ice cream on top.

"Wow. You really are a fairy godmother," Kenna said out loud.

"Darn skippy," Miss Violet replied with a grin lighting her face and making her look like a teenager again.

"Well, I guess I can't get out of it, can I?" Kenna said.

"Sure can't," Paige said. "I must admit, I want to know about Will too."

"Well, we came from the sales and then he fed me to the wolves here. But then he walked me to Miss Lily's and we talked about our past, playing catch-up on our lives. Then we were saying goodnight and Miss Lily swatted him with a broom," Kenna said.

"Oh, come on, gal. I know there has to be more than that. Lily Rae doesn't bring out the broom unless the young man is angling to get fresh," Miss Violet said and made a move to take the brownie away.

"Okay, okay, I'll talk. Just don't hurt the brownie," Kenna laughed and the others joined in a round of giggles.

"Well, he was moving in for a kiss. But we didn't get lift off because Miss Lily came out right before we could kiss. He tried to kiss me again but got another thwack from her. I must admit, I was really hoping for that kiss," Kenna told her avid listeners.

"I'm really surprised that Will moved so fast. He's usually so slow and he never has a girl around during the sales or Derby because of Whitney," Paige said, eliciting nods from both Miss Violet and Miss Daisy.

"Whitney?" Kenna asked and her stomach flopped as she waited to hear what Paige was going to tell her.

"Yeah, Whitney Amber Bruce Ashton," Paige said, impersonating a very snobbish person.

Ashton, Kenna thought, her last name was Ashton. It was true, he did have a wife. She couldn't believe she'd been so stupid. What a jerk to cheat on his wife. It made her so mad just to think about it. And, it seemed the whole town knows about his cheating. Apparently he only curbs it when his wife is in town.

Paige cut into Kenna's thoughts, "Though, I usually just call her Bitch."

"Wow, you're the second friendly person who said that today.

What's wrong with her?" Kenna asked. It seemed on cue, but the whole table rolled their eyes as if they didn't know where to begin.

"This soup is too hot," Miss Violet said in her snooty voice.

"This soup is too cold," Miss Daisy imitated.

"This jewelry is so cheap," Paige threw in.

"Don't you have any good service in this hole-in-the-wall town?" Miss Violet asked next.

"Oh, I got that one too!" Paige said. "Is that enough of an example? I'm sure we could continue for hours," Paige asked her.

"No, I see your point. She doesn't seem like a nice person," Kenna said.

"The worst part," Miss Daisy said, "is that no one will stand up to her. Her daddy is a senator, and Will is a local boy who coaches high school football for free. His farm brings in the tourists which helps the local economy. But, mark my words, someday she'll get what's coming to her. Karma's a bigger bitch than she is," Miss Daisy announced.

Paige scooted her chair back and stood up. "As much as I'd love to continue this, I need to get back to the shop. Kenna, it was such a pleasure seeing you again. I'm sure you'll ace your interview tomorrow." When Kenna looked at her strangely, Paige said, "Yes, we all know about your interview, too. Keeneston grapevine and all. Anyway, I'm hoping you'll agree to have dinner with me after your interview to celebrate you new job. We could meet here at six?"

"That would be great. Thanks, Paige. I guess I better get going too." She paid Miss Daisy and headed back to Miss Lily's. The Keeneston grapevine, as it was called, was something that would definitely take time getting used to. Thinking about Will being married brought her down. It was wrong to cheat, even though his wife was apparently the devil. And Kenna especially disliked being kept in the dark. But, as much as that brought her down, the fact that she had a new friend in Paige brought her up. It would be nice to talk to someone again.

Kenna started the short walk back to the bed and breakfast. She couldn't help thinking of her best friend. Paige and Dani would get along great. The last time she had seen Danielle, her face had been twisted in fear. She had been near panic as she raced out of the parking garage. Her life changed forever, all because of what Kenna had seen. The situation Dani was in was her fault. But she had no choice. After looking over that cubicle there was no other option.

She thought of Danielle and wondered where she was now. Everything had been quiet for a month now. She decided to risk a quick email to her to see if they could make contact. She hoped like hell that Danielle had found a place to hide.

CHAPTER 5

KENNA SAT in her room studying until a knock on her door interrupted her. Kenna had nearly worked her way to the end of Kentucky's criminal law book. She marked her place in the book and said, "Come in," as she tried to stack the books into what resembled neatness. June opened the door and floated in, her blonde hair pulled back into a sleek ponytail and a navy cocktail dress. It fit her curves and hung loose from her hips to her ankles, which were outfitted with silver spiked heels to finish off the outfit. Kenna was pretty sure that even though June was from Florida, she must spend a lot of time shopping in New York City.

"We were hoping to see you at dinner, but Miss Lily said you were studying. I just had to stop by and tell you all the horse world gossip before we hit the club to celebrate," June said, sweeping into the room.

"What are you celebrating?" Kenna asked.

"We bought the most beautiful colt. He's the perfect addition to our stable. Oh, and Will sold one for one point one million today, sired by last year's Derby winner." Before Kenna could even comment, June continued, "And that wasn't even his best horse. He's raking it in this year, that's for sure. But the poor dear, one of his stable hands had some kind of accident on the farm and Will had to leave right away. I guess it was kinda serious since he said he wouldn't be able to go out with us tonight. I think he said the man broke a leg, or was it an arm? I can't remember, but it really upset him. Oh, and I have to tell you about the drama today. Whitney Ashton showed up and caused such a stir. She wore the most outrageous white pantsuit to the sale. I mean, who wears white in March? And who wears it to a horse sale? Hay, dirt, and horse poop do not cry out for an all-white outfit. I'm sure Whitney was there to see how the sale went to see how much money she could get her grubby little paws on," June laughed as she remembered the day.

"You wouldn't believe what happened to her. I can't even say I feel sorry for her! She had on these white peep-toe shoes, and she was walking with some poor Keeneland employee, chewing him out for something, when *squish,* she stepped in a fresh pile of horse manure!"

Kenna's mouth fell open and she covered the laugh with her hand. She shouldn't laugh at someone's misfortune, really she shouldn't.

"But that's not all! She picked up her foot and started screaming. She's jumping around on one foot and loses her balance. She fell flat on her ass, the leg with manure on the shoe dangling in the air. And then, *splat!* A big glob of manure fell right in the middle of her white suit coat! Oh, it was priceless. But, enough of that," June waved her hand through the air as if clearing out a bad smell. "I wanted to see if you'd go to the sales with us tomorrow?"

"Normally, I'd love to, but I have my interview and dinner plans with a friend. Are the sales still going on the day after tomorrow?" Kenna asked, still laughing over the Whitney story.

"Sure are. We'll be here all week. We'll just go in two days, what is that, Thursday? That will be perfect. The sale ends on Sunday. Well, I'm sure Julius will be wondering what's taking so long. I never tell him though. It keeps the mystery alive! Toodles!" June said with a wiggle of her fingers, and disappeared out the door in a flash of navy and silver.

Kenna shook her head. It was as if she had been hit by a perfectly coifed tornado. As she opened her book, she hoped she wasn't making a mistake by going to the sales again. It was so interesting the first time that she really wanted to go. She had no claim to Will and thought him a snake for making a move on her behind his wife's back. But Kenna had to admit, she was curious about his wife.

Some hours later, Kenna woke with a page of the criminal procedure book stuck to her face. She had fallen asleep face first into the book and then drooled, making the page stick to her cheek. Too tired to walk across the room, she stripped and climbed under the covers in nothing but her panties. With a sigh, she fell asleep almost instantly.

KENNA STOOD in front of the courthouse and straightened the knee-length, black pencil skirt and matching fitted black jacket. She wore an ivory satin shell underneath and had almost killed herself getting into her pantyhose this morning. She wore simple black pumps and her long auburn hair was in a French twist. A car honked and she ignored it until it honked again. Thinking it was probably some idiot, she turned to give the driver the finger. She caught herself just in time from flicking off Pam Gilbert.

"Good Luck, McKenna!" Pam shouted as she drove by and they exchanged waves. That was a first, Kenna thought.

She turned back to the courthouse, walked up the steps, and pulled open the heavy front doors. She found the building directory and took the stairs to the second floor district attorney office, consisting of three rooms and the Keeneston Law Library. She entered a room that was a mix of old school attorney with a hint of criminal. The leather seats in the waiting room were bolted down, and a chest high desk separated the secretary from the waiting room. Overall, the room looked warm, but not so warm that the people swearing out warrants wanted to hang out. A woman who looked no-nonsense in khakis and a light-blue sweater sat with a pinched face, probably from the tight bun she had pulled her hair back in. Her age could be anywhere from twenty-five to fifty-five.

She looked up from the computer, "Can I help you?" she snapped at Kenna.

"Yes, I'm McKenna Mason. I have an appointment with Mr. Burns," Kenna answered with a slight smile on her face. She was pretty sure if she used charm, this woman would toss her out on her ass before she could even interview. The lady held up a finger to indicate she should wait, but didn't offer for her to sit down. So McKenna stood waiting while the lady picked up the phone and told the person on the other end of the line that "A Miss Mason is here for her appointment."

Kenna must've passed the first round because when the happy greeter looked up after putting the phone down, she pointed to a door behind the desk, "Go on in," and went back to her typing.

McKenna pushed through the swinging half door attached to the desk and walked to the back office. She knocked on the door and took one final deep breath to calm herself. She heard a gruff voice call for her to come in. She opened the door and walked in to meet her potential boss.

Very old school, Kenna thought, as she took a quick glance on her way across the room. She made her way to a set of leather chairs in front of an old massive legal desk. Mr. Burns was a man in his early fifties and had thinning brown hair turning gray. As he stood to greet her, Kenna realized he was actually much shorter than she thought. He probably stood at only five feet eight inches, and it looked as if he had worked hard on the pot belly that hung out over his belt. He had huge round glasses, a neatly trimmed gray mustache and looked to be friendly enough now, but Kenna could definitely tell he'd be a monster in the courtroom. Between him and his secretary, it was no wonder they had the lowest deadbeat parent standing in the state. Everyone paid because no one wanted to come pay child support to Miss Sunshine in the office, or go up against an aggressive Mr. Magoo in the courtroom.

"Miss Mason, it's nice to meet you. I'm Tom Burns," he said as he held out his hand over his desk. Kenna shook it and they both sat in their respective corners. He eyed her over his massive desk, and she sat as tall as possible in the old chair.

"It's nice to meet you, too. I've been looking forward to this since I received your email setting the date for our interview," Kenna smiled. She knew better than to use her fake happy smile. She figured both Miss Sunshine and Mr. Magoo saw enough bullshit to know when to spot it.

"I'll cut right to the point. You have an impressive resume. Top 25% of your class from Syracuse University. An elite job at one of the biggest firms in New York City. An impressive amount of wins and large settlements during your time there. But, here is what bothers me. There are two things. First, why you stated in your letter that I couldn't call and check your resume with your boss at GTH? And the second, why I should give you a job whose focus is on criminal law when your main area of practice has been in civil litigation and public relations?"

Boy, Mr. Magoo really could cut to the chase, she thought. She took a deep breath and answered, focusing on half truths to make the answer believable. "To address your first question, I don't know how things are done in smaller firms, and I don't know how they are done in Kentucky, but GTH was very much a good ol' boys' system. Women did not advance past associate. I was the first woman to make it to junior partner and that was only after bringing in a five million settlement fee in a class action. It was made very clear to me that I'd never be part of the club and that I'd never advance any higher. I had a hard time accepting that sort of sexual discrimination and decided to start looking for a different avenue where my day wouldn't just repeat itself."

"I didn't want to be stuck in civil litigation all my life. I wanted to branch out to other areas of the law. But because I was good at it, the partners refused me any cases in a different field. I asked for you not to contact my boss since I was still working there. And if this didn't work out, I knew I'd be fired on the spot. When I resigned and moved down here with the intent of taking this job, if offered, I knew it wouldn't do any good for you to call GTH. The partners were furious I left and aren't above telling you lies," Kenna finished. She kept it very close to the truth, but left out that the main reason they were enraged was because she had evidence that implicated them in a crime. She disappeared before they could make sure she didn't say a word to anyone ever again.

"To answer your second question, I've always been interested in criminal law. I received A's in my criminal law, criminal procedure, federal criminal law and federal criminal procedure classes when in law school. Although I have no courtroom experience, I was published in the law review for my research on the Brady Rule, which focused on the ethical versus legal duties of the prosecutor to turn over evidence to defense counsel if it helps the defense's case. Further, I have studied Kentucky's criminal law and criminal procedure and believe I'll be able to pass the Kentucky part of the bar exam in two weeks. And very quickly after that, I'll be prepared to handle the duties of an assistant D.A. in the courtroom and outside of it." Kenna had her hands clasped lightly together in her lap and was afraid to even re-cross her legs. It seemed to be a delicate time in Mr. Burns' contemplation period. He sat staring at her. The only noise in the room was the drumming of his thick fingers on his polished desk.

"I'm sure you have the school side of things down. But as you know from experience, law school does nothing to teach you what it's like in the courtroom. Also, things that happen in Kentucky are different than in New York. In New York you probably get a lot of public intoxication and people pissing in the street. Here we get some drunk bastard thinking it's funny to ride a John Deere Combine Harvester down the road. Or, for instance, what would you do if Joe Schmoe is brought before the court on a drunk driving charge? He blew two times the legal limit." Mr. Burns stared at her.

"I would follow the guidelines for violation of Kentucky Statute 189A.050, which prohibits the driving of a motor vehicle while under the influence of alcohol." Kenna re-crossed her legs then. She knew she answered the question correctly and was giving herself a mental pat on the back.

"First rule, Ms. Mason, is to make sure you get all the facts. You did not ascertain he was driving a car. In fact, what happened in this case was one of the grooms out at Stapleton Farm got drunk and his buddies dared him to ride one of the horses down Main Street. A Deputy pulled over the horse at one in the morning, right outside the courthouse. The boy failed the field sobriety test. The horse passed it. Now what would you do?" Mr. Burns leaned back into his chair, keeping his gaze fixed on hers.

"I would ask how old the drunken horse rider is and if he had any prior alcohol charges. Oh, and if he was a legal citizen of the United States." Kenna was already searching the pages of her mind for juvenile offenses, underage drinking laws and non-motor operations while intoxicated laws.

"Very good, Ms. Mason. He was twenty-two years old, no priors, and he was born and bred here in Kentucky."

"Then I would say under Kentucky Statute 189.520, he would be found guilty of his first offense of operating a non-motorized device while intoxicated. The horse would fall under the same category as a bicycle in this case. Depending on his attitude and the circumstances, I would say to give him the normal penalty or drop the charge down to public intoxication with one hundred hours of community service." Kenna maintained eye contact with Mr. Burns and saw the slight crinkle of his eyes that showed he was happy with her answer.

"You certainly have been studying, Ms. Mason. That is a very good answer. There are a couple more things I'd like to discuss with you that may be different here than in New York. First, it's just me as the D.A. There is one assistant job and then we have multiple part-time support staff. Mainly, it's Martha Schrader out in the front who runs things. The assistant's job is just part time. You'll be responsible for court all day Monday, Tuesday and

Wednesday mornings. When necessary, we can cover for each other. What it also means is that being just part-time, you can open your own practice or join one here if you'd like so long as your cases don't conflict with your prosecutorial duties. I'm willing to offer you the job on the condition that you pass the bar exam in two weeks. What do you say?"

Kenna smiled and stood up. She extended her hand over the desk, "I say you have a new assistant," and she took Mr. Burns' hand in a firm shake.

"You can call me Tom. Here," he said as he shoved a pile of books across the desk, "these are some study guides for the bar exam I got from UK's law school. They have practice questions and so on to help you study. After you take the exam, but before you get the results, feel free to come to court as often as you want. I'll want you to see the procedure in action and how the courthouse functions."

"Thank you. I'll do that. You can call me McKenna, or just Kenna. You said I could open my own practice, but I don't know the real estate around here. Isn't it hard to get an office close to the courthouse?" Kenna was already thinking of the things she needed to do to go out on her own. It was scary, but at least she'd have some money coming in with the assistant D.A. job, though, compared to her old salary, it was peanuts. It was a good thing she had paid off all her loans while working and saved a nice nest egg for rainy days.

"There is a solo attorney who handles a lot of defense work who had put the word out a couple of months ago that he was looking for someone to share the space with. His name is Henry Rooney. He's not bad for a defense attorney," Tom winked.

"That sounds promising. Where is his office?"

"It's about two blocks up from the courthouse on the right. If you pass the feed store, you've gone too far."

"That sounds wonderful. I'll talk to him. I'm really looking forward to working with you, Tom."

"Just keep in touch and let me know how the bar went. I'm sure you'll have no problems. Besides, I'm pretty sure if I didn't hire you, the town wouldn't re-elect me. Do you know my own father called me and told me I was a moron if I didn't hire you? Not to count my nephew, the Rose sisters, all three of them, the Ashtons... William even threatened to have me blackballed at the country club! Then Pam Gilbert called and threatened to have the PTA vote against me too. I don't know how you met so many people in such a short time, but your friends play politics better than the mayor does. And he wanted his nephew to get the job. But, I must say, you're a damn good reason not to hire that loser," Tom said as he escorted her to the door.

Kenna was slightly stunned that all these people contacted Tom just to support someone they only knew for a couple of days. Kenna gave a nod and a smile to Tom, then turned to walk out of the office. A scruffy looking man in what used to be a white undershirt stood at the counter, arguing with Martha about taking out a warrant on someone for assault and battery stemming from a fist fight. She couldn't see any evidence of bruising, but his right hand was swollen and wrapped in an air cast.

"Don't you pull this crap on me, Dwayne. You know perfectly well that your brother didn't hit you. He took your punch, turned around, and left." Martha nodded toward Dwayne's hand, "and apparently you got hurt as a result. The only assault and battery charges you can file are against yourself. You want to just go ahead and do that, Dwayne?" Martha asked in all seriousness.

"You don't know he didn't hit me. It's my word against his. I say he hit me and I was just defending myself." Dwayne's lower lip stuck out in a nice pout. Kenna was sure any minute this man-child in a dirty undershirt and jorts would stomp his booted foot and go into a full tantrum. Kenna enjoyed watching Martha work too much to ask Dwayne to get out of the way for her to open the swinging door. So Kenna propped a shoulder against the wall and decided to enjoy the show. Maybe Martha wasn't that bad after all.

"Dwayne, bless your heart, but you are one stupid man. Do you think no one would see you storming up the church stairs, grabbing your brother, and pulling him out into the parking lot? We all saw and we all heard you threatening to cut off his balls if he didn't cover your mortgage payment. Pastor Jacob even followed you all out there and saw the whole thing. Now, Dwayne, do you really think a judge is going to believe you over Pastor Jacob when he testifies he saw you hit your brother? I don't think so, and all because your brother has put his foot down and isn't allowing you to leech money off of him.

Dwayne, sober up and get a job. Now get! Get out of my office before I call Red up here to arrest you for stupidity." Martha lowered her head back down to her computer and started typing. Dwayne shuffled his feet as his mouth opened and closed like a fish. He then turned and walked out the door, mumbling some very nasty phrases about Martha.

Kenna opened the door and gave Martha a little golf clap. "Very well done. It'll be a pleasure to work with you next month," Kenna said as she walked out the door. All she heard in response was a grunt and figured it was better than nothing. She smiled and headed to see a man about a law office.

CHAPTER 6

KENNA WALKED UP THE STREET, passing the bank building, which she was pretty sure had been there for a hundred years. She came to a stop just past the bank. The building was a light tan with moss-green trim. In front of the building was a sign that read Rooney Law Office. There looked to be just the right amount of space to add Mason Law Firm underneath.

Kenna opened the glass door and stepped onto the thick tan carpet. The office was quiet and smelled of lemon oil. A welcome area stood over to the right with a brown leather couch and two upholstered, burgundy arm chairs. A coffee table held an assortment of magazines ranging from the *American Bar Association* to *Field & Stream* and, of course, *Southern Living*. A head popped around a door frame from behind the desk placed in the middle of the room, and a pixie of girl shouted, "Be right with you, hon."

Kenna looked around at her potential new office. There appeared to be a conference room right behind the waiting area. On the other side of the room was an archway that led back to more rooms. The room was painted the lightest of moss greens. The overall impression was very clean and professional but also very masculine. Kenna's eyes went back towards the pixie's direction when she heard a loud thump, accompanied by some odd phrases meant to convey frustration and anger. Kenna made a mental note to ask Will about "being as useless as tits on a wild boar." Kenna heard one more thump, which she was pretty sure was something being kicked. The pixie reappeared with a look of momentary exhaustion. The girl looked no more than twenty and had tousled blonde hair styled into a fashionable boy cut. She had a cute round face that still had a little baby fat in the cheeks. She was a couple inches shorter than Kenna and a good thirty pounds lighter. She looked a lot like Tinkerbell.

"Hi ya. Can I help you?" she asked.

"Yes, my name is McKenna Mason and I was hoping to have a word with Mr. Rooney about renting an office."

"Oh! That would be so cool. We have a ton of offices for you to choose from. Have a seat and I'll tell Henry you're here." Kenna watched as the pixie sat down and pushed some buttons on the phone. A couple of seconds later she was telling Henry there was someone interested in renting space.

"He'll be right out. I'm Tammy by the way. I'm the only employee here, so if you do rent the space you'd share me as your secretary. Oh, and here's Henry now."

Kenna looked to the left and saw a man not much older than her coming towards her. He was tall, probably close to five eleven, and had black hair slicked back and held in place with some kind of hair product. He wore olive colored pants with a little shine to them and a very sharp crease down the middle. A white dress shirt with monogrammed cuffs and shiny brown loafers finished off the look. Kenna knew exactly what type of person Henry was. He fell into the sleazy ambulance chaser category. Not all of them were bad, but it took a certain breed of people to be able to do that. When he leered at Tammy's breasts for a second before turning to leer at her own breasts, Kenna's suspicions were confirmed.

"Well, hello there. I'm Henry Rooney."

Kenna was a little skeptical about taking the hand he stuck out for her to shake. She fought the impulse to pull out the hand sanitizer from her purse. She took his offered hand and shook it. When he didn't let go right away, she squeezed it tighter, never taking her eyes away from his.

"Tammy said you were interested in renting some office space. I'd be more than happy to have you move in with me." He gave a wink and instead of dropping her hand, he started to make soft circular motions with his thumb.

Kenna smiled her 'sweeter than honey' smile and squeezed his hand tighter, digging her nails into the fleshy part of his palm. "McKenna Mason, and remember Henry, I'm from New York. I'll just pepper spray you and then kick you in the nuts if you don't let go of my hand right now."

Henry dropped her hand, and this time when he smiled, it was one of humor and not a sales pitch. Kenna heard Tammy give an unladylike snort from her desk and was pretty sure she had judged the situation correctly. Henry probably wasn't a bad guy. He just liked to see how far he could take things. She had a feeling that if she told him he wasn't half as bad as some of the attorneys she worked with in New York, he'd get his feelings hurt. At least she was on familiar ground here. Poor Henry, he had no idea who he was dealing with.

"It sure is nice to meet you, McKenna. Let me show you around." He reached around her, put his hand on the small of her back and guided her through the archway from where he had come. He led her to the first door on the left, which shared a wall with the lobby. "This is the second conference room. The bigger one is out front. And over here," he turned her to her right, "are the offices that are available. This first one is mine, but you can choose any of the other two if you'd like. There are some upstairs also, but I'd like to fill these first."

She took a peek into Henry's office as they walked by. It was a big square room with the normal office furniture. All the surfaces were covered with papers and folders as is typical for an attorney's workspace. As they continued down the hall, Kenna felt Henry's hand sliding lower until it rested just above her bottom.

She smiled and gave a slight shake of her head, "Henry, dear, this is your last warning. If you don't want to pull back a nub and lose your ability to have children..." Kenna said in a slight, sing-song voice.

She counted to three and then dug the heel of her pump onto his big toe with just enough pressure to get his attention but not enough to make him limp... well, only limp for a couple of hours anyway.

Henry yelped and pulled his arm back to its original location. He shook out his foot and then gave Kenna a full grin. "You're going to be so much fun as a roomie. Come on, let me show you the offices and the library. At the end of the hall on the right is the copy room. It circles around there and you come out behind Tammy's desk. If you agree to rent the space, Tammy will be responsible for answering your phone and taking messages. You can also leave things at the front desk for pick up." They had stopped outside the third office and Kenna took a peek into a nicely furnished library next to it. Old leather chairs sat around a coffee table and a larger conference table. The room ran the length of half the building. From what Henry told her, on the other side of the far right wall was the kitchen that was accessible through the copy room. She looked over to Henry, who now had his hands in his pockets and seemed completely harmless. He was a bit of a snake, but she still liked him. "So, what do you think?"

"I'll take it." Kenna held out her hand and Henry took it and shook it enthusiastically.

"This will be great. Come on, let's celebrate. Tammy! Go get us some drinks, love. We have a new tenant." Tammy gave off a squeal and a couple of minutes later ran back into Kenna's new office with three glasses of champagne.

"You have champagne in the refrigerator at the office?" she asked.

"Sure do. Bottles of it for just this reason. Also have a nice assortment of bourbon. Since you're a Yankee, I don't think you'd be up to handling that. We'll save it for when you want to seduce me," Henry winked. It was delivered so smoothly that Kenna couldn't help but laugh.

KENNA LEFT an hour later after deciding what furniture she needed and signing the lease agreement. She had assurances from Henry and Tammy that they'd order the new sign for out front. Kenna couldn't keep the smile off her face as she left the building. She looked up the street and saw Southern Charms. She thought about stopping to pick up Paige for their dinner date when she heard the courthouse clock chime once, indicating it was now six fifteen. Realizing she was late, Kenna turned down the street and hurried to the Blossom Cafe.

As she approached the cafe, she noticed the street was filled with cars. The cafe was packed. She was hopeful that Paige was able to get a table. Kenna thought of the homemade food, and as if on cue, her stomach growled. As she entered the cafe, cheers broke out as all the patrons turned to Kenna and clapped. Kenna's brows knit together, and she realized her mouth was hanging open a little.

"What's going on?" She looked over the happy crowd and saw all the people she had met the other night and some faces she didn't recognize. But there was one face she noticed wasn't in the crowd, Will's. Well, fine. He was with his wife anyway. Grr! It made her mad just to think about it.

Paige made her way through the crowd and held up her arms, "It's your celebration party, Assistant D.A. Mason! Congrats on the new job and welcome to Keeneston!" The place erupted with cheers, whistles, and an array of welcomes.

"But, how do you know already? I haven't told anyone except Henry and Tammy? It's only been a couple of hours since I left Tom's office."

"You can't keep anything a secret in Keeneston. Besides, Martha called," Roger Burns said as he slowly made his way up front to shake Kenna's hand. "Glad my son did the right thing and hired you instead of that sniveling brat. You'll actually do a good job. Now, let's eat." Roger made his way back to his table, and the rest of the patrons found their seats, happy conversation flowing through the room.

Paige led Kenna to a table in the middle of the room where Miss Daisy and Miss Violet had already placed some food. Kenna looked at it and couldn't really figure out what it was. There was something underneath some kind of thick cream sauce. Cheese sat on top of that, accompanied by a couple slices of bacon and topped off with a slice of tomato.

Miss Daisy bustled over full of congratulations, "Now sit yourself down for a spell. You must be exhausted after all the excitement."

"Thank you, Daisy. It looks great, but what is it?" Kenna asked as she pointed to the plate in front of her.

"That is a Kentucky Hot Brown. It's an open-face turkey sandwich covered in a yummy rich Mornay sauce, then topped with bacon, tomato and some parmesan cheese. Tradition around these parts. Thought it would be the perfect dinner for you tonight considering this is your new home."

Kenna felt her eyes start to sting. After an initial interrogation that stopped just short of waterboarding, Kenna was now being accepted as a true member of the community. She felt like she was finding a family again. "Thank you so much, Daisy. And you too, Violet. You all have made me feel so welcomed."

"You just eat up now. We need to get some meat on your bones. And save room for dessert. Violet made you a bourbon pecan pie." Daisy gave her a wink and then hurried off to serve the other tables.

Kenna cut into the sandwich and took a bite, "Oh my God." She couldn't help it. It just slipped out as she chewed the first bite of the Hot Brown. "This is amazing. It's like a cheesy heart attack on a plate and worth every artery-clogging bite," she said as she popped another bite into her mouth. Paige laughed and they dug into their dinners.

They sat in a comfortable silence while they ate. But as they lingered over the pie, Kenna wanted to learn more about her new friend.

"You know all about my family. Tell me about yours."

"My parents have a farm out in the country. I grew up helping harvest corn, soy beans, and a little tobacco. Went to school here, but then as any teenager thought I just had to get out of this town. It takes getting used to, people knowing all my business and everyone else's too. It wasn't until I was in L.A. at design school that I realized how much I missed it: the support of the people, the ribbing, the rivalries, and the community gatherings. It was my junior year and I sat in my dorm feeling lonely. It just hit me, how much I missed Kentucky. I missed church pot lucks after the service, I missed everyone in town knowing who I was dating and giving me unwanted advice. I missed men opening doors for me." Paige gave a little laugh, "I was once walking to a building with a man on each side of me. Both looked to me to open this heavy metal garage door to the studio. One even asked me what's wrong and why I wasn't getting the door. I realized what I thought of as macho by my brothers and boyfriends was just good manners. I thought they were patronizing me when they offered to carry things for me, as if I couldn't do it myself. But out there, it hit me that it was done out of respect. I missed the food too. I missed the farm and the open air. As a teenager it seemed like nothing but wasted space. Then, after two years in smog, I couldn't wait to run through fields again. So, I decided to load up on classes and I graduated by the end of my third year. Moved back here, designing clothes and hats for a couple of years, selling them at church functions or online before I saved enough to open my shop. And the rest is history, as they say."

"That's really amazing. How big of a family do you have?"

"A big one. My parents still live in the main farm house. I have four older brothers and one younger brother. We're all two years apart, except for the youngest. He's three years younger than me. They all continued the farming tradition. The oldest Miles started a farming corporation and bought up land around my parents' farm. He lives on the neighboring farm and is currently building a house there. Number two Marshall thought it was a good idea and bought some property to the south. He and numbers three and four, Cade and Cy, live there, even though they both bought property connected to either my parents' farm or one of the brother's. But Marshall's place is the ultimate bachelor pad with the three of them there. Then Pierce is the baby. He's at UK getting his Master's in agriculture."

"I can't imagine having that many brothers!"

"Even though they are all wildly overprotective, it was a lot of fun. They never let me get away with screaming and freaking out over spiders, worms, and muck. And boy, can I fight, swim, and throw mud with the best of them! They still laugh at the fact that I own this really girly shop yet have a rifle in the back of my truck," Paige snickered. "It's always fun to confuse men, isn't it? Speaking of men, I thought Will would be here. Have you talked to him at all?"

"No, I haven't talked to him. Tom did tell me that Will talked to him about hiring me. That's all I was hoping for, so I'm sure I won't be seeing him too much, especially with Whitney here to see him. I'm not the type of person to get in the middle of that. I'm pretty sure I'm going to be too busy setting up my own practice and studying for the bar to have time to worry about men and their intentions. So," raising her glass of ice tea, "here's to girls, their rifles, and law degrees."

Paige raised her iced tea and they clinked glasses, "Here, here," Paige said before taking a sip.

The tinkle of the bell over the door had everyone turning to see who was coming in. John heaved his pot belly through the door, and before anyone could even wave, he bellowed out, "You won't believe what happened out at the Ashton Farm."

The previously boisterous place went quiet in a heartbeat. Kenna's stomach clenched with worry. Even though she knew she had no claim to the Ashtons, she couldn't stop herself from worrying about them.

John took a deep breath, "Someone let all the mares out of the pasture, about twenty of them. They were wandering all over the farm and a couple of them were even spotted wandering down the road. Pam was on her way home from a soccer practice and had to slam on the brakes and swerve around a horse just standing in the middle of the road. Thank God she saw it in time. You all know how much damage a horse can do to a car." Kenna and Paige shot a glance at one another. They knew firsthand the danger of a horse in the road.

"Took every hand on deck to round them up. There's something going on out there. One of his grooms breaks an arm, the mares being let out of the pasture, the tractor parts that were stolen, fences that were in perfect condition having nails removed, barn doors being left open... I'm telling y'all, I think someone is trying to run him out of town," John told his friends, his eyes wide, and his face turning red.

Roger spoke up from his table, "I say it's that no good prince. He came in here last year and bought up both the McKinney Farm and the Bush Farm. I bet he'd want to get his neighbor's farm and Will is the unlucky guy to be his neighbor." Kenna noticed several more heads bobbing in agreement and then the noise level rose again as people started talking amongst themselves about the trouble at the Ashton Farm.

Kenna turned to Paige, "What is going on?" She hadn't heard such heated debates and such a strong dislike for someone as she was witnessing about this prince.

"Last year both the McKinney and Bush Farms were seconds away from foreclosure. Sheik Mohtadi Ali Rahman is a wealthy kid, although I guess I can't really call him a kid. He's in his mid-thirties, but he has been spoon fed his whole life. Anyway, he comes over from some little oil country in the Middle East with all this money. He buys out both farms, but is very nice about it. He could've given them pennies, but he gave them a fair shake, even if no one likes to admit it. He builds a huge mansion on it and is determined to start a Derby winning stable. He bought some horses from the Ashtons and brought some from the Middle East. This will be the first year to see how he does when the races start at Keeneland in April. There are two prevailing theories. One, he's an evil outsider and everything he does is wrong. And two, that he isn't so bad. He's brought a lot of money to the town and hired a lot of people to work out on the farm. More importantly, he's keeping it a farm and not trying to develop it."

"It sounds like he's not so bad. I don't understand the unwelcome response he's received. You all have been great to me."

"It's a little different. You have a connection to Keeneston in the form of the Ashtons. If old lady Ashton liked your granny, that's good enough for everyone here. Also, you came in and met people. He hardly ever comes to town, and he didn't have a local showing him the ropes. That, and there is this steady stream of different women out there that some of the old guard doesn't like. Most importantly, everyone was willing to give him a shot until all these accidents started a couple of months ago."

"So, people are just assuming it's him. It seems kinda strange to me. I mean, if he has all this money he could just buy out the Ashtons if he wanted."

"Rumor is, he tried that and failed. About two months later is when these accidents started happening."

"Oh," Kenna scrunched up her nose as she mulled it over, "What do the people who work on the farm think?"

"They all love him. He pays great, hires locals, and gives them benefits."

"I think I'll have to reserve judgment. But I'm inclined to agree that he shouldn't be held accountable until there's proof."

"That's what I think too. I've seen him a couple of times and he always seems like he's trying to fit in. Anyway," Paige said, indicating the change of topic, "I need to head into Lexington to get some supplies for the store. I'll probably head out there in the next couple of days, so give me a call if you want to come to the big city," she said laughing.

"Thanks, I will. That may be a good study break." Kenna stared down at the empty pie plate. She felt full and tired. The excitement of the day was starting to wear off and she was ready for bed. "I think I'm going to head back to Lily's and go to bed." Kenna gave Paige a hug goodbye and waved to the remaining patrons on her way out.

Her thoughts kept returning to Will. But she redirected them, reminding herself that Whitney was there for him and she couldn't be drooling after a married man. She turned her thoughts to what a fun night she had. Paige was turning out to be a great friend, but that made her miss Danielle even more. The last time she'd seen her best friend was in a dark parking garage while they were fleeing the GTH offices. They had agreed to toss their cell phones and contact each other via web email, hopeful that the GTH private investigator couldn't find them.

Kenna walked up the hill to the bed and breakfast, trying to push both Will and New York from her mind. Instead she filled it with

thoughts of how to design her new office and the best way to prepare
for the bar exam. Kenna opened the door to her room and changed
into her pajamas. She washed her face and brushed out her hair. Her
eyes kept darting to the laptop sitting on top of the dresser. Finally
giving in, Kenna grabbed it and sat in the middle of her bed. She
signed onto her free email account and saw one message in the inbox.
She clicked on the new message and brought it up. It was from Ron
Fox, not Danielle. But then Kenna laughed, "Clever Danielle." Ron
Fox was this sweet old man who had been a client of Kenna's at GTH
and as her paralegal, Dani would know that. He was a low profile
client, so the big wigs wouldn't recognize the name. Kenna looked at
the body of the letter and read,

"DEAR MS. MASON,

    *I seem to be in need of your legal services again. I have recently retired
and believe my company is trying to get me to come back. They appear to
have put a tail on me and are trying to track me. I've moved to using only
cash and tossed all electronics I previously had. But I can feel that they are
getting close to trying to force me to come back to the company. So far, no
direct contact has been made. There have been shadows outside my door
and they've knocked at my new apartment door. I had to leave through the
back once when they were persistent and I found a new place to sleep.*

    *I'm hopeful you aren't having the same problems. Please let me know
how you are and if you think you can help me.*"

KENNA PROCESSED THE EMAIL. It appeared that Danielle was safe, for
the moment. But they were closing in on her. She hit reply and
started typing,

"DEAR MR. FOX,

    *I'm always available to help such a loyal client. I am happy to report
that I still have a good relationship with my firm. I would advise you to*

leave the area immediately. Maybe take a vacation to one of the places you always wished to travel to. I can wire funds or mail a cashier's check to assist you on your vacation if needed. Please let me know if you require anything further and know I'm always here to help."

KENNA TOOK a breath and then logged off the internet. Neither message gave away a location, but she was sure that Danielle was still in the city and hoped she'd get out soon. GTH hired the best and they would track her down in the city sooner or later.

Kenna got up, put away her laptop, and turned off the lights. She pulled back the heavy comforter and climbed into the huge bed. Just an hour ago, she felt love and support. Now, she felt cold and alone. She closed her eyes and hoped sleep would come.

CHAPTER 7

KENNA LOOKED up from her desk and if she leaned far enough to the right she could see into the reception area. Danielle De Luca was sitting at the desk in front of the elevators answering the phone. Kenna's office was on the ninth floor of the huge office building. The seventh floor was the lobby and client conference rooms. Floor eight housed the associates. Floor nine hosted the junior partners and the attorney conference room. The tenth floor housed the senior partners. On the sixth floor, there was a kitchen and a private gym for the members of Greendale, Thacker and Hitchem, GTH for short, to help keep them sane.

Kenna looked down at the signed settlement agreement in her hands and smiled. She had just settled a mediocre pharmaceutical neglect case for five point five million dollars. It was a good day. Even the fact that GTH was hosting one of their "guys' nights" didn't bother her. GTH hosted a poker night once a month with the equity senior partners who liked strippers, or as she was informed by Bob Greendale, the senior partner of GTH, she was being politically incorrect to refer to them as strippers. The 'professional clothing removal experts' hosted these poker nights and entertained the private VIPs, including local and federal judges, as well as certain higher ups in the city and state offices. Kenna never approved of these events and was pretty sure laws were being broken. They were undeniably in breach of ethical rules. But the senior partners made it clear. If she wanted to keep her job, then she had to keep her mouth shut. In order to do that, Kenna made sure to be out of the office well before their night started.

Tonight that was going to be easy to do. It was her twenty-ninth birthday. Kenna stood up and straightened her red designer business suit and slipped her matching Manolo Blahniks back on. She shut down her computer and carried the settlement statement out to Danielle.

"Hey, I just finished the Raymond case. It's ready to be closed. Settled for five point five mil."

Danielle turned from the filing cabinet and gave Kenna a high five. "Congrats, girl! I thought you'd only get a million out of them. I don't know how you do it. Are you sure you didn't sleep with opposing counsel? He was definitely doable," Danielle winked. "If not, girl, you gotta get me his number!"

Danielle was a twenty-seven-year-old knockout, a teen beauty queen. She stood just under six feet and had the most amazing olive colored skin and piercing blue eyes under her fashionably cut, black hair. Her mother was a professional skier from Maine and had met her father at an Aspen event. Her mom had fallen in love, given up skiing, and moved to Italy where her father owned a small vineyard. When Danielle turned thirteen, they had moved to New York City where Danielle attended school and did the beauty pageant circuit. She went to college part-time while working as a model for car lots and supermarket openings. She managed to get her degree in paralegal studies when her parents moved back to Italy. Danielle was the lead paralegal for the junior partners and in charge of fifteen other junior paralegals. That meant that she got to pick and choose whom she worked for. Danielle chose to work for the one female breaking rank, and Kenna was forever grateful.

"You excited about your birthday tonight?" Danielle asked as she went to file the Raymond case away in the wall of filing cabinets that sat behind her desk.

"I can't believe I'm entering the last year in my twenties. You're coming to The Zone, right?" she asked Danielle.

"You bet. That's the only way I can get into that club!"

Danielle moved to close the file cabinet and Kenna chuckled, "Yeah, right. All you would have to do is wink at the bouncer and you'd be in the place so fast the line wouldn't have time to moan and complain!"

"So, is Chad going to be there tonight?" Danielle asked. Chad Taylor was the vice president of one of the largest lobbying firms in the City. He was everything a boyfriend should be: six feet tall, athletically fit, and blonde hair cut short to show off his perfectly sculpted face. Danielle liked to call him a pretty boy. Kenna just thought him attractive and someone who got her schedule. He was friends with Bob Greendale and had lobbied for special interests for the firm before. Bob had introduced her to him at the celebration party after winning a class action lawsuit against a long term care facility in February. They had hit it off instantly and had been seeing each other once or twice a week for the past two months.

"Yeah, he is. It'll be nice to see him again. The Raymond case has kept me so busy that I haven't had time to see Chad all week," Kenna answered as she pulled on her coat and gloves. It was the beginning of February and that meant more freezing weather in the City.

"Well, let's not keep him waiting! Are you heading over to The Zone now?"

"Yup, you need a ride?" Danielle was notorious for mooching rides off of people. Her own 1997 Chevy Lumina was starting to rust out and had a muffler that even the loudest Jay-Z music couldn't cover up. But it was the first thing Dani had bought with her own money. Being a symbol of her fierce, independent nature, Danielle just couldn't come to terms with trading it in yet.

Kenna and Danielle rode the elevator down to the parking garage and walked to Kenna's car parked in her reserved place by the door. They got in and took off for the hottest new club in town. She and

Danielle were the last to arrive at The Zone. Cheers went up as Kenna walked in and took a bow.

"That's right, ladies and gentlemen. I'm getting older and wiser, and so we must drink to my dotage!" Another round of cheers went up from the associates, junior partners and a lot of the support staff. However, none of the partners had bothered to show up. Kenna caught Chad's eye as he smoothly rose from the VIP table and walked over to plant a chaste kiss on her cheek.

"Hey, Sweetheart, we were wondering if you were going to stand us up for that case you've been working on." He smiled and his straight, dentist-bleached teeth twinkled.

"Sorry to keep you waiting. I was able to settle the Raymond case just an hour ago." Chad led her through the crowd where she greeted all her co-workers. Chad ordered her favorite drink, a sparkling peach martini. As they sat at the reserved table with Danielle and some friends from the office, they chatted, laughed, and talked office politics. Kenna finished her drink and frowned, "The birthday girl can't have an empty drink. It's against the law. Chad, why don't we both get another round for the table?"

"I'm sorry to do this, sweetie. I got a text from the office. Something has come up and I need to meet with a couple of senators. I'm taking the late train to D.C. and will be out of town until Monday." Chad faked a pout and gave her knee a squeeze. Kenna managed to hide her eye roll. She hated the pout. It just rubbed her the wrong way.

"Can't you stay longer? I've only been here an hour and I haven't been able to see you much recently," she asked with a hint of a whine to her voice. She stopped and cringed. She was not a whiner, so she decided to blame that on the sparkling peach martini.

"Sorry, but it can't wait. I'll call you when I get back in town. I only have twenty minutes to get to the train station, so I have to go, babe." He leaned over and kissed her goodbye, his hand sliding up her skirt and around her thigh. "Think of me and miss me."

She watched him slide out from behind the table and turn to give her a wink, "Happy Birthday," he said as he put on his coat and left.

Kenna sighed. Maybe it was time to cut Chad loose. Maybe it was time for her to just have a good time. This wasn't the time to think about it, though. It was a Friday night. It was her birthday. She had just settled a big case, so she was going to have another drink and hang with her friends.

Kenna and Danielle hit the dance floor, dancing together until they got separated by two hunks. Why not? This was her birthday, after all. Danielle and Kenna made their way back to the table after getting worn out from a couple of crazy dances.

"Damn!" Kenna guessed the look of dismay was easy to read on her face because she knew the music was too loud for Danielle to hear. Danielle raised an eyebrow to her as if to see what was wrong.

Having to raise her voice over the music, she yelled to Danielle, "I left the Lawrence file at the office. I need to take it home with me tonight so I can start work on it tomorrow. That means I have to go back to the office tonight." She stuck out her lip in a pout and for dramatic measure she stomped a foot. She broke out laughing, not being able to keep the facade going.

"Bummer. Hey, when you're ready to leave, do you think you can take me back to the office so I can pick up my car?" Danielle asked.

Kenna nodded yes in response and picked up her third martini.

Two hours later she was ready to go. She signaled Danielle and the two of them linked arms as they went outside to wait for the valet. She turned to Danielle, "I think I'm going to break it off with Chad." She knew she caught Danielle unaware by the way her head snapped around.

"Dude, what? You were just gushing over him at the office this evening. What happened?"

"I think our schedules are too crazy. Besides, he texted me eight times in the last hour. Apparently the first text came when I was dancing and I didn't answer back. So I got three more texts wanting to know why I wasn't responding and what was I doing. Then they just got a little weird, saying things like I was punishing him for going away. It wasn't that at all, I was just having a good time with you and my friends. I didn't want to text him the whole time he was on the train. I just think he's insecure and clingy at times. Maybe I'm rushing the break-up and maybe it's the three martinis speaking, but I just feel like I want my life to go off in a new direction."

Kenna pulled into the parking garage beneath the building and heard Danielle cursing under her breath. "Such ugly words from such a pretty girl," Kenna said to Danielle in the snootiest voice she could manage.

"I must've left my car keys in my desk, because I can't find them in my purse. I'll just come up with you and look for them. They have to be up there somewhere," Danielle said as they both got out of the car. Kenna and Danielle rode the elevator to the ninth floor, amusing each other with stories from the club. When the doors opened, Kenna noticed that the lights were still on.

"I guess I forgot to hit the switch when I left," Danielle murmured.

"I'll get that file from my office while you look for your keys and I'll meet you back at the elevator in a couple of minutes," she said to Danielle as she walked across the marble entranceway. She turned to her right and made the short dogleg to her office.

She unlocked her door and sat at her desk, searching for the file buried under stacks of messages and notes that were piled around. Finding the file, she turned off her lamp and picked up her keys. As she was locking her door, she cocked her head. She could've sworn she heard a scream coming from the back conference room. She shook her head. Deciding she was hearing things, she locked her door. Before she could turn back to the lobby, she heard it again. This time she was sure it was coming from the conference room. She went further down the hall, her Manolos not making a sound on the thick Persian carpet as she passed cubicles on the right and the other junior partners' offices on her left.

The steady thump of dance music assaulted her ears as she approached the conference room. It was a glass-enclosed room that ran the length of the building. It hosted the company meetings where all hundred plus attorneys tried to squeeze in for meetings. Not knowing what she'd find, she slowed her steps as she approached the last cubicle. Once she got to that point, she'd be able to look into the conference room. Knowing it must have to do with the equity partners' guy night, she didn't want to be seen, so she ducked into the cubicle and slowly raised her head over the top. Her heart was pounding and her palms were starting to sweat. Her breathing seemed to be so loud she thought they'd be able to hear her. Bob made it clear to everyone that these nights were privileged. If you weren't invited, then you better not be seen there.

When she looked in to the conference room, she saw a professional clothes removal expert up on the table with Bob and about 15 other men leering at her while they were watching her dance. "Ah, poker night," she mumbled as she let out a breath. Nothing too serious besides the dents the stripper was leaving on the table. She marched her way up and down the table like a runway. Kenna was about to turn around and duck out of the cubicle to head home when the girl on the table screamed again. Kenna popped her head back up and saw the stripper backing away, shaking her head as if saying "No." The sea of men parted and Chad approached the dancer.

"What the hell?" she said under her breath. She stopped herself from going in and cussing him out when she saw him reach up to grab the dancer's legs. He jerked them toward him, making the girl fall onto her back. The table shook and the air was knocked out of the girl. She lay still on the table, her blonde hair fanned out on the dark mahogany wood. Her legs were spread and dangling off the table, Chad's hands still on each calf where he had pulled them out from under her. The conference room erupted. Not in outrage like she thought, but in whistles, hoots, and cheers. Chad ran his hands slowly up her legs and stopped at the waistband of her black g-string. The dancer was struggling to breathe again, and then she started to thrash her arms and legs, trying to shake Chad off of her.

This was not right. Waves of panic came upon Kenna as she realized what was going to happen to the girl. The worst part was the smile she saw on Chad's face, his fake tan making his bleached white teeth look animalistic. With one hand, he ripped the g-string off and tossed it into the crowd of men. She recognized some of the partners, a couple of sitting judges from the appeals court, and even one from the Supreme Court. She was also pretty sure that one of the men was a U.S. Senator. Chad used one hand to cup the stripper's bare mound and his other hand went to her breast where he squeezed it so tightly that it elicited another scream from the girl. He ripped off the silver sequined bikini top and used both hands to squeeze her breasts so hard that even Kenna cringed. The dancer screamed again and started to struggle.

She couldn't help it anymore. She had to do something. She looked around the cubicle and found the phone. Hoping no one would notice the line light appear on the conference room phone, she picked it up and dialed 9-1-1. When the operator came on, Kenna gave the address and the location of the conference room in a whispered voice. She told the operator she was witnessing a rape. When the operator asked her name, she gave it. The operator asked her what was going on. So she raised her head again and looked into the room. Chad had one of his big hands around the girl's pale throat. She was kicking and trying to hit him with her arms and legs, but a couple of the men had moved up to pin her flailing arms down. Kenna looked around the room for some help. They all stood still, smiles coming onto their faces as they started talking excitedly amongst themselves. The girl, sobbing and begging to be let go, tried to fight one last time. Chad pulled his hand back and slapped her so hard the girl became dazed. Chad's hand went to his zipper. His voice rose above the music as if making an announcement, "Okay boys, I won the pot tonight. I get to go first, but it's up to you all on who goes next."

Kenna's face went white. They weren't going to rape her just once, they were going to gang rape her. Fear mixed with anger and overcame all thought. Kenna placed the phone face up so the operator could keep recording. She knew it was a long shot that any of the talking would be picked up over the music, but she knew the screams of the girl had a chance to reach the receiver. She rose and ran from the cubicle with a stapler in her hand. She ran to the door and pushed it open so forcefully it slammed into the wall. The occupants of the room froze. Chad raised his head from where it was buried in the girl's breasts. With that same twisted grin on his face, he looked her right in the eye. "Sweetie, what are you doing here?"

The girl looked up to her with pleading eyes. "Help me," she whispered.

Chad raised his hand and backhanded her across the face. "I told you not to speak."

That was enough of a distraction for Kenna, and she lunged for the table, trying to grab the girl's arms that were being pinned down. The men holding the girl down just shoved her away.

Chad looked up from where he had slapped the girl, "Kenna, would you care to join us? You could go next." His voice was so even and calm that it sent shivers down her spine. Her grasp tightened on the stapler and she threw it as hard as she could, hitting Chad in the head. Chad staggered back, his erection protruding from his pants. Instead of getting mad, his smile widened. Kenna started to shake as she realized his eyes were clear and she was staring into the heart of evil.

"Chad, take care of this little problem. We'll see to the girl," Bob said as he glared at Kenna and moved over to yank the dancer up by her hair.

"Let her go!" Kenna was amazed the words came out at all, and even more amazed they were clear and that her voice didn't shake.

"Oh sweetie, she likes it. Just like I know you will. She's a special hire for rough... entertainment." Chad started to walk around the table towards her. He reminded her of a predator stalking his next kill, and she didn't want that to be her. She started to back out toward the door when he spoke again, "Now, now. Don't run from me, Kenna. Running only makes things worse. We just need to talk. You and me."

"You were supposed to be in D.C.," she stupidly mumbled as she pushed the door open and backed out of the conference room.

"Yes, well, change of plans. Just got invited for a little guys' night out."

Kenna bumped into the cubicle where the phone was still off the hook. Her back was pressed against the rough material, and she instinctively tried to grasp the material for safety. She felt around trying to find something to defend herself with. She looked both ways and tried to take a quick step around him so that she could run back to the hall. But Chad was quicker. He grabbed her right arm hard enough to leave bruises and shoved her back against the cubicle. His arms moved to pin her against the cubicle while his body loomed over her. He pushed his erection suggestively against her. She looked over his left shoulder, back into the conference room where Bob was dragging the dancer out of the room through the second doorway at the far end of the conference room. Her toes were dragging the floor and tears were streaking down her face. The other men had already scattered like the cockroaches they were, no evidence of anyone being there except the silver sequined bikini top lying on the floor of the conference room.

Kenna turned and spat in Chad's face as she started to struggle for all her worth. Chad's grip tightened, and it seemed his erection grew more as he started rubbing it against her skirt. He used his hips to pin hers against the cubicle. She let out a sob and he just laughed, "If I had known you'd be so much fun, I would've fucked you like this two months ago. Imagine all the fun we could've had. I guess I'll just settle for fucking you now. I think you'll like it. I can train you to like it."

Pulling her arms behind her so that they felt like they'd pop out of their sockets at any moment, he pinned her wrists together so that he was holding them both in the same hand. His other hand ripped open her suit coat as he reached up to the top of her silk blouse and tore it down, exposing her ivory lace bra.

"I think it's time to have a talk about what a girlfriend's responsibilities are to her boyfriend."

Kenna knew she couldn't back down. She hoped the police were on their way, and if she could just prevent being raped a little longer, maybe Chad would be scared away by the sirens. "Well, maybe you can have that talk with your bitch in jail because I think it's pretty safe to say I'm no longer your girlfriend. But then again, when I put you in jail, maybe you'll like being the bitch," she said with anger boiling up to the surface. She had taken self defense. She was a confident woman and she could protect herself. She balled her hands into fists and tested the movement of her legs. Unfortunately, her skirt was too tight to allow her to kick him. Before she could test her range further, Chad slammed her against the cubicle, lifting her feet off the ground so that her Manolos fell off. Her head snapped backwards as he repeatedly slammed her back.

"No one speaks to me like that, you little bitch. I'll just have to teach you a lesson." Chad lowered her so her feet could once again touch the ground, and still gripping his right arm, pulled back with his free hand and slapped her hard across the face. Kenna's ears rang and she tasted blood in her mouth. Now wasn't the time to lose it, she thought. She felt his hand at the hem of her skirt, shoving it up around her thighs.

She felt his hand groping her body when all of the sudden she heard, "Kenna, where are you? You ready to leave yet?" Danielle was calling for her. From the sound of her voice, she was moving down the hall toward them.

Chad pressed his mouth to Kenna's ear and whispered, "I always wanted a threesome. Now I get to have you both."

Kenna didn't think it was possible, but she overcame the fear and flew straight into adrenalin fueled anger. When Chad shoved up her skirt, he had freed her legs. She swung her leg back as far as she could and used momentum to increase the power of her knee as it swung up to hit him in the balls. He bent at the waist and lost his breath. She took full advantage and threw another knee straight up. She heard the satisfying sound of his nose breaking. He let go of her, so she pulled her right hand back and swung with all she had downward to land a punch on the left side of Chad's face.

Turning, she ran as fast as she could. Danielle was halfway down the hall and froze when she saw Kenna running right at her, her lip bleeding, her shirt hanging in shreds and the skirt pushed up over her waist.

"Kenna, what the fu..."

"Run!" was all Kenna could scream before she reached Danielle, grabbing her arm without slowing down.

Danielle spun around with the force but didn't take off. Instead she started yelling, "What happened to you? Kenna stop, tell me what happened."

"Kenna!" Danielle and Kenna turned toward the name being bellowed.

"It's Chad. We gotta go now," she said to her friend. Chad turned the corner around the cubicle at the end of the hall. Danielle's eyes widened as she started putting the pieces together. They both turned and took off at a dead run toward the stairs. The sound of Chad's heavy breathing and feet hitting the thick carpet echoed in the office as he closed in on them.

"We gotta haul ass, girl!" Danielle said as she flung open the door to the stairs.

"You have to be careful. He's dangerous, and so is Bob. I'll explain when we get out of here. Just get to your car and get home. I'll call you," Kenna huffed as they flew down the stairs heading to the underground garage.

They looked at each other when they heard the door opening four floors above them and pushed harder to make it to the garage. Kenna's stockings ripped as her bare feet slapped each concrete stair. They hit the door to the garage, and Danielle took off to the left to the general parking area half a ramp up. Kenna pressed the unlock button on her keys when Chad burst through the door. She looked over the trunk of her car as she rounded it to get to the driver's door and saw him running towards her. The garage was lit by an eerie yellow light, enough for her to see the blood staining the front of his shirt from his broken nose. His left eye had begun to swell shut. Knowing she only had seconds, she wrenched open her door as fast as she could and hurled herself into the front seat. She didn't bother with a seatbelt and pushed the engine start button at the same time as the auto lock. But she could already see Chad behind her car. He stood there with his hands on his hips and the twisted smile was back. Apparently he thought she wouldn't run him over. Boy was he wrong. Before she could put her car in gear and have the satisfaction of flattening him like a bug, car lights appeared from the level above and an engine roared to life. Tires squealed and a brown Lumina rounded the corner on two wheels.

Kenna could see Dani's eyes narrow as she gunned it in Chad's direction. Kenna heard a thud and saw the Lumina race past her with a honk. She looked back but could no longer see Chad. Not caring if she was going to run over him again, she put the car in reverse and floored it. She didn't feel a thump, so she looked into her rearview mirror and saw Chad's body lying motionless in an empty parking space.

Her body shook as she navigated her car to her apartment, trying to figure out what just happened. Who was Chad? What was this poker night? What did Bob do with the stripper?

She reached her apartment and parked her car in the private garage. She told the footman to allow no visitors and went up the elevator to her apartment. She approached her door slowly and listened before opening it. She walked into her apartment and stood quietly. She listened, just to make sure no one was going to jump out before locking the door.

Placing her purse on her Queen Anne chair, she jumped when her cell phone rang. "Hello?" Her voice trembled.

"Kenna, sorry for any disturbance our party caused you tonight. I'm guessing you were working late?" She recognized Bob Greendale's voice immediately.

"I don't think I'd call that a party. I think I'd call it a felony. What happened to the girl? Is she okay?"

"Oh, fine, fine. She does this kind of thing all the time for VIPs. The senator really enjoys the ladies, you know. Did Chad explain everything to you?"

"Explain what to me? There's nothing to explain, he was going to rape her, and you all were just going to watch and maybe have a go at it too!" Her voice was starting to rise with each word. She knew she had to move. This was a firm phone and they could track her on it.

She was breathing heavy again and darting glances around her apartment, half expecting to see Bob walk in from the bedroom.

"Kenna, you misunderstood the whole thing. It was just guys hanging out. I hope we aren't going to have a problem, are we?" Bob asked in a very patriarchal voice.

"Um, yeah, I think we have a major problem." Did he think she was going to believe his story of her wanting to be raped?

Bob's voice took on a hard edge, "What are you going to do, Kenna? You better think real hard about your answer. There were powerful people in that room who could destroy you."

Bob was right. The judges could easily fix any trial. The senator could put pressure on the police chief or D.A.'s office to dismiss any lawsuits against them. Actually, they could bring attempted murder charges, or maybe even murder, against her or Danielle for the hit and run since Chad could be dead. They had enough power to circumnavigate the judicial system to see to it that she was the one who spent time in jail. But, could she allow this to continue? Did they do this every month? She thought of all those victims, all those potential victims. Tears threatened and Kenna shook her head regaining control of herself.

"Kenna, what are you going to do?"

"Bob, I'm going to destroy you and everyone there tonight. Every minute from now on you won't be able to think of anything but me. Am I going to report it to the police? Am I going to go to the media? Will I file a civil suit on top of a criminal one? Will I take everything you own? Just remember this. You know I'm a damn good lawyer, which means I know how to protect myself. If anything happens to me, Bob, people will still find out about you. It'll make it even worse for you. Missing body and all, after the evidence comes to light with a nice note penned by me, you will be exposed. Touch me and you'll go down. Leave me alone and then there's always a chance. You like to gamble, Bob. What are you going to bet on?" Kenna moved to her closet and pulled out her set of suitcases. "So Bob, what are *you* going to do?" Kenna waited for an answer but only heard the click of the phone. Knowing she had no time left, she dialed Danielle as she carried her bags to her bedroom. She had worked so hard to live in all this luxury and now she was leaving it all behind. She was stuffing her clothes into her Louis Vuitton trunk when Danielle answered.

"Kenna, what the hell just happened?"

"Danielle, listen we don't have much time. There was this stripper and Chad was going to rape her in front of all the VIP's, including Bob. They were cheering him on. They were going to go next. I couldn't just stand there and do nothing. I called 9-1-1. There should be a tape. I barged in and tried to stop it, but Bob just dragged this young girl out of the room. It was horrible. Anyway, Bob sent Chad after me while those bastards dragged the girl out the other door. Chad knocked me around but with your interruption didn't get a chance to do anything else."

"Shit. I mean, *shit*, Kenna! What are we going to do?" She heard Danielle's voice start to show evidence of her calm veneer cracking.

"Bob just called here. We both threatened each other. We gotta get out of here, and I mean now. I'm packing right now. Withdraw cash, toss your firm cell phone, and get out of town, Danielle. You have my private email, and I know no one else has it. Email me on that when you get a new address so we know how we're doing. Keep it vague until we know what's happening here." Kenna finished with her trunk and had filled a second bag with her toiletries and her family photos.

"Okay, girl. You stay safe and I'll get in touch with you. I'll pack up and leave within the next twenty minutes. Legal Sisters?"

"Always." Kenna closed the phone and tossed family heirlooms and anything meaningful into the last bag while calling for the footman. Minutes later, she had her car loaded and watched the footman disappear back into the building as she slid into the front seat.

A knock at the window elicited a scream from her throat. Chad's face was pressed against her glass window, his hand slowly rapping against the glass...

CHAPTER 8

"KENNA, YOU UP YET, DEAR?" asked a familiar, friendly voice.

Kenna bolted upright in bed. Sweat ran off her face as she looked around. "It was a dream. It was a dream," she chanted to herself.

"Kenna, did you still want to go to the sales today?" June's lyrical voice floated through the door, scattering her remaining dark thoughts.

Kenna jumped out of bed and started peeling off her clothes, "I'll meet you downstairs in ten!"

"Okay, take your time. We weren't planning on leaving for another thirty minutes."

Completely stripped, Kenna hurried to take a quick shower to wash the remnants of the nightmare away. She knew she'd have to do something soon about the situation. So far, she'd penned a note and had given it to her parents' estate attorney for safe keeping. Soon, but not now, she'd have to start gathering her evidence.

Kenna blasted her hair with the hairdryer and deftly put it into a French twist while it was still somewhat damp. March in Kentucky was hit or miss on the weather. It would be spring one day and winter the next. Opening the window and sticking her head out, she discovered a nice spring day. So she pulled out a jungle-green, wrap dress and dug around her trunk for her brown, high-heeled sandals. Twenty minutes later, dressed and with at least some make-up on, she hurried down the stairs and met June on the porch.

Looking around the patio, she noticed they were missing someone. "Where is Julius?"

"Oh, he hitched a ride this morning with one of our friends. He wanted to see this one horse have its early morning workout. He's debating whether to buy it or pass on it."

Kenna opened the passenger door and slid in beside June. June kept up a steady stream of conversation on the drive to Keeneland. Kenna was sure she was caught up on all the gossip, who did what, and who said what for the entire sale. So much so that she could likely pass as being a regular horse person by dropping a couple lines such as, "Can you believe he tried to pass that horse off as yearling? You know him, he tries it every couple of years," and so on.

Walking into the paddock area, the sale seemed busier. There were more people milling around and certain passageways were shoulder to shoulder with people. As Kenna and June tried to slide through the crowd by the railing surrounding the sales pit, Kenna saw some men dressed in black suits approach. Everything from the shiny black shoes to the reflective dark sunglasses screamed hired guns. They couldn't have found her. Not here, not so fast. She looked in every direction but was walled in by the crowd. Just as she was getting ready to push her way back towards the exit, the lead man walked by her as if she weren't there, although, it would be more accurate to say he walked through her. Kenna felt the man's shoulder hit hers which spun her back with such force that she stepped backwards and stumbled into a man along the rail. She reached out to steady herself and found herself being saved from landing ass first on the brick walkway by a very handsome and well-groomed man. His arm reached out and caught her around the waist as she was falling back.

"Are you okay?" His accent was heavy and obviously Middle Eastern. Kenna took a breath, relieved not to have landed on her bottom, more relieved he didn't seem to want to kill her. "Please let me apologize for my man running into you. A beautiful woman like you should never have to put up with such vulgar behavior. Please, let me assure you it will never happen again." With a nod to a dapper man standing slightly behind his shoulder, the man immediately left and approached the offender. Quiet words in a language she didn't understand were had. The offender's head hung low as he nodded finally.

"Thank you for making sure I didn't take a tumble. But I'm all right now. You can release me." He dropped his arm from her waist and stepped back to allow her some room to stand upright and straighten her dress. "Again, I appreciate your help very much. Thank you." She took a step forward but was stopped by a hand laid gently on her forearm.

"Madam, it would please me greatly if you allowed me to make up for this unfortunate accident by taking you out to dinner tonight. Please, allow me to introduce myself. I am Prince Mohtadi Ali Rahman. But, please, call me Mo."

"It's a pleasure to meet you, Mo. I'm McKenna Mason. And this is my friend June Kranski." She gestured to June who was approaching them.

"It's all my pleasure to meet such beautiful women." Mo tipped his head slightly, allowing Kenna to study him.

He was thin, but from what she could tell from his arm when he caught her, very well muscled, more like a marathon runner's than the thick muscles Will had. His skin was a handsome shade of light brown and his slightly long, wavy hair was slicked straight back. He didn't have a beard, more like a five o'clock shadow. When he raised his head and looked at Kenna, she observed his black eyebrows and amber-colored eyes. He was very handsome. But more than that, he gave off the friendliest of airs.

"Please, allow me the honor of escorting you to dinner tonight."

"That is very kind of you, Your Highness?" June questioned him.

"Mo, please," he said with another slight bow of his head.

"Oh, that's so nice, Mo. We'd love to, but I had promised a friend of ours I'd bring Kenna back to Keeneston for dinner tonight," June quickly inserted.

Kenna shot a questioning look to June who politely ignored her.

"I would never dream of interfering with your plans. However, I'm so pleased to hear you mention Keeneston as that is where I live. Maybe I can take you to lunch sometime this week."

"Thank you. That would be a lovely study break for me. How about the day after tomorrow?" Kenna noticed that when he smiled, he smiled with both his mouth and his eyes.

"Perfect. I will send a car for you. Where are you staying?"

"At Miss Lily's Bed and Breakfast on Maple Street. It was such a pleasure to meet you." Kenna and June said their good-byes and watched Mo walk off with a confidence she figured was bred into royalty.

"Well, that doesn't happen every day." June was still watching Mo walk toward the sales arena.

Kenna just laughed. "True. And I didn't think royalty would be so nice." Kenna smiled again.

In all her life there had only been real sparks with Will. Life was playing one hell of a joke on her by placing a nice, handsome, wealthy man in front of her and then giving off the friend vibe. "Let's go find your husband," Kenna said to avoid thinking about it any longer.

June and Kenna finished walking past the paddock and headed towards one of the barns. Kenna heard a sharp whistle, the kind she made when hailing a cab. Reflexively she looked around for the source and saw William Ashton walking toward her with a beautiful woman on his arm.

"Oh, it's William and Betsy!" June squealed as she raised her arms in a wave to make sure they were heading her way.

Kenna was instantly impressed with Betsy upon introduction. She was about Kenna's height. Her once dark blonde hair was now starting to lighten with age. She had it pushed back with a headband, and it ended at her shoulders with a neat flip. She was dressed in a gorgeous, pale blue pantsuit accented by her diamond earrings that were outshone by her sincere smile.

Betsy placed her hand on top of Kenna's. "I've heard so much about you over the years, my dear. I feel as I'm seeing a long lost friend again. Granny would talk about you constantly." She patted Kenna's hand and then let go. "You simply must join us for dinner soon. Mustn't she, William?"

"Of course, my dear. Any time our new assistant D.A. has to spare, we'd love to have you," William winked at her.

"Everyone is tuned into the grapevine then. I probably don't even need to have cards made up! Of course, I won't jinx myself by doing that before I take the bar exam in two weeks. June is being nice enough to give me my last day of freedom before I lose myself in the study guides and textbooks."

Betsy gently took her hand again and the warmth made Kenna want to hug her. When she met William for the first time, it struck her how much of a father figure he instantly took on. Now, she found it was the same with Betsy.

Betsy opened her mouth to speak when Kenna noticed her eyes dart to over her shoulder, and she felt Betsy's hand tighten on her own. "Damn! Double damn!" Betsy cursed. Everyone turned to see what elicited such a response from Betsy when Kenna felt her right shoulder being knocked forward by a large leather bag.

"So, you're the one trying to replace me. Moving on to the parents already? Boy, do you move fast." Kenna turned and encountered the most beautiful woman she'd ever seen. She was everything Kenna wasn't. She was tall, and her platinum blonde hair fell in perfect waves down her back to her shoulder blades. Her make-up was perfect, and she had a body straight off the catwalk. Suddenly, self-conscious of her curvier figure, Kenna didn't know what to say. She just took in the perfect nails, the designer miniskirt with lace-up boots, and the light tank that left nothing to the imagination. "I can't believe you had the nerve to show up here and then move in on William and Betsy. He won't give you a dime, you squatty little tramp."

Kenna's mouth fell open, shocked by being attacked by someone she had never seen before.

"That's enough, Whitney. Will's expecting you down at the barn," William roared.

So, that was Whitney Amber Bruce Ashton. Kenna knew there was no way she'd ever compare to her physically. But June was right. She was a witch. Whitney's nose went up in the air as she floated past Kenna and strutted to the Ashton Barn. Kenna closed her mouth and watched Whitney as she disappeared into the Ashton Barn. Guilt for flirting with Will hit her, causing her cheeks to turn bright red.

"Don't worry, dear. You did nothing wrong. She's just, well, she's just not a nice person." Kenna knew Betsy had mistaken her red cheeks for embarrassment, but she still felt bad. "I know there's that cliché about mothers-in-law and daughters-in-law not getting along, but in this case it was true. We clashed on everything from turkey or ham for Christmas to her continual whining about my son. She was so mad when he stopped playing football. She enjoyed the photos of her in the wife box and the fame she got through Will. Her daddy is in D.C. too, Senator Bruce. She got to hobnob with sports figures, politicians, and celebrities on a daily basis. Then Will wanted to retire and move to the middle of nowhere. At least that is what Whitney considers Kentucky. But that doesn't stop her from coming here a couple of times a year to annoy us," Betsy sighed and looked to the barn. "Oh, here comes Will. I thought for sure she'd have him by the ear by now."

Kenna turned and watched Will's easy gait as he walked towards them, a smile lighting his face and showing off the adorable dimple on his cheek, his broad shoulders tapered so nicely to a trim waist. And how those jeans fit his legs! Kenna had to mentally shake herself. The man's wife was here and she was still drooling over him!

"Hey, Kenna! I see you met my mom." He came up to Betsy and slung his arm around her shoulder and gave her a peck on the cheek. Betsy all but glowed for her son. "Congrats on the job. I had no doubt you'd get it," he winked at her. "You want to catch dinner tonight to celebrate? I'm sorry I couldn't make it last night. As I'm sure as you heard, we had another accident at the farm."

Was she misreading signals? Maybe he was such a snake that he'd hit on her in front of his mother with his wife yards away. No, he just didn't seem like the type. She was pretty sure it was just meant to be friendly then.

"Sorry, Will. But you have to get in line," June laughed. "I already have a girls' night planned starting with some shopping at Paige's and then we're taking her to dinner at the Blossom Cafe."

"Well, I don't mind being next in line then," he said with an easy smile.

"Oh? How about third in line? The Sheik has already asked her to lunch. But, I'm sure you don't mind waiting until after that." Kenna observed that June had a devilish glint in her eye, and if she hadn't been watching closely, she wouldn't have noticed the subtle look between June and Betsy.

"That's right, dear. Kenna is the toast of the town as we used to say," Betsy said. She and June were definitely up to something, Kenna thought. She just didn't know what.

"William! I need you, now!" A shriek came from the Ashton Barn. Everyone turned to see Whitney standing by the barn doors, arms crossed and pushing up her huge, yet plastically perky boobs. Her foot was tapping to demonstrate her annoyance at being kept waiting.

"*Shit!*" Will blurted. "Sorry about this. I have to take care of something. I'll see you all later." He turned toward the barn and took off with his pace reflecting his agitation.

"Well, I think this is the perfect time to go see a man about a horse. Come on, Kenna. Let's go spend some money. I'll even let you name the horse. Then it's off to Southern Charms!"

A COUPLE HOURS LATER, Kenna had helped June buy a beautiful filly, and they had discussed names all the way to Paige's shop. Southern Charms was a beautiful old house turned into a boutique. It was a two story, brick building, painted a cheery pale yellow with highlights of white and light pink. Blue accents on the window treatments finished off the welcoming vision. Upon walking into the shop, the bright colors and arrangements had Kenna flitting from one item to the next. Quilted purses trimmed with beautiful ribbons and embroidered initials drew her attention until she saw the hats.

"What are these?" Kenna walked over to a room full of nothing but hats. They ranged from small to large, plain to elaborate, dark colors to near neon. She picked up a white, wide brim straw hat, tightly woven, with a black satin ribbon tied around the base of the hat. The ribbon ended on the back in an elaborate bow with the ribbon then hanging down almost like a train.

"I love designing hats. Some are for everyday, like this one." She held up a tan cowboy hat any man would like. "Some are for church," she said pointing to a small brimmed hat simply decorated. "And then some are for the Derby," she said pointing to a hat beside Kenna. Kenna turned to look at it. It was a massive hat with a brim that started on the left at a normal height and then looked like a rolling wave to where it ended at cheek level. The hat was covered in bright pink silk and decorated with a couple of huge black feathers mixed in with what looked like pearls along the black silk trim. It was outrageously gorgeous, and she could just imagine it with the perfect little, black dress.

"So, are hats big for the Derby?" she asked as she eyed some of the more elaborate hats.

"Huge. The bigger, fancier, and more complex, the better," Paige said as she pointed to another hat that had to be over a foot tall with red roses all over it and a horse featured on the front, looking as though it was running to the roses.

"Wow. These are all so cool."

"Come on, girls, let's get down to the cafe and talk. We have a lot of gossip to cover." June walked over to where Paige and Kenna stood looking at hats. "Kenna met Whitney today." June looked pointedly at Paige.

"Eww. Sorry, honey. For that kind of trauma, I say we skip dinner and order a whole bunch of desserts. Let me just race upstairs and get my coat." Paige turned to head up the ornate staircase that sat in the front of the shop.

"What is upstairs?" Kenna asked as Paige started up the stairs.

"I am. I live upstairs. Very convenient. Almost never late for work."

THE LADIES ARRIVED at the cafe and were shown to a booth in the back by Miss Daisy. "I heard that Henry ordered your sign today, Kenna. Should go up next week."

"How on Earth could you know that?"

Miss Daisy just smiled and patted her head like a little girl, "I never reveal my sources. Now, what would you ladies like to drink? You know what you want for dinner yet?"

"Kenna got to meet Whitney today," June piped in.

"Then I know exactly what you want. Be back in a jiffy." Daisy took off to the kitchen, stopping at every table to spread the word of what was being called 'the meeting.' Heads turned toward her as people gave her sympathetic looks. Daisy trotted back out with three tall glasses of what looked like iced tea. "Bless your heart. If you had to meet Whitney, then you need this. Now, what would you like to go with it?" Daisy set down the glasses and took out her pad.

"We were thinking of a dessert dinner. Let's start with the bread pudding with bourbon butter sauce as an appetizer. Then move to chess pie for dinner. And peach cobbler with ice cream for dessert." Paige looked to Kenna who stared blankly at her and to June who was just nodding her head in approval of the choices.

Feeling slightly overwhelmed with the dinner menu for tonight, Kenna took a sip of her iced tea and choked. "Daisy Mae, what on earth is in this ice tea? It's kinda burning a little."

"That's the bourbon, dear. Now ladies, may I also recommend the chocolate silk pie for an appetizer, freshly made this afternoon?"

"Sounds great." June took a sip of her drink. "Ohhh, this is heavenly. I love the touch of mint you added."

Daisy nodded her thanks and took off to the front of the café, spreading the news of 'the meeting' and the fact Kenna needed a stiff drink, bless her heart, and dessert. Seeing that she was once again the focus of most of the patrons, she took another big sip of the bourbon spiked ice tea. This time it wasn't nearly so bad.

Kenna looked down at her glass and realized it was almost empty. "Wow. It does go down smooth after the first sip. And it feels good. I'm all warm, and I think I'm already tipsy. Why haven't I had bourbon before?" Paige and June looked at each other and then down at their glasses. All three broke out into giggles as they realized each glass was now empty.

Miss Daisy came out with a slice of chocolate silk pie and a big bowl of what looked like bread under whipped cream, sitting in some kind of creamy sauce.

"Another round of Daisy Mae's special iced tea, please!" Paige giggled.

"Coming right up as long as you promise to not drive. And don't get into any strange man's car. One of the boys will walk you home. I could call Noodle. He'd escort you."

"Cross my heart and hope to die," Paige said, making an X over her heart and looking at Miss Daisy with all the seriousness in the world.

Kenna snorted, "Did you say Noodle? Noodle would walk us home?" She succumbed to another round of the giggles.

"That's one of our trusty deputies. I'll go get you another round, but just because you had to deal with Whitney, bless your heart." Miss Daisy went back to the kitchen where Miss Violet had anticipated the need and made a whole pitcher that was quickly brought out to the table.

Kenna looked at the bread pudding and decided to give it a try while Paige was pouring another round of drinks. She scooped up a piece, making sure to include some whipped cream and a good coating of sauce.

"Oh my God!" Kenna blurted out. Paige, June and most of the cafe turned to her, "This is so good. I have never had anything so good. This definitely makes up for having to meet Whitney." The patrons laughed and Kenna took another sip of her now full glass before plunging in to the rest of the bread pudding.

"So, now that you're liquored up and starting on desserts, tell me what happened when you met the wicked witch from D.C.," Paige said as she topped off Kenna's glass of iced tea.

Kenna leaned forward and whispered, "It was so embarrassing."

"Speak up, dear. We can't hear you," an anonymous older lady's voice said from the depths of the cafe. Kenna looked out of the booth and found the whole cafe had gone quiet and people were all looking at her expectantly.

"All of you want to know? Why?" she addressed the crowd.

"We'll just find out later, hon. So you might as well tell us. Besides, most of us have had our own run-ins with Whitney," Miss Violet said as she came out of the kitchen and took a seat at a table.

Kenna took another big gulp of her spiked iced tea, "Fine. You all want to know?"

As the entire crowd nodded, she slid out of the booth and stood up, swaying slightly. Wow, that ice tea really packed a punch.

"Okay, so here goes the whole embarrassing story." She heard chairs scrape the floor and turn to her. Silverware was laid down, food pushed aside, all to focus on her. A piece of her hair had escaped from behind her ear and she shoved it back in place. "Will was my first crush. We met and spent a week together in Liverpool, New York. My grandma and his were best friends at the retirement village. Miss Alda read all of her letters from home to my grandma, and then she told me all about them. I was half in love with Will one summer when I was almost thirteen and he was fifteen. We met while we visiting our grandmas. To make a long story short, he was my first kiss and it was amazing."

She heard some 'oohs' and 'aahs' go up from her crowd.

"Then our grandmothers interrupted and it kinda killed the mood." When the crowd laughed, she took another sip of her drink.

"Anyway, almost seventeen years have passed and as we've already established, I needed some help moving into a new town." More chuckles arose from those who were there the night they interrogated her. "And thanks to many of you, I now have the job I so desperately wanted."

Cheering went up and she took another drink, the iced tea leaving her pleasantly tingly. "Well, I arrived and Will brought me here for dinner as you all know. But did you all know that he walked me back to Miss Lily's? I thought he was going to kiss me, and I was going to let him. Then I find out about Whitney and am totally confused as to why he's making a pass at me. Then I met Whitney and I don't want to ever again."

She realized she was rambling but couldn't stop, "So I go to the sales with June today and we're talking to Betsy and William. They are so nice. They make me miss my parents, but in a good way that reminds me of them. Anyway, sorry, back to the story. Everyone stops talking and they look right behind me. Before I can turn around, I get hit in the shoulder by this really nice bag. Miss Supermodel starts accusing me of trying to replace her and moving on Will's parents. Then she accused me of being after Will's money. She even called me a 'squatty little tramp.'"

There were angry murmurs and Kenna felt a little better.

From the crowd someone called out, "But what about Will?" People nodded approval of the question.

"What about him? I left and he was with Whitney. He's married and I'm not a squatty little tramp who breaks up marriages. I don't care if he was my first kiss and if he thinks it's okay to put the moves on me. I refuse, no matter how much I dislike his wife." She sighed and climbed back into her booth. The crowd was silent, maybe she'd said too much.

Paige turned to her, "Honey, don't you know? Whitney is...."

"He's coming!" Daisy put down her phone, "Will's on his way. He just left Lily Rae's. He was there looking for Kenna and she directed him down here. He'll be here any minute! Everyone, act casually."

Kenna buried her face in her hands and shook her head. She was thinking of banging it against the table when the bell tinkled over the door. Please, please, please, let it be someone else, Kenna thought.

Anyone else... well, maybe not Whitney. But anyone else would be fine. She knew she was wasting her wishes though. The place was still dead quiet and she had goose bumps. Her nerves always went into high drive when he was near. Could anyone die of embarrassment? She heard his boot steps get louder as he came closer.

"Kenna!" Paige whispered sharply and kicked her under the table. "You need to know that Whitney is...."

"Hi, Kenna." Will had arrived and when Kenna looked up she first saw Paige doing a little wave and pointing to her ring finger and than making some other motion.

"Hi, Will. Did you have a good day at the sales?" There, nice and polite she thought.

"I heard about Whitney. I'm so sorry. She is not a nice person anymore. It seemed as soon as I married her, her true greedy self came out." He was now at the front of the table with his back to Paige and June looking right at her. Paige was waving wildly and doing something that looked like cutting her throat. Kenna shook her head and focused back on Will.

"It's okay. You don't have to apologize for your wife, Will. I don't hold you to her actions."

"But that's just it, she's not my wife. Well, not my wife anymore." Will looked relieved and hopeful.

Kenna was just confused, "What?" was all that she could muster up.

"We've been divorced for two years. My mother thought you had the impression that we're still married, but we're not. I'm happily divorced and am not seeing anyone. I am completely free, free to ask if I can walk you home so we can talk some more." He looked at her and she felt her heart speed up.

Paige exhaled, threw her hands up and flopped against the back of the booth. June and the rest of the patrons sat nodding their heads and smiling and then went back to their dinners. Apparently all was right in the world again.

"So, you're really not married?" She couldn't believe it, all the guilt she had been suffering, all the pulling back, all because she thought she was wrecking a marriage.

"I'm really not married, and now the only woman I want to be with is you. Will you let me walk you home?" He looked so nervous. He was usually so confident that she couldn't stop from reaching out and taking his hand in hers.

"Sure. I'd like to go home now." Will smiled and squeezed her hand. He let her step in front of him as they walked towards the door. As Will reached to open the front door for her, she looked back and saw June high five Paige. She shook her head at them and then shook for a completely different reason as she felt Will's hand slide along her waist and pull her against his side.

Will guided her across the street and too soon they were on Miss Lily's porch. Will cleared his throat and brought her to a stop turning her to face him. "I know I'm not royalty, and I know I come with baggage in the form of a nasty ex-wife. But what I want to know is... do I have a chance? Kenna, do I have any chance to be with you?"

Her heart was thudding so loudly she knew he had to hear it. She couldn't believe what she was hearing. He didn't think he had a chance with her, Will, who was her first kiss and was so kind, so caring. He looked after his parents, the farm and all the employees. He coached kids for free, helping them achieve their dreams. And he thought he wasn't good enough for her because he wasn't royalty.

Kenna smiled slowly and took a step toward him, placing her hand on the ridges of his abs, gently running it up his chest and around the back of his neck. She took another step closer and pulled his head down to hers. She gently touched her lips to his and tasted his shock. It only took a second for him to comprehend her meaning. She felt one arm come around her waist and the other reach up her back to pull her flush against him. He deepened the kiss and Kenna was lost to the feeling of her breasts pressed against his chest and his erection pressed against her stomach. His fingers were dancing down her spine as he opened her mouth further and found her tongue with his. She didn't know how long the kiss went on and felt the vast space between them as he pulled away. A slight moan came from her. She opened her eyes and realized the porch light had been turned on. Miss Lily, with her broom, was at the window by the door and looking out at them.

Will rested his forehead against hers, "We've been busted." This time, both laughed and saw the curtain fall back as they heard Miss Lily open the front door.

As KENNA GOT ready for bed that night, she thought about all that Will had told her and that Whitney had showed up at the sales and had wanted half of all the money Will had earned. She didn't seem to care that money went to the payment of his employees, training of horses, payment of vets, trainers, jockeys, and the upkeep of the farm. Nope, she just wanted money. It also didn't matter to her that they had been divorced for two years and their settlement was all she'd ever get from him.

Will had told her the reason she was so greedy for his money was that he had listened to his mother about getting a prenup. His parents said they would leave the farm to charity before giving it to him if he didn't protect the revenue and property of the farm. They had also pressured him into a clause protecting all the money he had made prior to marriage. And finally, they made Whitney agree to a cash payout in the event of divorce.

Whitney had been sweet, attentive, and talked on and on about wanting children, which Will told her he wanted. The thought of Will as a father brought a sense of peace within Kenna, especially if she were the mother. But she decided not to look at that too closely right now. One week after Will and Whitney returned from the honeymoon, she approached him with a reality TV deal, similar to those of other athletes and their wives. The show would revolve around how hard it is to be the wife of a pro-athlete. They would pay to have her redecorate his bachelor pad. They asked to put him in situations where women where throwing themselves at him so Whitney could talk about infidelity among players. And worst of all, they wanted to set up cameras all over the house, in the cars, and even in the locker room at the stadium. When he had told her there was no shot in hell of his agreeing to this, he began to see the shift from sweet girl next door to greedy bitch. She whined, pouted, and spent ungodly amounts of money until he had to close his credit cards. They had only been married six months when Will got news of his father's heart attack. It had been the easiest choice he ever made. He let the front office know it was going to be his last season, and he started packing up to move back home to take over the family farm.

Whitney had asked for a divorce the second he told her he was retiring and moving back to Kentucky. He finished the season out with a Super Bowl appearance. The next week, he handed over one hundred thousand dollars to Whitney in front of a judge to finalize the divorce. He told Kenna that he had never been happier. It had taken a couple years, but he had learned how to run the farm. He was able to profit on what his father had started. The result of his work, combined with his dad's efforts, produced Spires Landing, a colt his dad bred, but was ready to sell because he was slightly smaller than others. Something had drawn him to Will and Will decided to outvote his dad. Will began training the horse to race. As it turned out, Spires Landing was small but quick. Spires Landing turned out to be a Derby winner and near Triple Crown champion. Last year Will had turned the runt into a Derby winner and was only one race from winning the Triple Crown. Spires Landing had come in second at the Belmont in New York by a nose. Affirmed was the last horse to win the Triple Crown in 1978, and this year Will hoped to finish what Spires Landing had started last year.

Kenna was still amazed to learn that Spires Landing finished off a racing career earning over three million dollars. He was now happily providing stud service at two hundred thousand dollars each go-around.

Everything had been looking great for Will until four months ago. The farm was making money. His employees were happy. His mares were pregnant. And training was going well for all his new horses. Then the accidents started happening. Stall doors mysteriously opened in the middle of the night. A trainer had come in at five in the morning to discover the door open to Spires Landing's stall and his tail peeking out the feed door. He was happily eating a pile of fresh apples and sugar cubes. He had thought it a fluke until the fence in the stallion pasture fell down. A whole section of the four plank fence was found lying on the ground, conveniently moved to the side so Spires Landing could just walk right on out. Luck was again on Will's side as Spires Landing was scheduled to be bred that day and had never left the breeding barn.

Will hired additional guards to patrol at night, but they turned up nothing. Accidents continued to happen though. The engine on one of the tractors was damaged so it was unusable, and more fences were torn down. He was left with having to drive the fence lines, over fifteen hundred acres worth of fence line, every morning before the horses were let out. But that still didn't do anything to protect the hundreds of horses that were kept in pastures day and night. He had almost one hundred employees all trying to figure out who was doing this.

That was where Will thought Prince Mohtadi Ali Rahman came in. He had approached Will just two months before the accidents started, wanting to buy his farm and horse operation. Will and his family turned him down. He tried once more, offering an ungodly amount of money. But this was Will's family heritage and they couldn't sell it. Mo seemed to take it in stride, buying the two horse farms next to the Ashton Farm instead. It was after he moved in that the accidents started. Will figured Mo didn't like losing. When money didn't work, he had his security force start these attacks on the farm in hopes that they'd change their minds and sell.

Kenna didn't agree with his theory of Mo being behind the problems. But she knew not to argue until she had proof, one way or another.

Will's parting words still caused heat to flood her belly though, "Mo isn't going to get the farm and he sure as hell isn't going to get you."

Kenna closed her eyes and dreamt about sweet kisses and horses eating apples.

CHAPTER 9

THE NEXT FIVE days flew by for Kenna. She woke up at six in the morning, took a hot shower to wake up, and started studying. At eight, Miss Lily would send a tray up with breakfast and orange juice. Kenna ate while studying Kentucky law. She studied property law, criminal law, civil law, ethics, family law, court procedures, tax law, estate law and so much more that it was all starting to run together.

Paige or Betsy would come over with a late lunch, giving Kenna a thirty minute break. Kenna bored them to death with conversations based on what she was reading. Then it was off to take a practice test and review the incorrect answers before Will arrived for dinner around eight at night. After studying for twelve hours a day, she made herself stop when Will came over. They would go out on a date at the cafe or drive into Lexington for dinner and a movie. They talked, laughed, and kissed whenever out of sight of the Rose sisters.

It became a joke between them to see how long they could kiss good-bye on the porch before Miss Lily turned the light on or came out to sweep imaginary leaves off the steps. She'd then usher Kenna inside, asking about how the date had gone and how studying was going, all while scolding Will for being fresh.

. . .

KENNA PUT on a spring skirt and polo shirt. She spun around the room. Today was her last break. She had studied all morning and now Mo was sending a limo to pick her up for their lunch date. Will wasn't thrilled when she told him about her lunch, but she swore it was strictly friendly. He trusted her, so he didn't even try to stop her. Maybe he knew if he had tried, their relationship would be damaged. Working in a male dominated field made it real easy to have male friends, and Will was trying to accept it. McKenna knew the reason wasn't because Mo was male. It was because Mo was Mo. And Will thought he was responsible for the accidents on the farm. What Will didn't know was that she was going to this lunch primarily to find out if Mo was really behind all of the damage to Will's farm.

Kenna applied her pale pink lip gloss and then looked out the window. She liked watching the gentle breeze over the daffodils and the new leaves trying to make their way to the light. She took in a deep breath of country air, smelling some horse feed from the seed store and the fresh cut grass from the house next door. A slight tingle of worry washed over her, but she pushed it back. If Danielle needed her, she'd contact her. She had written Danielle a couple of quick emails to check in but hadn't heard back yet. Just as she started to pull in her lower lip to nibble on it over what horrible possibilities were occurring to Danielle, a huge black limo stopped in front of the house. A uniformed man she recognized as Mo's security guard got out of the passenger side door and confidently walked up to the house. She grabbed her purse and gave herself one last look in the mirror before heading downstairs to have lunch with royalty.

"Madam, I am Ahmed. I'll escort you to lunch today," he said with a slight bow of his head. He stood only about four inches taller than she, but she was pretty sure his uniform hid a cache of weapons that he knew how to use. He was friendly, but there was alertness in his eyes to everything around them.

"It's so nice to meet you. I'm sorry I didn't get to introduce myself the other week at the sales," Kenna said.

Apparently not used to such attention, Ahmed blushed slightly. "I am used to staying in the background. Most people don't notice me.

Madam is very attentive." He opened the back door and held it open for her. When he went to close it, she stopped him.

"Please, no need for me to sit back here by myself. Please join me. I'd love to talk to you some more. And please, call me McKenna or Kenna. Either works for me!" Surprising to her, he looked unsure of himself momentarily before he decided it would be okay to join her. "Ahmed, what do you do for the prince?"

"Oh, this and that. Mostly I head security because that puts me in the most contact with the Sheik. I also act as an assistant when needed."

"Sounds very exciting. I bet you've traveled all over the world and seen amazing sights. It was very nice of you, as head of security, to pick me up today. I'm sure you have more important things to do, what with all those accidents at the Ashton Farm. I'm sure you have to work really hard to make sure the vandals don't start tampering with things on your property." As subtlety went, it was a poor effort. But she hoped she pulled off the innocent face well enough to disguise her interrogation.

Her hopes were squashed when Ahmed let out a sharp bark of laughter. "McKenna, you are very direct. I know all about your relationship with the Ashton family, and I am very aware of their belief the accidents are being ordered by my boss. You are very brave to attempt interrogation on an interrogation expert. Of course, my interrogations usually involve certain... tools, shall we say." He shook his head as if fully amused by her thought of interrogating him.

"Well, we could go back to Miss Lily's. She has a wonderful watering can for her flowers that would be perfect for waterboarding if you're feeling my form of interrogation is inadequate," she dead panned. That ought to shut him up, she thought, when she saw his mouth momentarily drop.

But then he grabbed his side and doubled over in his seat with big belly laughs. Well, there goes being the tough chick. Ahh, now she knew what to do... Kenna slipped her sunglasses on and turned away from Ahmed, shaking her shoulders as if racked with tears. She threw in a couple of sniffles and a repressed sob or two.

Ahmed immediately stopped his laughter, "Madam, I am so sorry I insulted you. You are too kind-hearted and innocent for such talk. I offer you my humblest apologies."

Kenna turned her head, letting out a little sob. With a slight lip tremble she said, "I was just trying to look out for my boyfriend, you know?" Hiccup. "It's been very stressful on him and his poor father with his heart condition. You know, I lost both my parents." Hiccup. With her lip trembling again she added, "and Betsy and William are like surrogate parents to me." Full on sobs began. Kenna turned her head and gave more body-shaking sobs.

"Please, Madam, McKenna. Please, I am so sorry I made you cry. I know you were looking out for them. Please, let me assure you, it is not we who are causing these problems. Actually, I have been put in charge of trying to find out the culprits. As you've mentioned, we fear they will move on to us next."

Kenna cast a glance out of the corner of her eye and saw Ahmed fidgeting with his tie and lacking his normal composure. She turned her head to him and let a smile overtake her face as she removed her sunglasses, exposing tear-free eyes. "Thank you for letting me know, Ahmed. I'm very relieved you had nothing to do with it." She smiled wider as Ahmed's mouth dropped and started making fish faces as he stared at her. "I'll convey my belief to the Ashtons that you have nothing to do with the accidents and hopefully you can work together to solve this mystery before anything else happens."

Ahmed took a good thirty seconds to recover. Slowly, a smile crept up his face, "You, Madam, need to come work for me. I will pay you more than you can ever dream of. Well played. Well played, indeed."

Kenna returned his smile, "Thank you. You have your interrogation techniques and I have mine," she winked.

By the time they arrived at Mo's farm, Ahmed and she were joking easily together and acting as if they were lifelong friends. Kenna enjoyed Ahmed's dry sense of humor. She loved that she could replace the seriousness that sat so far back behind his eyes with a little laughter. Ahmed opened the door to the limousine for her and she was met by Mo as she stood up. Dressed impeccably in a black pinstripe suit, he kissed both of Kenna's cheeks as he escorted her up the stairs and into, what she could only describe, as a palace. White marble outlined the black marble floors in the center of the room. Furniture she knew was specially made for his home filled the entrance way. They walked a quarter of the way down a hallway and turned right into a sitting room twice the size of her apartment in New York.

"Sir, I feel as your head of security, I must warn you to be careful when alone with Miss Mason," Ahmed said as he signaled the wait staff to bring in the meal.

"Do you believe she would harm me, Ahmed?" Mo asked with a faked look of fear.

"I must warn you, she has unprecedented interrogation skills." Ahmed looked sternly at her.

She raised one corner of her lip in a look of deviousness.

"And how do you know this?" Mo was now looking at her, taking note of the side games going on between her and Ahmed.

"She interrogated me in the ride over here."

"Surely you mean she *tried* to interrogate you." Ahmed turned to Mo and lowered his head in shame.

"No, Your Highness. I mean she interrogated me thoroughly. She asked me about the accidents at the Ashton Farm. I told her everything I knew and all we were doing to try to figure out who's behind them."

"Really? She broke you? I don't mind you telling her, as I figured the subject was going to come up. But, I was hoping I could seduce her before we got to serious conversation. But, my curiosity is piqued now. How did one little woman get you to talk about a confidential matter? After all, I know when you were a commander in the Elite Service, you were captured and tortured for three days before rescue, all the while, never revealing any classified information. So how on earth did Kenna get the information out of you?" Mo asked, truly confused.

Ahmed cleared his throat and looked down at the floor, "She cried, Your Highness."

Mo looked at Ahmed's lowered head and then over to her. She knew she was the picture of womanly innocence, except for the huge smile across her face. She saw Mo fight the laugh coming, but he couldn't stop it. She and Ahmed soon joined in.

"Please, let us sit and have lunch. You may tell me all about this interrogation technique. Then I thought to seduce you with my charm, have you agree to marry me, and we can look around your new home."

Kenna laughed even harder. She knew Mo was only partly teasing, and she also knew he was aware of her relationship with Will. Anything Ahmed knew, she was sure Mo did too. "Lunch sounds great and so does the tour, but you know Will already thinks you're causing the accidents. Do you really think it's a good idea to move in on his woman, too?"

"Sadly, it is not. That is too bad. We could have had beautiful children together. Ah well, let's eat!" Mo approached her, slung a friendly arm around her shoulders and led her out the French doors to the table the wait staff had prepared on the patio.

Kenna enjoyed lunch so much, she thought about reconsidering his offer for marriage. The chocolate soufflé for dessert almost tipped the scales. She knew he wasn't responsible for the accidents. Maybe she could be the one to bring him out, so to say, into Keeneston society so people could change their opinions of him.

After lunch, Ahmed led them off the patio to two golf carts. She had no idea Mercedes made golf carts! Ahmed took the first one while she and Mo climbed into the second one. Mo turned to her, "Are you sure I may not seduce you? I am good at it you know."

She smiled at him, "I know you are. And it's very tempting, especially after that dessert. But there's just something between Will and me."

"Too bad. A nice seduction after lunch sure hits the spot. But, at last, I am bested," Mo joked. "However, I would ask your permission to talk about a sensitive topic."

Confused about what topic he meant, she nodded her head, giving her approval.

"I know there is something going on in your life that you are not telling anyone."

She felt the blood draining from her face. No, there was no way he could know about New York. "What are you talking about?" She tried to plaster a smile on her face while wiping her now sweaty palms on the hem of her dress.

"Ahmed runs a full background on anyone I invite over. I know you were an up and coming attorney at the largest law firm in New York City. I know about two months ago, on the night of your twenty-ninth birthday, you went off the grid and didn't show up again until you came to Keeneston. You haven't touched your gold card, and you haven't withdrawn any cash, except for a large sum during your last night in New York."

Not knowing what to say, she took the advice she had always given her clients and kept her mouth shut.

Not seeming to be deterred by her silence, Mo continued, "I know it must be something bad if you felt your only option was to disappear. Just know that I am a very good friend to have if you need help. Being a lawyer, you must know too, it is nice to have a friend with diplomatic immunity." With that, he turned and pointed out the foaling barn. He spoke of his hopes to develop his stables into a Derby winning one.

As he talked about the farm, she thought about what he had said. It would be nice to tell someone why she was here and the fears she had. She still hadn't heard from Danielle and was getting nervous. Not now, but someday, she knew she'd be able to trust Mo enough to tell him the truth.

"Mo, what about you? What brought you half way around the world?"

"My parents. I turned thirty about four years ago. Ever since, my parents, especially my father, deemed it necessary for me to marry. However, it was my dream to live on my own and marry whom I wanted. I worked out a deal with them that I had until I was thirty-five to enjoy my freedom. I started a racing stable in my home country and it prospered. I figured in the last year or so of my freedom, I would establish a stable in Keeneston, the heart of horse racing."

"Will your father force you to marry next year?" This was the first time she had considered how life was so very different for him. It made her want to get him more involved in the community she had already fallen in love with.

"Yes, and no. If I am not married by thirty-five, I must return home to choose one of the eligible ladies my father picks out and marry within the year. I hope to have my stables established by then. After the marriage, we'll move back here to live."

"Then, you asked me to marry you for no reason. I'm so hurt!" She gave him a nudge with her elbow.

"Actually, that is part of the arrangement between my father and me. I have the final and only say in whom I marry before my time is up. Unfortunately, I am not very good at meeting women who are not after a name and position in a royal family. I am third in line for the throne, and many women see it as a way to live a fantasy life. I don't want that in a wife. But my time will soon expire and I will end up married to a boring woman of good breeding." Mo drove the golf cart around to the front of the mini-palace and pulled to a stop. "I am sure you are eager to get back to your studies. I will have Ahmed drive you home. I do hope you know I am sincere when I say I hope we can be friends. It was lovely sharing the day with you."

"I enjoyed it, too. I'm sure there will be a party when the bar exam is over. You must promise me that you and Ahmed will come."

"I promise." The sound of tires on the crushed stone made them turn to look at the taxi coming down the long drive. "Oh, no! Not another one," Mo groaned and put his fingertips to his forehead as if trying to relieve a headache.

"You have a problem with solicitors? Are they Girl Scouts trying to sell cookies?" Kenna joked.

"I wish. I've developed quite a taste for those cookies. Sadly, this is my father's hand. He keeps sending women to me in hopes that I will not marry whom I choose but find one of his choices attractive enough to marry after I examine her."

"You mean he ships eligible women over here to be paraded in front of you in the hopes that you give in to marry one. Doesn't he know women aren't horses?" She knew there was a cultural difference, but she felt bad for these women.

"No, he doesn't know that. I do though," he said before she had a chance to go off on a women's rights tangent.

"But, for a bride to be considered eligible, she has to pass a physical and mental examination to make sure she can have children." She and Mo turned to see the taxi door open and a woman in a beautiful, navy silk, flowing pantsuit and a fuchsia silk head wrap step out. She was stunning with high cheek bones and a slim figure.

"Geez, Mo, you must hate having beautiful women mailed to you. I wonder what the postage is on that." She saw the corners of his lips tip up. "Well, I'll leave you to it. Thanks for a great lunch," she said as he waved good-bye as she climbed into the limo with Ahmed.

THREE WEEKS after lunch with Mo and Ahmed, Kenna sat on the porch at Miss Lily's, staring at the envelope from the Kentucky Bar Association. The mail came about an hour before, but she was too nervous to open it. June and Julius had gone back to Florida a couple of weeks ago, promising to stay in touch. She had spent long hours studying and then sat for the six hour state portion of the bar exam two weeks ago. After taking the bar, she had filled her time putting her office together, drafting an announcement for the paper, and slipping in to watch Tom in court. She was also lucky enough to be able to see Will every day. She cherished every moment she had with him. She was falling hard and she knew it. But she couldn't help but enjoy the newness of the relationship: the laughing, the small touches, the talking.

Kenna heard footsteps running up the path. She looked up to find Paige running toward her. "Well, did you pass?" Paige asked, sucking in a deep breath.

"How did you know I got it today? And no, I'm too nervous." Kenna turned the envelope over and over in her hands.

"Ronnie told me he gave it to you." Upon seeing Kenna's confusion, Paige clarified, "Ronnie, the weekday mailman."

"Oh here." She shoved the envelope at Paige, "Open it and put me out of my misery." Unlike Kenna, Paige didn't hesitate for a moment and ripped it open. Kenna watched as Paige pulled out a sheet of paper.

"You passed!"

Kenna jumped up and joined Paige for a little dance. "You get sworn in next Friday up in Frankfort by the Kentucky Supreme Court. How cool! I totally want to come."

"Me too!" Miss Lily opened the screen door and came out to do her own little dance.

"We must celebrate!" she said to Paige and Lily.

"Don't worry one bit about that. Paige and I have already been spreading the word that it came in the mail today. We were all confident you'd pass, so there's going to be a party at my sisters' tonight at six."

"Ronnie needs to keep his mouth shut. What if I had failed?"

"Then you'd definitely need a party to get drunk at," Paige joked.

Kenna nodded. What could she say, Paige was right. "Make sure you invite Mo."

"Who?" Lily asked.

"The prince. Mohtadi is his first name, but he wants to be easier to approach. So he thought to go with Mo. That, and he said it sounded more American. Paige, he's really nice. And make sure to tell him to bring Ahmed, his head of security. I'll give you the phone number."

"I'll call him, but do you think that's wise with the Ashtons coming?" Paige asked.

"I know you all don't believe it, but I believe it is someone else causing the problems at Will's farm. They're both really nice and I consider them friends. I really want you all to meet them."

Paige nodded, "Fine, I'll invite them, and I'll be nice just because you like them. After all, they can't be worse than Whitney." At her name, all three women shivered.

AT FIVE THIRTY, Will showed up at Miss Lily's to pick Kenna up. She walked down the sweeping staircase and saw his smile beaming up at her. Her stomach flipped, and even though her heart sped up, she felt a wave of calm and rightness settle over her. Will met her at the bottom of the stairs and extended his hand to gently take hers. His thumb rubbed gentle circles on her skin.

"Congratulations, honey! I knew you'd have no problem with passing the test. Sorry it took me so long to get here. I was detained for a bit of business."

Dread filled her, "Not another accident?" She noticed his normally confident gaze had turned to examining his shoes. "Will, was it bad?"

His chocolate eyes moved up from his shoes to look her in the eyes once again, "Yeah, it was bad. One of the grounds men got hurt by one of the balers. Someone had loosened a blade. When it was turned on, the blade collapsed on him. Cut up one of his legs pretty bad. I'm sorry, McKenna, I wanted today to be all about you and celebrating your accomplishments."

"Nonsense. You are important to me and therefore anything that affects you is important to me. Is the man okay?"

Will gave a clipped nod, "Yes, after a lot of stitches and a big tetanus shot, his wife was able to take him home. So, no need for you to worry. I'll get to the bottom of this soon. I have someone watching the border between my farm and the Sheik's. I think if we protect that area the attacks will stop." Will looked out the front door and shook his head, "I just don't understand why such a rich man would do something like this. He could just buy some more property on the other side of his land. It must be plain revenge motivating such acts."

Kenna knew she had to tread carefully with this topic. Will was so sure it was Mo, just as she was sure that it wasn't. "Will, I know you think it's Mo. But maybe you should consider who else it could be.

You know, in case it's not Mo." She knew she had said too much as soon as she saw a red line literally climb from his neck up his face. She saw him look away and take a deep breath. Ugh, men... Why couldn't they look at all the scenarios instead of zeroing in on one and refusing to let go?

"I know you like the Sheik, but your infatuation with him has to stop. Of course it's him. The accidents started just after I turned down his offer to purchase my farm. I think that's a little too coincidental even for a lawyer to ignore."

She knew there was little chance at getting him to change his mind so she figured she'd change the subject, "We will have to agree to disagree. How about we just head down to the cafe?" Obviously relieved, she saw him blow out a breath and relax. It was a problem, but there was plenty of time for her to work on it, she thought to herself, with a quick smile. After all, she wouldn't be very good at her job if she couldn't persuade people.

The party was already in full swing when Will and Kenna arrived at the Blossom Cafe. She was happy to see the Rose sisters in their element. They were flitting from group to group, their white hair perfectly helmeted and they in their Sunday best. They were so very close to being adopted grandmothers. She had to smile to herself as she watched them fuss over John Wolfe. They had been welcoming but with old school beliefs and mannerisms that reminded her of her own nana. Along with Paige and the Rose sisters, she spotted Pam, Henry, Tammy, Roger and his nephew Paul, all of whom had called Tom to say he needed to hire her. She thanked every one of them, and her heart grew a little more with each person she talked to.

Will was by her side the whole time, with either a supportive arm slung over her shoulder or a hand resting lightly on the small of her back. But now, he had been cornered by John wanting to know the details of the latest accident. Kenna had excused herself, no longer being able to tolerate the speculation, and walked across the room toward Paige. However, once she was no longer with Will she had been ambushed.

Kenna first saw Violet Fae head toward her coming from the

kitchen. Lily Rae converged from the front door area and Daisy Mae closed in from behind her. It was a well-planned attack, she thought, as they surrounded her before she could reach Paige.

"About time we got you alone. We thought he was never going to leave your side," Daisy complained. "We wanted a chance to talk to you. Alone."

Kenna managed to suppress an eye roll as Daisy turned to Violet for part two of the confrontation.

"We know Will is a good young man, and you've been seeing him for a while now. Well, we wanted to give you our approval."

This time Kenna skipped eye roll and went straight for open mouth.

The group looked toward Lily. "You see, we know you don't have any family to look out for you. Well," Lily gestured towards her sisters, "we kinda feel responsible for you. We know that from your neck of the woods, you probably don't care much for approval from anyone. But down here, family is important and approval from them clears the path towards a happy relationship. When things are going well, you'll have us to share those times with. When things get hard, you'll have us to lean on."

Kenna felt her eyes start to tear up and turned to look away for a second to stop herself from crying. She saw the Rose sisters' eyes were similarly affected, their wrinkled eyes filled with love for a stranger practically. Kenna took a deep breath and turned back toward the sisters. She didn't say a word. She didn't need to. Instead, she just opened her arms and the elderly sisters filled them.

Kenna pulled back from the group hug when she heard the tinkle of the bell over the door and heard the collective gasp of the crowd. Knowing only two people could elicit such a response, Kenna said a quick prayer that it was Mo and not Whitney.

The partygoers moved aside allowing Mo and Ahmed to walk directly to Kenna. Taking a quick glance around the room, she saw heads leaning together and hands rising to cover mouths as the gossip and speculation spread like wildfire. She caught the scowl on Will's face right before Mo made it to her side. Determined to show

Mo and Ahmed that these folks were good people, she refused to let go of the Rose sisters and pushed them forward.

Raising her voice to courtroom level, she met Mo's hesitant eyes. "Mo, Ahmed, I'm so happy you could make it tonight! This party wouldn't be complete without two of my best friends here to share it with me." Giving the sisters a nudge, she started introductions, "Mo, Ahmed, these are the famous Rose sisters. I'm staying at Lily Rae's bed and breakfast. And Daisy Mae and Violet Fae own and operate this cafe. Ladies, this is Mohtadi Ali Rahman and his chief of security Ahmed. They were generous enough to give me a wonderful study break and have promised to be one of my first clients now that I can legally practice."

Mo and Ahmed gave identical bows of their heads to show their respect to the elderly trio, "Ladies, believe me, this is entirely my pleasure. My cook from France came in to the cafe when we first moved in. He had your bread pudding with bourbon sauce and has been trying to recreate it ever since. Please, do me the favor of calling me Mo. So much easier and less formal. In my life, I have had too much formality. I enjoy being able to, how do you say it, let my hair down."

The ladies gave each other a look. Through wordless communication only seventy years of being sisters could form, they turned in perfect unison and smiled. Kenna felt some of the tension leave the room as the obvious acceptance of the Rose sisters was won.

"Well, young man, you should just send your cook over to visit me. I'd be glad to show him how to make it. Is your cook a single man?" Violet asked, looking eager all of the sudden.

Mo chuckled, "Yes, Madam, he is. You must excuse the French. They are a paranoid lot. I am afraid he would never have presumed you would share such a treasure so freely. I thank you."

Impatiently waiting for him to finish his conversation with her sister, Daisy jumped in as soon as possible, "More importantly than your cook, are you single?"

"To my parents' despair, I am."

Kenna looked away from the group when she sensed Will

approaching. Will came to stand behind her, placing a hand on her hip, his fingers applying subtle pressure that sent a suggestive blush up her neck and to her cheeks.

"In fact, I tried my hardest to win Kenna's hand but am content with losing her to someone who has such obvious feelings for her." She noticed the slightest tilt of Mo's head in Will's direction and felt Will relax behind her. "Luckily, I am blessed with her friendship in its place."

Kenna felt Will shift behind her as she saw him extend his hand to Mo. "Will Ashton, it's nice to finally meet you." Mo took Will's hand and shook it. Kenna knew this was the closest Will would get to changing his beliefs toward Mo. It wasn't what she had hoped for, but at least his estimation of Mo hadn't gone down. This meant she still had some time to change his mind.

Miss Lily cut into her strategic planning and reached out to grab Mo's arm. Before Kenna could blink, Ahmed had moved directly in front of Mo to protect him from the attacking little old lady. Just as quickly, she saw Ahmed realize Lily was just reaching to take Mo's arm and wasn't a potential threat. At the same time, the sisters sucked in an air of protest. Ahmed took Miss Lily's hand and brought it to his lips.

"I just had to introduce myself to the wonderful lady taking such good care of our McKenna. She has told us so much about your wonderful establishment." He looked Lily right in the eye and let loose with a full smile. This elicited another gasp from the ladies for a totally different reason. When Ahmed smiled, it tended to cause women to faint on the spot. And being in the South, Kenna was sure the women would swoon with grace and elegance.

For the first time in a month and a half of being with Lily, she had seen her blush. Good manners soon took over and Miss Lily got herself under control, "Well, shut my mouth, aren't you sweeter than apple pie! And are you single too?" Not even waiting for Ahmed to answer, she placed her hand in the crook of his arm and reached around with the other arm and placed it in Mo's arm, "Well, boys, we'd better do something about that. Let me introduce you to some of my friends." With that, the Rose sisters took Mo and Ahmed away to break ground and start the process of building them up in the community.

Later that night as Will walked her back to the bed and breakfast, Kenna couldn't help but feel slightly at peace. She knew it wouldn't last though. Her thoughts turned back to the cold night just a couple of months ago when her boss had called her in the New York apartment. Now she realized it was a ploy to find out her location. She shivered, despite the warm spring night. Will mistook the shiver and put his arm around her as they walked up the hill. She knew she should stop right now and tell Will all about what had happened and why she was here. But every time she talked herself into it, she couldn't force her mouth open. There really was no good reason to remain silent on the issue, but she just couldn't stir up the courage. Maybe it was because she still hadn't worked it all out in her mind yet. Or maybe it was the fact that she was used to being on her own and taking care of her own problems. Either way, her mouth stayed shut as they walked up the stairs and onto the porch. Her secret would stay another day - hell, who was she kidding, at least a week.

Not wanting the darkness to creep in and flood the happy memories of tonight, she did the one thing she knew would push them into the back of her mind. She looked up at Will, who was quietly looking down at her. Despite not knowing what she was contemplating, he knew he didn't need to fill the quiet with worthless chatter. She ran a finger over his masculine jaw line. Her finger glided over the stubble as she reached his chin and moved up to trace her finger gently over his lips. He opened his mouth and gently sucked her finger into his mouth, his darkening eyes never leaving hers. His tongue swirled over her finger as he sucked on it.

Kenna placed her other hand on his stomach and traced the muscles running down to the waistband of his jeans, her fingertips sliding under the waistband as he forcibly removed her finger from his mouth and replaced it with her lips.

This time he wasn't gentle. He hauled her up against him so that she was standing on her toes, his hands kneading her ass as his tongue plunged into her mouth. Her breasts were smashed against his chest and yet she couldn't get close enough to him. Kenna hooked her leg around his waist and tangled her hands in his short hair, trying to pull him closer. The apex of her thighs rode the hard denim clad length of his erection. As she moved up and down it, he used his hands on her ass to pull her tighter against him. She couldn't hear the moan coming from him, but she felt the rumble in his chest and knew she was echoing it.

Will removed one hand from her bottom, and she about jumped out of her skin in anticipation as she felt him move his hand to her stomach and slide it upwards to her breasts. He was going so slowly that the anticipation had her shaking. His thumb brushed the underside of her breast, and she sucked in a breath and held it, waiting for him to explore further. A flood of light hit her eyes just as he was moving to cup her breast, and suddenly, she was hit with something cold and wet.

Sputtering, she and Will jumped apart. "Oh dear. I didn't know you two were out here. I was just emptying this flower vase. Well, since you're home, my dear, let's get you inside and get you dried off. It looks plenty warm out there, but we don't want to take a chance of you catching a cold, now do we, William?"

Will shook his head as droplets of water went flying, "No, ma'am." He smiled and gave her a wink. "Goodnight, Kenna."

Before she had a chance to tell Will goodnight, Lily had ushered her in the house while clucking like a mother hen the whole way.

CHAPTER 10

KENNA ARRIVED at the courthouse twenty minutes early for her first day of work. She had woken up that morning hot and sweaty from reliving last night's make out session with Will and decided to get a jump start on her first day. She had on her most professional outfit: a black fitted suit with a white silk shirt underneath. She had on killer four inch heels that made her legs look as if they went on for miles, which, for any woman, justified the six hundred bucks she had spent on them last year. Sexy shoes also made up for the fact that it was hard to tell a group of male attorneys from a group of morticians. Apparently, when men founded the legal system, it was necessary to be somber to be taken seriously. The only way they thought they could do so nowadays was to dress in dark suits and look serious. One of these days, she swore she'd go to court in her scarlet red suit just to see what would happen.

Just this past Friday, she had stood in the Kentucky Supreme Court and sworn, "To support the Constitution of the United States and the Constitution of this Commonwealth, and be faithful and true to the Commonwealth of Kentucky so long as I continue a citizen thereof, and that I will faithfully execute, to the best of my ability, the office of attorney according to law, and I do further solemnly swear that since the adoption of the present Constitution, I, being a citizen of this State, have not fought a duel with deadly weapons within this State nor out of it, nor have I sent or accepted a challenge to fight a duel with deadly weapons, nor have I acted as second in carrying a challenge, nor aided or assisted any person thus offending, so help me God."

She did get a chuckle out of swearing to have not participated in a duel, but something about the language fit this Southern state where men were still gentlemen and old ladies with brooms guarded women's virtue.

She gave the Courthouse one last look and started up the stairs. She went up to the fourth floor and stood in the security line.

"Miss Mason, come on through. You don't have to wait in line. You're not carrying a weapon are you?" a deputy sheriff asked.

He was dressed in the standard brown uniform. He was tall and lanky. She guessed he could be around forty. The two deputies working the security line looked to be retired, twice, but were much more pleasant than she was used to. They also seemed to know most of the people making their way through.

"Thank you, Deputy," she said as she cut around the line.

"Noodle, ma'am," responded the deputy.

She stopped and could feel her brows drawing together. "Noodle? Oh, you're Deputy Noodle? I've heard about you. Can I ask? Is Noodle your actual name?"

"Heavens no! It's Eugene Miller."

"Where in the world did Noodle come from?"

He moved beside her and walked her through the waiting area and toward a set of double doors. "Everyone on the force has nicknames. The sheriff is Red. My partner is Dinky. And there's Biggy... the list goes on and on. I got mine because I like to noodle." They had stopped in front of the closed double doors that went into the courtroom.

"You cook a lot of Italian?"

Noodle let out a belly laugh. "No, ma'am, noodling is when I try to catch catfish with my bare hands. I find their nest and try to lure them out with my fingers. When they open their mouth to bite, I grab them just like a hook and pull them out."

He was joking, right? Kenna gave the smile she gave to the crazy people she met on the subways with a standard, "Oh, that's nice," response.

"I'll have to bring you out to our next competition. There will also be a carp shoot. There's usually a big turnout for that. Well, you'll want to get on in here. I'll be in there with you today, so just signal me if you need anything." He opened the doors before she could ask what the hell a carp shoot was.

Kenna walked into her new home and looked around. She'd be spending a lot of time in this room. It was large with an ornate ceiling and crown molding. A large, polished wooden bench stood at the far end. She had come in a few times to observe, but now she felt like she was part of the room. part of what the flags stood for, part of the Great Seal of Kentucky hanging above the bench. She had to walk through the public seating, then past the front tables and jury box where attorneys sat for motion hour. It surprised her to notice that there were fewer women here than in New York. In fact, there were no other women besides the clerks. Heads started turning to check out the new girl, and she saw many sly smiles from attorneys who assumed she was an easy target.

Henry gave her a little wave from where he was sitting at one of the tables. Henry suddenly became the cool kid in class that all the other kids wanted to sit by. Kenna waved back and went to meet Tom at the podium slightly to the right of the bench. He had a table placed slightly to the side piled with files he was putting in order.

"Good morning, Tom."

"Ah, good morning, McKenna. I thought we'd try the sink or swim method. I'm sure you're used to it."

Kenna nodded. Unfortunately she was familiar with it. The sink or swim method was when an older attorney would hand off a case, or in this instance, lots of cases. They stick you in front of a judge and tell you to go at it with no instruction or explanation. The lawyer either ends up making a huge mistake that gets her in trouble with the judge, or the lawyer manages to bullshit long enough to read the case file to figure out what is going on. In Kenna's opinion, the practice was horrible. But for some reason, it was commonplace for a partner to be running late for a tee time, hand an associate a file in the courtroom, and say "handle this" just before the case is called before the judge.

Kenna looked at the stack of about twenty files and sighed.

"Come on over here and meet Judge Cooper. He's back in chambers but is expecting you." Tom led Kenna around the bench and through a door. She entered a room filled with law books and saw a bushy man in his late sixties sitting behind a huge desk.

"Good morning, Tom. So this is your new girl." Turning to Kenna, he introduced himself, "Bert Cooper, nice to meet you."

"McKenna Mason. It's nice to meet you too, Judge Cooper." Kenna looked him over and liked what she saw. He had big, bushy gray brows that sat over thick glasses that made his eyes appear to take up his whole face. His rounded belly gave him both a jovial and authoritative appearance at the same time.

"We'll get along fine as long as you do just a few things," he said as Kenna nodded in response. "Don't interrupt anyone. I know big city lawyers like to come in here and espouse some great legal theory in long prose. But it's for me to interrupt, not you. Secondly, know your law, Miss Mason. I won't tolerate your adding incorrect charges or citing the wrong statute. I know you're new, so I recommend you bring your copy of the penal code with you. I'll give you a moment to consult it if needed and prefer you to do so instead of guessing. Lastly, if you don't know something, say so. Nothing I can abide less than someone making shit up to see what flies. If you can manage to do that, then we'll get along just fine. You have any questions for me, Miss Mason?"

Kenna had to bite the inside of her lip to stop from laughing. While Judge Cooper was giving the speech, his eyebrows were wagging and flopping around, making him look like an excited Old English Sheepdog.

"No sir, I'm sure I'll think of some questions after I get my feet wet. Thank you for helping me adjust to your courtroom."

Tom led her back into the courtroom and over to the stack of files. "From nine to nine thirty is plea bargain time. Come by the office when you're done and let me know how it went."

Kenna glanced at her watch and saw that it was just a couple of minutes to nine. The men in the room were looking anxious to begin. She got the docket from the clerk and started putting case files in order.

"You about ready for us, little lady? We don't have all morning, you know," a defense attorney said from his slouched pose in a chair.

"I don't know, Randy. You know women can never be on time. The more you hurry them along, the longer they take," a man from the jury box shouted.

"You running on big city time?" yet another man called out.

Sink or swim. "Listen up, boys. I'll call you up in order of the docket to discuss any plea bargains. Come prepared and come quickly, something many of you should have no problem with. So, it shouldn't be too hard for you all to get used to. We'll discuss the case. You will put forth any argument for a reduction in sentence, and then I'll decide if we'll take it. If so, we'll go before the judge with the agreement. If not, you and your client will stick around until after the agreements and we'll have a hearing. Got it?" She looked out over the sea of men and found some scoffs but quite a few nodding heads.

"ALL RISE!" Noodle yelled. The thirty minute plea bargain time had flown by, and before she knew it, Judge Cooper stepped up to the bench and sat down. The plea bargains were addressed rapidly, leaving only a couple to be heard before the judge. The first case was a simple destruction of property case involving high school seniors spray painting the school. Some of the boys had accepted pleas, but one wanted to present evidence that he was at the school running on the track at the time and had nothing to do with it, though some of the boys caught red-handed still pointed fingers at him. The result was three months probation with 75 hours of community service. His record would be cleared at the end of the three months if he completed the terms of the court order. Kenna was pleased, but her pleasure was short lived as she picked up the last file. One more to go, then she could take a breath.

"11-C-A190, State versus Tony Chapman. All parties and witnesses come forward to be heard," Noodle announced and gave a little wink to Kenna.

The parties were sworn in and Kenna knew this was going to be interesting. Her witness was a priest and a fourth grade special needs teacher. The defense's witnesses were the alleged criminal, who looked a lot like a twenty-five year old version of the geeky characters Anthony Michael Hall played, and his wife, a very stern looking woman with black hair pulled tightly into a bun. She was pretty. But with her baggy clothes and no make-up, she looked more like fifty than thirty.

"Miss Mason, you may begin your questioning," Judge Cooper said with a flick of his wrist.

"Good morning, Mr. Chapman. Could you tell us where you were at twelve o'clock on the afternoon of March 4th?"

Tony looked down at his feet. "I stopped by St. Francis for my lunch break."

"What were you doing at St. Francis?"

"I went for confession."

"Did you get to speak to Father James?

"No, he wasn't available."

"So, what did you decide to do then?"

"I waited for him in the confessional until he showed up."

"That's all you did, Mr. Chapman?"

"Um, yes?"

Kenna waved to Father James and had him step forward. "Father, do you remember the day Mr. Chapman came to see you for confession?"

"Yes, ma'am."

"Can you tell us what happened that day?"

"I was giving a tour of the church when we approached the confessional. I was going to demonstrate how confession was done when I opened the door to find Mr. Chapman occupying the room."

"And what was Mr. Chapman doing in the confessional?"

"He had his pants pulled down and was, um. How do I say this? He was enjoying his own company, so to say."

"Then what happened, Father?"

"One of the children screamed, scaring Mr. Chapman."

"Excuse me, Father, children?"

"Yes, I was giving a tour to the special needs children of the St. Francis Middle School."

"And one of the children saw Mr. Chapman exposed?"

"More than one did. One of the children screamed when she saw a man in the confessional. He jumped up, his pants falling to the floor and fully exposing himself to all the children and the teacher."

"What did Mr. Chapman do then?"

"He took the Lord's name in vain and asked the teacher Miss Benson if she wanted to take his confession. He took off when I told him I was going to call his wife if he didn't leave right then."

"Thank you, Father. Do you have any questions?" she asked as she turned to the defense council.

"Actually, your honor, we would not dispute the testimony from Father James. But we do offer a defense."

Judge Cooper and Kenna simultaneously turned to the attorney.

"You have a legal defense that allows your client to whack off in church in the presence of a priest, a teacher, and special needs children? I would love to hear it if you do," Judge Cooper said, bushy eyebrows wagging.

"I would like to introduce Mrs. Chapman as evidence," said the opposing counsel.

Kenna couldn't contain a snort and noticed Judge Cooper's eyebrows bouncing as he repressed his laughter.

"Mrs. Chapman and Mr. Chapman married five years ago. She refuses Mr. Chapman sex. Refuses to allow him to masturbate at home. Refused to pay for internet service after she discovered him watching porn and has created a hostile living environment, leaving Mr. Chapman no other option but to seek his pleasures elsewhere. Mrs. Chapman has even tried to have him committed for an addiction to sex, all because she found one magazine in his car. Mr. Chapman has not had sexual relations with his wife in three years, and masturbation is the only way to stay true to his vows. By his wife taking away all sexual stimuli, Mr. Chapman has not been in his right mind. And as such, cannot be found guilty."

Kenna noted the silence in the courtroom, "State rests, your honor." She took a big step back and decided she'd let Judge Cooper handle this one.

Judge Cooper stared at Mr. Chapman and his attorney.

"Son, that's the stupidest thing I've ever heard. Your wife withholding sex isn't an excuse just to whip it out whenever you want. Hell, if that were the case, every married man would expose himself in public at some point. In this case, it's just you. I sentence you to three days in jail and counseling. Obviously, I can't order your wife to attend with you but would strongly advise it. A word of advice: I'd make sure you keep it in your pants for those three days. Also, I want a letter of apology written to the teacher and also to the parents of the children within two weeks. That's all folks. Let's go to lunch."

Kenna wanted to check in at the office before going to lunch, so she crossed the street at the stoplight and waved to the courthouse patrons filling the Blossom Cafe before turning left and heading up to her office.

"How'd it go?" Tammy was sitting on her desk, her pixie hair highlighted in pastel purple this week. Kenna leaned against the desk and told her about her plea deals and the two trials. "You mean Father James, accompanied by a whole group of children, caught him with his pants down?" Tammy placed a hand over her mouth and tried to stop laughing. "I know I shouldn't laugh, but I just can't help it."

Tammy's laughter was contagious, and Kenna found herself trying to imitate Judge Cooper for her. It reminded Kenna of the days she'd come back from court and dissect the case with Danielle. Quieting some, Kenna made her excuses and went back to her office to check her email.

HEY GIRL! I'm guessing since our last communication went undetected, we'd be safe contacting each other this way. Hope poor Mr. Fox doesn't mind me using his identity a little longer.

I've been moving all over town, trying to find out what happened to the girl you told me about and to keep an ear out for what all these people want with us. I thought about going to Italy but am pretty sure my passport has been flagged because every time I use my metro card some mean-looking guy in sunglasses and a black suit shows up.

Somehow, I'm managing to stay one step ahead of everyone. When I say everyone, I mean everyone is after us. One person in the room was a senator. I haven't been able to figure out which one, they all look alike – old, wrinkly, dark suits, white hair! Anyway, I found some very dour men trying to follow me. And when I looped back around and came up behind them, they kept mentioning 'The Senator.' Chad has come close a time or two, and old Bob is pulling some major strings behind the scenes.

Thank goodness you told me to pull out all my money because my account is frozen. I assume yours is too. Also, we are wanted! Yup, there are arrest warrants out for us. I'm having trouble figuring out what for. All I can get when I call and put on a wonderful attorney-like voice is that we are witnesses, and the police want to ask us some questions.

But, hey, maybe becoming a wanted girl will do something for my love life. This little event here has put one hell of a dent into it! Maybe I should get some leather studs and trade my Lumina for a motorcycle. Hang out with other wanted criminals at that one little hole-in-the-wall we've heard about from the Gebbino case!

Please let me know how you are doing. Were you able to save all your shoes? Girl, if you didn't, I will risk jail to break back into your apartment to get them. Especially those purple Pradas!

XoXo,
Dani

. . .

KENNA WAS SO RELIEVED she almost started crying right there in her office. She didn't know what made her want to cry more, that Danielle was safe or that there were so many legal difficulties arising in New York. She looked up and shook her head. These were high players with lots of resources. How could they not have found her by now? The Kentucky Bar would contact the New York Bar to get her federal test scores. Her name and social security number are listed for her job in the D.A.'s office. Her only guess was that they were monitoring her credit cards and probably didn't think she was so far out of state. They probably assumed her being close to Danielle. Taking a deep breath, Kenna hit reply.

I'm so happy to get your email! I am safe and have had no run-ins with any men in dark suits and sunglasses. But I'll be looking for them from now on. I can't imagine why I haven't. I've made new friends and feel relatively safe in this great town I'm in. I'll tell you all about it when we are free to do so.

Even in the midst of panic, I was able to save my shoes. But if we get through this, the purple Pradas are yours. I think you are correct in saying there are more forces at work than we thought. I'll start doing some research as well. Maybe, between the two of us, we can gather enough evidence for when the time comes that we're found by the police.

Let me know what you find out. Stay safe.

LOVE,
  KVM

KENNA HIT send and looked up when she heard Tammy knock at the door.

"Hey, I didn't know if you wanted to see a potential client. There's this walk-in who didn't want to wait for an appointment. She said you'd have her business if you'd see her now."

Her first client! Kenna was so excited she hit her knee against her desk as she stood up. "Have her seated in the conference room, and I'll meet her there in just a moment."

Tammy nodded but didn't move.

"What is it, Tammy?"

"I don't think you should see this client. The only reason I'm back here is because she threw such a fit when I said no one was available and she demanded to see you."

"Why wouldn't I be available? This is my first client!"

Tammy's head snapped up. "Because I'm trying to protect you from that demon spawn!"

Kenna felt her face quickly lose all color. "Is the client Whitney?" she all but whispered.

Tammy nodded.

"I can see why you wanted to protect me. No one should have to deal with her. But if she wants me for a lawyer, then I can at least find out what this is all about." Kenna straightened her skirt and put on some fresh lip gloss.

Kenna walked into the conference room a couple of minutes later, her head held high and with her best attorney-client mode going. Whitney, splendid in a pale pink shift dress, gracefully uncrossed her legs and stood up. Whitney held her hands out to Kenna, and when she took one, Whitney kissed each cheek.

Kenna smiled and gave elegant smooches back on each cheek. She had hobnobbed with the elite of the elite in New York. If Whitney wanted to try to play the game of who's the biggest debutante, she was prepared to outperform Whitney if it was the last thing she did.

"Whitney, dear, so nice to see you again. That dress is just divine, last season? I have some outfits from this season's runway show in New York that are just to die for." Kenna gave her hand a little squeeze and broke out in a huge smile, "Now, what can I do for you today?"

Kenna's smile faltered just slightly when she saw the one Whitney pulled out. It was a smile, but instead of conveying warmth, it conveyed a chill with icicles attached. It was the kind of smile that made Kenna worry that she had just walked into a trap.

"Well, I have the most glorious news. But I think I need an attorney to protect myself. With this difficult situation, I just knew I had to have an attorney who understands a woman's perspective on relationships."

Kenna gave a business-like smile as Whitney dug around in her purse. She saw her pull out the largest diamond ring she had ever seen and slipped it onto her ring finger.

"Will and I are engaged!"

Kenna felt her heart stop. It literally stopped, and she was sure she was going to drop dead right there at Whitney's matching Dior heeled feet. She was sure of that until she looked up from the huge diamond engagement ring to Whitney's face. Kenna looked into her eyes and saw ice staring back at her.

Lifting her chin a notch, she kept her eyes on Whitney. "Congratulations. What can I do for the blushing bride?"

"Well, as you know, Will and I have already been married once before. I want to make sure I'm financially protected if he changes his mind again. I want you to do my prenuptial agreement."

"Oh, how wonderful of you to think of me for that service. However, I'm sorry to say that since I'm friends with Will and his family, that I can't represent you as it would be a conflict of interest. I'd recommend Henry Rooney though. You can make an appointment with Tammy on your way out." Kenna closed her notebook and stood up, "Again, thank you so much for thinking of me. Please feel free to come see me about anything that comes up in the future."

Whitney stood up and flashed her ring once more to make her final point. "That's too bad. Maybe when we have kids we'll come in for you to do our wills."

Kenna sucked in a breath but didn't show the pain she was feeling as she walked Whitney out the door. After her meeting with Whitney, Kenna held it together long enough to reach Miss Lily's. She got out of the car and walked up to the porch where Miss Lily was sitting on the porch swing.

Miss Lily jumped up as soon as she saw her. "You poor dear! How could he? I've been so upset since I found out about Whitney that I almost took myself down to the sheriff to see if Red could arrest him for what he did to you!"

"I've learned by now not to even ask how you know, just seconds after I find out from Her Bitchiness."

"I found out from John, of course. He said he talked to one of the drivers of the moving company. They were packing up Whitney's belongings and taking them to Will's house. She told them to move her back into his wing." Miss Lily shook her head and opened her arms.

It was all the invitation Kenna needed as found herself enveloped in Miss Lily's strong embrace. She felt the tears coming, and with Miss Lily murmuring comforting words to her, she didn't hold them back. She was ushered in to Miss Lily's private sitting room.

"Now, you just kick off those heels and relax a minute while I make us a drink and bring in some cookies. Your friends will be here soon," Miss Lily said as she made her way to the kitchen.

Before Kenna could ask who she meant, she knew. Miss Lily would've called Paige and Mo. If John knew about the move, then so did all the Rose sisters and the rest of town. Violet and Daisy would be at the cafe, but she knew she'd hear from them some way. Through the heartbreaking pain of the situation, she did feel a sense of peace and warmth. She had friends, real friends.

She kicked off her heels and peeled off her pantyhose. She had just curled up onto the couch when the door to the sitting room opened and chaos ensued. Mo came in carrying a tray of chocolate chip cookies. He was wearing his typical fitted suit. This one was dove gray. Paige came in next with a pitcher of what she was guessing was the Rose Sisters' Special Iced Tea as she had nicknamed it. Then Ahmed came, carrying plates. Finally Miss Lily came in with chocolate pecan fudge that she learned was just sent over from Violet and Daisy. Everyone was talking at once. Paige wanted to beat Will up. Ahmed was strongly agreeing and suggesting some very painful methods to pay him back. Lily was ranting about Whitney. Bless her heart, she was a soulless creature. Mo was morally outraged anyone would toss out someone as wonderful as Kenna.

Kenna felt her tears start again. But this time it was because she had so many wonderful people looking after her. As soon as the first tear trickled down her cheek, all conversation stopped and she found four pairs of eyes go wide.

"Group hug!" Paige said as she came toward her with her arms open. Before she could explain to all of them that these tears weren't for Will, she found herself being hugged by all her friends.

"Thank you all for coming. I don't know what to say. This is all just a shock to me." Kenna wiped away a tear.

"Nothing fudge, cookies and a stiff drink can't fix." Lily pointed to the trays and herded everyone to sit down. The group was quiet for a minute while sampling the goods.

Several suggestions on revenge plots started again, but Kenna just laughed at each of them.

"I don't want revenge. I want to just forget him and move on." She looked over to the table and noted the pitcher was empty and it was dark outside. "Did we drink that already?"

Paige giggled, "We didn't just drink one. We've had three!"

"Three!? Maybe that's why I feel like doing something. I feel like I have all this energy now."

Mo looked down at his watch, "It's only ten o'clock. Why don't I call for the limo to take us into Lexington? I hear a popular band is playing at one of the clubs. Been sold out for months."

"Let me guess. You have tickets?" Kenna stated more than asked.

"Of course," Mo winked at her.

"Ohhh, let's go! Kenna, I'll have to raid your closet though. I don't think jeans will cut it."

Kenna smiled, "Give us ten minutes." She grabbed Paige's hand and ran upstairs.

. . .

EIGHT MINUTES later Kenna came downstairs in a brown miniskirt with a tight white tank top and espadrille wedge sandals with a tan ribbon crisscrossing its way up to her knees. Paige followed in a cute jean mini she wore with her white peasant top. Miss Lily kissed them goodnight, told them not to do anything she wouldn't do, and gave Kenna a curious wink. The wink made Kenna think there was something Miss Lily wasn't telling them, but the thought died as a black Mercedes stretch limo drove up.

"Really Mo, you didn't have to do this. But I'm so glad you did!" Kenna squealed as she and Paige jumped into the back seat. Mo and Ahmed slid in after them.

Twenty minutes later the limo pulled to a stop in front of Classic's. Classic's was a live dance club that featured up and coming artists and occasionally paid big money to bring in the big names after they played gigs at the arenas in Lexington or Louisville.

Tonight was one of those nights. A local country band had played in arena downtown and were going to rock out at Classic's in a couple of minutes. The limo door was opened by a valet, and the group was ushered past the huge waiting line. They headed to the back of the club and up to a private box overlooking the stage and standing room only floor. Mo purchased a bottle of Woodford Reserve and some Cokes. Ahmed mixed the drinks for them as the club began to fill up.

"Oh, I don't know if this is a good idea," Kenna said as she took the glass. "I have court in the morning."

"Trust me, if you show up at all, you'll be a point ahead in the game. By now, everyone knows, even Judge Cooper. I'm sure he'll think you're off crying your eyes out and couldn't possibly make court. Just watch. I'll make sure you get there, even if I have to drag you." Paige gave a salute with her glass to Kenna and took a big swig as the band made their way out onto the stage to the deafening cheers of the fans.

Paige and Kenna immediately started dancing. They laughed at Mo and Ahmed as they stood still, giving each other a curious glance.

"Come on, guys, don't tell me you've lived here this long and haven't gotten into country music? I've lived here for just a couple of months and I'm hooked." Kenna grabbed Mo's hand and tried to get him to dance.

"It's not that, you see. I've been taught how to dance since I was four years old. However, I was taught how to dance at formal functions where I was representing my country. I can waltz with the best of them. But I don't know how to do this," he said, pointing to the people dancing below.

"Oh, it's easy. It's just not structured like a waltz. Something I had to learn too. Just find the rhythm with your foot. Tap it along and then start moving your hips. Before you know it, you'll be a foot stomping country dancer!"

After trying for another thirty minutes to teach Mo how to dance, Kenna felt she accomplished a great feat by just having Mo swaying to the music. Paige had had more luck with Ahmed, which was enough to have Kenna cracking up. Mo and Ahmed were being good sports though and seemed to be truly enjoying themselves. The band was great and the drinks flowed. Kenna had more fun than she could remember while dancing and laughing with her friends. All too soon, the band stopped, and they had to make their way back out to the limo. Kenna glanced at her watch as Paige's head fell onto her shoulder. It was already one thirty in the morning. Court started at eight thirty. Kenna groaned, knowing she'd hate herself tomorrow. But she couldn't quite feel guilty over the fun she had had tonight.

The limo stopped at Paige's first, and Ahmed helped her to her apartment. He returned shortly after and had the driver go to Kenna's. Mo helped her out of the car and walked her to the door. "Do you know that you, and now Paige, are the only female friends I have ever had? I am too much of a 'catch' in the international royalty marriage market that I have never been able to just enjoy friends of the opposite sex. I know we were supposed to be cheering you up, but I wanted to thank you for showing me some fun too. I want you to know that means a lot to me. If you decide you need me, just call. I will always answer the phone for you, especially if you want me to seduce you." Mo gave her a wink.

Kenna felt the tears start again and wiped her eyes. "What are you trying to do, make me into a blubbering idiot?" She rose to her toes and kissed his cheek. "Thank you."

BRIGHT and early the next morning, Kenna pulled her sunglasses down to shield the glare from her bloodshot eyes as she stepped out onto the front porch. Miss Lily made sure she got up and showered. She also supplied her with coffee and a bacon, egg and cheese biscuit with a side of aspirin to help the hangover. The throbbing and spinning had stopped, but the headache was a killer.

As she walked to the courthouse, she waved to the neighbors and tried not to process the remorseful looks they were throwing her. She thought about the docket for the morning and knew it would go until lunch by the amount of cases on it. It was her day to handle domestic violence. After her encounter with Chad, she didn't think she'd ever look at the issue the same. She reminded herself that because some men were assholes, it didn't mean they all were. It was her job to make sure the guilty were punished, but the innocent cases were dismissed.

She got off the elevator and bypassed the line. Today, Deputy Noodle wasn't there. But a man no more than twenty-two was checking bags and keeping the victims separate from the accused. He gave a slight wave, indicating he wanted her to wait. After he informed a man that shirt and shoes were required in order to enter the courtroom, he came over to her.

"Hi ya, ma'am. I'm Dinky, Noodle's partner. Today is my day in the courtroom and I wanted to introduce myself." Kenna removed her sunglasses and put them into her briefcase. "Geez almighty, ma'am! You okay?" Kenna touched her puffy, bloodshot eyes and winced at the bright overhead light.

"It's nice to meet you, Dinky. Can you make sure I have water in the courtroom?"

"Sure, ma'am. He's not worth it you know."

Kenna couldn't help but laugh and then grabbed her head to stop the throbbing it caused. "I won't ask how you know about my relationship, or lack thereof, with Will. I assume everyone knows?"

"Yes, ma'am. There was a pool going that you'd be in too delicate of a condition to come in this morning. Martha is sitting in the courtroom waiting to find out, collect the money, and then call Tom to fill in this morning."

"Where did you put your money?"

"I put a twenty in that you'd not only show up but be able to work." He gave her a broad smile that even managed to bring a little smile to Kenna's face.

"I'll let you in on a little secret. The bloodshot eyes are from drinking too much at Classic's last night. But, I think I better go put on a good show for the gallery, don't you think?" With a wink to Dinky, she put her head down, grabbed some Kleenex out of her purse, and started the slow, downtrodden walk into the courtroom.

As soon as she entered, she stopped and blew her nose. Looking out at the occupants in the courtroom from underneath her eyelashes, she saw everyone take note of her, and some hung their heads in defeat. Others bragged about their soon-to-be winnings. Kenna gave one more breathless sob and dabbed her eyes again. Holding onto the benches, she slowly made her way to the front table where Martha sat with a look of disgust. Kenna took the seat next to Martha and let out a shuddering breath.

"Well, it appears I better call Mr. Burns to come down and cover for you. You're obviously in no condition to do your job." Martha turned the office chair away from Kenna and was about to stand when Kenna put both hands on Martha's shoulders and laid her head on Martha's shoulder as if needing the support.

"Appearances aren't always what they seem. Where did you place your money?" Kenna said in a soft, confident voice with a hint of her own displeasure in it.

Martha went still, as if caught with her hand in the cookie jar. "You know about the pool?"

"Of course I do. You think anything can stay secret around here. I'm just giving everyone a show for their money, seeing who supported me and who thinks I'm too weak to go on. I have, at quick glance, about fifteen who thought I couldn't handle a tough relationship. I want you to organize the cases in the following order so that I can wipe those smug little smiles off their faces. I'm also guessing you bet against me. For that, you get to stay here and handle all the paperwork. And tell everyone who bet against me, never to do so again." Kenna let out another sniffle and slouched back into the chair. She looked over at Martha and saw she still hadn't moved. Kenna fought back a smile. Today she was going to be the victor.

Dinky called the court to order and Martha called the first case. The attorney handling the matter was as smug as they came. It was clear he thought he could take advantage of Kenna's downtrodden spirits to get the case thrown out against the boyfriend. The boyfriend was a twenty-one year old thug involved in the prescription drug trade coming in from Eastern Kentucky. He was skinnier than Kenna but wore XXL sweatpants that only stayed up if he kept his legs a yard apart. Tattoos covered his pale arms and were easily seen since his sleeves on his once white t-shirt had been torn out. Kenna knew they were building a case against him for drug trafficking, but it wasn't complete. However, if his girlfriend would testify against him, then he'd be locked up for decades. Kenna stood in between the boyfriend and girlfriend. It was customary for both lawyers to stand between the accuser and accused. But Mr. Sleazebag Attorney wanted to scare the girlfriend, so he put his client as near to her as possible. Kenna faced the victim, her bruises still fresh on her face and arms, while Mr. Sleazebag made his case that the boyfriend would never do anything like this. He blamed the bruises on an ATV accident in which she was thrown from the vehicle.

When the boyfriend spoke about how crushed he was his girlfriend would do this to him, Kenna saw the tears trying to escape from the girlfriend who was shaking so hard now her teeth were chattering.

Judge Cooper turned in his chair to Kenna, "State's witness."

Kenna immediately straightened and turned aggressively toward the boyfriend. "Do you actually think anyone would believe your story? I move to introduce into evidence, the security footage from the Keeneston Road First Bank."

Caught off guard, Mr. Sleazebag couldn't come up with an objection fast enough and the security footage was played. It showed the couple walk up to the ATM and trying to withdraw money. The ATM was either broken or, more likely, there wasn't enough cash in the account. Instead of trying a different bank, the boyfriend grabbed his girlfriend by her arms and slammed her face into the ATM. He grabbed her hard enough around the arms to bruise. When she fell back from the ATM, he punched her in the face one more time before walking off and leaving her there.

"Does your client have anything more to add before I make my ruling?" Judge Cooper gestured to the video frozen on the huddled and bloody form of the girlfriend.

"Yes, your Honor. We move for a recess to discuss a plea with Ms. Mason."

At the request, the boyfriend let out a scream and launched himself at his girlfriend, "You BITCH!" Before anyone had the opportunity to move, the prongs from a stun gun were implanted into the back of the flying boyfriend who was given a nice long jolt by Deputy Dinky. Everyone stared at the twitching mass lying on the ground and then with awe at the quick draw of Dinky.

"You need a new nickname," Kenna said to him as he leaned down to cuff the inert body. Dinky just smiled as some more deputies ran into the courtroom. "Your Honor, the State has no intention of settling this matter with the Respondent, and we ask the Court to enter its judgment now."

Mr. Sleazebag's complaints fell on deaf ears as his now drooling client was carted off to jail for five years while his girlfriend promised to go with Martha to give all the evidence necessary to put him away for even longer on the drug charges.

Kenna pushed through the docket efficiently and ruthlessly. Today there would be no plea bargains. She even moved for sanctions against those that falsely filed domestic abuse reports to improve their case in a custody or divorce matter. It was becoming all too common for a spouse to claim abuse during a divorce to obtain a better settlement from the other, in exchange for their dropping the abuse claim. These people made her so angry. She not only asked for sanctions but lectured them on the abuse of the system. Towards the end of the docket, those who thought her too weak to stand a break-up were scurrying out of the building as fast as they could.

Henry Rooney approached the bench and asked for a quick conference. "Well, I was hoping for some mercy for my client, but it seems today isn't the day to ask for it."

"Sorry, Henry, domestic abuse isn't a matter I will ever bargain on. Tell your client tough luck. If he did it, he'll go to jail."

"She. It's a she."

"Doesn't matter. If she did it, she's going to jail."

"You won't even hear my offer?"

"Nope. Not in domestic abuse cases. If there's something exceptional, it will come out during the hearing, and I'll move to reduce charges or sentencing."

Henry let out a breath. "Okay." Henry looked at the benches and shook his head at his client.

Kenna was already up to the podium calling the case. She heard Henry and the accused stop at the opposing podium. She skimmed the file and saw that the wife had attacked the husband with a frying pan that resulted in a 9-1-1 call and stitches to his head. Should be pretty cut and dry. She looked over her shoulder to motion the victim to stand closer and had a moment of 'what the...' She was expecting a 20-40 year old, not an octogenarian! His white hair was neatly trimmed and slicked back, showing the scar from the stitches. He was dressed in a suit that was probably older than she was but still clean and pressed. He had a slight stoop to his back yet seemed to be pretty spry. She waved him up and then turned to the frying pan wielding wife. She, too, looked to be in her eighties with tightly permed, gray hair. She wore a floral print dress and had a purse clutched between her hands. Kenna looked up at Judge Cooper who was also looking back and forth at the two parties. "Miss Mason, why don't you have Mr. Browston tell us what happened."

Mr. Brownston looked up, "What?"

Kenna raised her voice and said to him, "Mr. Brownston, will you please tell us what happened the night of April 3rd?"

"No, ma'am, I will not." Kenna was about to ask her next question when she realized he hadn't answered.

"Excuse me? You won't tell us?"

"What?"

Kenna raised her voice again, "Why won't you tell us what happened?"

"It's none of your beeswax, that's why."

"Oh, Harold, just tell them. I'm ready to go to jail." Mrs. Brownston turned to the judge. "I hit him with a cast iron skillet I was going to make cornbread in. He doesn't want me to go to jail, so he won't say anything."

"What did you say, Adele?" Mr. Brownston said to his wife who just pooh-poohed him with a wave of her hand.

Kenna turned to Mrs. Brownston, "Why did you hit him with a frying pan?"

"Harold had gotten a free sample of Viagra. He said it would make us feel like teenagers again. We've been married for sixty-four years. I don't want to feel like a teenager again. I want to sit and watch *Wheel of Fortune*, bake, and enjoy the grandkids. But, noooo, Mr. Stud has to get Viagra. Well, not to get too personal, but for a month he chases me around the house like a horny teenager. He starts watching that pornography and even talked about going to a strip club in Lexington. Well, I wasn't going to have him finding his pleasure somewhere else after all these years. So, I made an appointment with my doctor and got this new prescription patch to wear. It's supposed to do what Viagra does to men, but for women. I was being a good wife."

Kenna nodded and saw that everyone else was too.

"Well, a couple of days after wearing the patch, I started to feel frisky. I got myself gussied up and made a romantic dinner while he was at the Lodge with his buddies. I had the cornbread all mixed and ready to put into the skillet when he walks in from the garage and right past me. Not even a hello. He walks by and plops down in his recliner and yells into the kitchen for me to bring him a beer. Well, I still had that skillet in my hand and walked into the living room to talk to him. I told him I was making his favorite dinner, but I got a grunt in response. I told him I was feeling frisky, and you know what he did?"

Mrs. Brownston looked at Kenna and she shook her head. "That bastard told me he stopped taking Viagra. Said he realized he wasn't a kid anymore. Said if we continued, he might break a hip. So, here I am on a frisky high because of him, and he doesn't bother to tell me he no longer wants to do it. Well, I was just so angry and so frustrated that without even realizing I was doing it, I whacked him with the skillet. I know what I did was wrong. But it did make me feel better." She placed her purse back into her hands and held them together at her waist.

Kenna wasn't quite sure what to do. She noted that it seemed Judge Cooper didn't know either. "Mr. Brownston, is it your intent to not testify against your wife?"

"That's right. It was my fault and Adele shouldn't have to pay for it." Kenna couldn't help the smile this time.

"Your Honor, if Mr. Rooney has no objection, I would like to ask the Court to enter a suspended sentence to be dismissed upon proof of anger management counseling within thirty days."

"My client will agree to that," Henry stated.

"Very well. Mrs. Brownston, the charges will be dismissed against you if you submit a certificate to this Court within thirty days that you have completed anger management counseling. Ladies and gentlemen, that concludes this morning's docket. Court is dismissed."

CHAPTER 11

THAT NIGHT KENNA decided to sit on the porch swing and read a book Miss Lily had given her. She was only a couple of pages into it when a sporty little car pulled into the drive and parked next to her seldom used M6. Mo stepped out of the car and waved. Kenna smiled, knowing her friend would be here to cheer her up.

"My dear, I have a proposition for you."

"Seduction with a hangover, I don't know, Mo," Kenna teased and enjoyed the sight of the faint blush on his cheeks.

"I've come up with a wonderful idea to make the recuperation from your heartbreak complete. How about I fuel up my private plane, grab Paige, and we'll fly anywhere in the world you want."

"Oh, that's tempting. Very tempting. But, I'm not going to run from a little embarrassment. I'm strong enough to handle it. However, the next long weekend I have, I may take you up on that. How about a glass of wine for now?"

Mo sat next to Kenna on the swing and poured himself a glass of wine. She told him about her day at court and was even able to laugh when she told him about the Brownstons and about how happy Dinky was with his winnings.

Kenna thought she heard the rumble of a truck in the distance and quit talking when she saw the truck turn into the driveway. Will stepped out of the truck, and Kenna knew there was going to be trouble. She could practically see steam coming out of his ears. His eyes never left Mo's, and his agitated stalk up the walk was the final clue that something else had happened at the farm. She squeezed Mo's hand and stood up, blocking him from Will's menacing gaze.

"You have a lot of nerve coming here tonight when I have my friend over. What can I do for you, Will?" Mo had stood up and was now placing Kenna behind him. Will noticed the move and a shadow of doubt clouded his eyes before they snapped back to Mo.

"I can't believe you, you arrogant bastard. Did you think being here tonight with Kenna would provide you a solid alibi? I know it was you. Don't even piss me off further by denying it."

"I'm sorry, Will, but I don't know what you are talking about. I assume something else has happened at the farm?"

Through gritted teeth, Will answered, "You know it has. What I don't understand is why you had to kill her."

"Kill her? Who was killed?" Mo dropped the combativeness from his voice and Will took note.

"One of my old mares. She was a nanny for one of the horses who hated to be alone. I found her shot to death just a while ago. It was in the field nearest your place. When I went over there, your man denied involvement but said he was looking into it. I found out where you were and decided to come to the source." Will shoved Mo back, and Mo moved back in front of Kenna, making sure to protect her if Will decided to do more than push.

"I would never kill an innocent animal!" Mo stood toe to toe with Will. "I think it's about time we settled this. I understand that you think I am behind all of this, but I am not. In fact, I am trying to discover who is. So far my people have found some evidence of professionals being used, both in the instruments they use and from their movements. It's also clear that they want me to take the fall for it."

"Will, listen to me. Mo didn't do it. He was with me all last night, and so was Ahmed. Then he's been here for just over an hour before you came. I've come to know him really well. He loves horses and would never kill one." Instead of helping, Kenna was worried she only made things worse when she saw Will's jaw tighten.

"And what exactly were you doing with Mo last night? What is he to you, Kenna?"

"You have no right to ask me that anymore," Kenna hissed out. She couldn't believe his jealousy when Whitney was rearranging their house as they spoke.

"I was under the impression you gave me that right the other night, right here on the porch when we were climbing all over each other."

Kenna's face turned bright red, and she saw Mo move forward again.

"Will, I will not tolerate you hurting Kenna any further. Haven't you done enough to her without embarrassing her? I will be happy to discuss the problems at the farm tomorrow over lunch. I will bring the evidence my security team has collected. However, for now, I insist you leave before you cause any more pain to Kenna."

Will stepped forward and with his finger pointed at Mo asked, "Just who are you to her?"

"Her friend."

Will's head went back and he took a deep breath, "Why do you think I want to hurt her?"

Kenna stepped around Mo. "Because, yesterday your blushing bride came to tell me all about your engagement. Then I find out from everyone, and I mean everyone, that Whitney has been moving in with you, in preparation of the big day. Christ, it was so well known that I was heartbroken that the attorneys and courthouse staff had a bet going this morning to see if I'd be too upset to make it in today. A bet I won, by the way."

"Shit, shit, shit. Seriously, everyone knows about that stunt Whitney pulled? Wait, did you say Whitney came and told you we were engaged?" Will had both hands on the back of his neck and was squeezing them as if to relieve tension.

"Yes and yes. Nice taste in rings you have too."

"Let me explain."

"Oh, this will be good." Kenna rolled her eyes and sat back down on the swing.

"Whitney and I are NOT engaged! How come this continues to come up?"

"Maybe because she told me and because everyone saw the moving trucks at your house." Kenna crossed her arms and narrowed her eyes.

"Okay, I don't know what she told you, but I can tell you the why. I can also explain the trucks. Yes, she brought all her stuff and moved lots of it in while I was out in the fields working. My parents were down at the practice track watching Naked Boot Leg workout. By the time I was alerted to the situation, the first truck was already unloaded. I've spent the last day trying to get everything shipped back to her townhouse and trying to get her to stay away from me. The only reason she's around now is because Naked Boot Leg is a contender to win the Derby. I told you this before. She's greedy. She wants the spotlight. What better way to get in the magazines than to be on my arm at the Derby, and in the private box which will be shown all the time on TV. I'm suddenly becoming famous again, and she wants that spotlight. I just didn't realize how badly she wants it." Will ran his hand over his head and through his short hair.

Mo stepped forward and placed a kiss on Kenna's cheek. "I will leave you two to discuss this. Call me if you need me." He turned to Will, "Kenna's not alone anymore. Hurt her and you have many people to answer to. As for your other problems, let's meet tomorrow at Kenna's office at noon to discuss them. And bring a picture of Whitney for my security staff. If she's that nuts over your money, I would hate to see what she would resort to if she saw the numbers in my bank account," he winked at Will and walked off to his car.

Will approached the swing as Kenna reached for her wine glass. She was getting tired of this reoccurring theme of Whitney invading their relationship. She watched as he slowly sat down next to her as if expecting her to make him leave. She closed her eyes and felt the night air skim over her face with just enough cold in it to make her happy she had on her Syracuse sweatshirt.

"Kenna, I swear. There's nothing going on with Whitney. It's just so frustrating. She didn't want me anymore. And, well, I didn't want her either. But she just won't let go of the fame. I don't care if she sees someone else. In fact, I'd shout for joy if she were to get remarried." Kenna opened her eyes and took another sip of wine. "I know that she's a lot to deal with," Will continued, "but I really want this relationship to work. Please, tell me you do too."

Kenna turned her head to look Will in the eye. His chocolate eyes were filled with worry. She knew he was under a lot of stress and apparently Whitney was adding to it. "I won't be made a fool, Will. Promise me that you have no more feelings for her."

Will turned toward her and took her hand in his. "I swear, the only feelings I have for her are anger right now. And pity. I feel pity for her. I can't imagine what it would be like to think everyone is after you and wanting nothing but more. I promise you, I'll do right this time around, Kenna. I just fear that with me comes the trouble of Whitney. Please, say you're willing enough to try it, knowing you're the only one I have feelings for,"

She gave a slight nod and hoped she wasn't making a mistake in trusting him again.

"We have a spring practice game tomorrow at the high school. Why don't you come by after work and watch? Then we can go out to dinner. How does that sound?"

"That would be nice. I'd like to see you coach."

"Thank you, Kenna."

"For what?"

"I know this isn't the ideal situation for me to try to date you. I must be making one hell of an impression between the accidents on the farm and a crazy ex-wife trying to keep us apart. But I just know it'll be worth it. I need to get back to the farm tonight. I'll see you for lunch and then tomorrow evening for the game. I know a great place in Lexington you'll just love." Will stood up and dropped a gentle kiss on her cheek. "I'll see you tomorrow."

"Bye, Will."

Kenna watched as he made his way to his truck and drove off. She was about to argue with her feelings when the screen door opened and Miss Lily tumbled out.

"Miss Lily! Were you listening to our conversation?"

"Oh, heavens no. I was straightening the public sitting room for the weekend visitors and well, with the door open, I couldn't help but hear. But since you asked, I think you did the right thing."

"I didn't ask, but go ahead and tell me why you think so." Kenna patted the seat and before Lily had started her explanation, a car with tires screeching turned into the drive.

"What did I miss? Tell me everything!" Paige screamed as she got out of her car and ran to the porch.

Turning to Miss Lily, she shook her finger as if scolding her. "Did you call everyone in town?"

"No, I'd never do that. I just called my sisters and Paige."

"So, give it another ten minutes and everyone in town will know Will was over here trying to win me back."

Paige couldn't wait any longer, "Is that what he wanted? Then what was the deal with Whitney?"

With Miss Lily and Paige hovered around Kenna shooting off questions, Kenna filled them in on the conversation with Will. Miss Lily brought out a tray for dinner and a pitcher of lemonade. The ladies discussed Whitney and what they thought of the situations.

"I just don't understand her. Why would she put on this charade? Does she really think it's a good way to win Will back?" Paige asked as she took another bite of apple pie.

"Only because she's demented." Miss Lily's raised voice, along with her arms waving in the air, was enough to bring another round of laughter to the group.

Some time around the apple pie being brought out, the ladies decided to turn their discussion into a comedic enactment. Miss Lily had the best impersonation of Whitney between them. Their laughter died when they saw the sheriff pull to a stop in front of the house.

"Ladies," Red said as he tipped his hat, his red hair having faded to more of a strawberry blonde as he aged.

With her nose lifted into snobby perfection, Miss Lily let out her best impersonation of Whitney yet, "Officer, is there something we can do for you this night?"

Kenna saw Red's lips twitch. "Let me guess, you ladies broke out some spiked lemonade and decided to celebrate the downfall of Miss Bruce?"

Miss Lily's eyes got wide and then they narrowed onto Red. "I'll have you know I'm a good Christian and would never partake in spirits. And I don't want to hear you spreading that gossip, Red. Are you trying to get me in trouble?"

"It seems you've gotten yourself into enough trouble. One of your neighbors called, complaining about the loud ruckus going on out here so late at night."

"That would be Linda. It's barely ten o'clock. That old bat, bless her heart, she sees smiles and it's her mission to stomp them out," Miss Lily huffed.

"After the other night, I think it's a good idea all of us get to bed a little early," Kenna said as she stood and stretched her arms above her head. The fatigue from the last day washed over her. She said her good-nights and climbed the stairs up to her room.

Kenna changed into an old Syracuse Lacrosse t-shirt and climbed into bed with her book. Before she could open it, she spotted her laptop, and the urge to check her email hit her. She opened the laptop and turned it on. Every time she checked her email, her stomach tightened into a knot and she broke out into a cold sweat. She opened her browser and logged into her account. She stopped breathing when the screen went blank to load the page. When she saw the new email from Danielle, she wasn't sure if she should breathe quite yet. She made herself exhale and clicked to open the email.

K-

Beware! I think they found you. I don't know exactly where you are,
   but the men in black have stopped trailing me and left town. I really think
      they've found you. Please be careful. Let me know you're okay.

XoXo
   D

SHIT. Shit. Shit. Kenna tossed the laptop onto the bed and turned off the lights. She went over to the door and slowly opened it. Miss Lily tended to leave the front door unlocked so she quietly made her way down the old creaky staircase in the dark to the front door. She could see that the deadbolt wasn't thrown. As she approached, she peeked out the window. There were no cars on the streets or people lurking in the bushes. Kenna locked the door, ran back upstairs, shut her own door, and locked it. Breathing hard now, she got back into bed and picked up the laptop.

DANI-

DOORS ARE LOCKED and no creepy guys outside. I'll keep my eyes open and let you know if I see anything. Make sure you stay out of sight too. You never know if they pulled back to lure you out.

KEEP SAFE,
   K

~

THE NEXT DAY dragged for Kenna as she sat in a constant state of paranoia. In court, she looked back every time the door opened, so much so that Noodle even got anxious. She quickly walked back to the office, checking out everyone on the sidewalk to make sure she recognized them before jumping into her office at the last possible moment. She managed to get some paperwork done after she told Tammy that no one was to know she was there. Tammy had agreed although her confusion was plain.

She managed to get home knowing no one saw her and dressed for a night out with Will. The last thing she wanted to do was go into Lexington. But knowing she'd be with Will made her nerves calm down enough to talk herself into not canceling. She needed to tell Will the real reason she was in Keeneston. However, just the thought of doing so made the terror seem more real. It made the men looking for her real, and closer to her.

"Come on, McKenna, you can do it. It's easy," she rehearsed in the mirror. "Will, I'm really here running from some powerful people. Saw something I wasn't supposed to that would get them into a heap of trouble. Please tell me if any strangers are looking for me. Thanks," and she finished her practice speech. "There, simple. Just a couple of quick sentences and it'll all be out in the open," she told herself.

Kenna heard the sound of a car pulling into the driveway, grabbed her purse and started downstairs. As she rounded the curve in the staircase, she saw Miss Lily at the front door with Will. He was holding a bouquet of pastel colored tulips in his hand and looked so handsome in black dress slacks and a French blue dress shirt that Kenna almost stopped to stare. She was glad she had dressed up in a little black dress with half inch wide straps that crossed to form an X in the front and then crossed in the back as well. She chose to wear her purple Prada heels as a silent toast to Danielle.

"You look amazing," Will said, his voice a little huskier than normal as he handed her the flowers.

"Thank you. Miss Lily, would you mind if I borrow a vase for these?"

"Just give them here. I'll put them in a vase and take them up to your room for you. You two get going and have a nice time." Miss Lily took the flowers and headed to the kitchen as Will placed Kenna's purple shawl over her shoulders. She noticed his hands linger for a moment on her shoulder as he trailed a finger down her arm.

He held out his arm for her, "Shall we?"

Kenna placed her hand in the crook of his elbow and felt his muscles tense in response. "What do you have planned for tonight?" she asked as he led her to a silver Corvette parked in the driveway. "Is this yours? What happened to your truck?"

"I do own more than one car. I thought you deserved a nice car for a romantic night out on the town." Will stopped by the passenger door and opened it for her. He waited until she was seated and closed the door. She let out a nervous breath. She wasn't quite sure why she was nervous. They'd seen each other countless times in the past couple of months but this felt different. This was all or nothing, and she knew it. Either she was going to fall head over heels in love, or she was going to need to find the strength to walk away from Will forever. As she watched Will make his way around the car, she had a feeling she'd already made the choice.

Will opened the car door and reached into the back seat. "I got you something for tonight."

He handed her a box with a blue bow on it. He'd already gotten her flowers. She didn't know what else he could've gotten her. She opened the box and pulled out a black sweatshirt with KHS Football written across the front in royal blue.

"Thank you! It's great. Now I'll be part of the team." She took off her shawl and pulled the sweatshirt on.

"We have to get there a little before the scrimmage starts so I can talk to the boys. But you shouldn't have to wait too long. Cade Davies, one of Paige's older brothers, is my assistant. He's going to show you around some and then Paige will be there after she closes up to watch the scrimmage with you."

"You didn't have to drag Paige out to babysit me. I would've been fine watching by myself."

"Paige comes to all of the games to support her brother. Also, I think football games provide an outlet for her normally undetectable aggressive side."

They pulled into the parking lot at the high school. As Kenna waited for Will to open her door, she saw the steady stream of young men walking into the locker rooms. Some were laughing and joking around. Some were seriously discussing game plans with each other. Yet others were just listening to music and paying no attention to anything around them. Will opened the door and gave Kenna his hand to help pull her out of the low riding car.

Her breath caught and her heart stopped when she heard the sharp whistle. "Looking good, Coach! You're pretty dressed up for a game." Trey Everett nudged the guy next to him as they both broke out into laughter. Kenna released her breath and smiled.

"That's how you get women, Trey. Of course, by your record, you haven't learned that yet," Will shot back, a smile making his dimples stand out as he put his hand on the small of Kenna's back. Trey's friend pointed at him and broke out into a new fit of laughter.

"Wait here. I'll get Cade to show you around. Then I'll see you after the game and we'll go out to dinner at Marabella's," he said as he came to a stop outside the locker room entrance.

He slid his hand from her back to her hip and pulled her toward him. As he lowered his head, her lips raised instinctively to his. She sighed when he placed his lips on hers, gently brushing them back and forth before settling in for a heartbreakingly sweet kiss. He ran his hands up her back so softly that it felt like a whisper.

"That was for luck," he whispered into her ear before heading into the locker room.

Kenna turned away from the door and stopped dead. Two young boys stood with their mouths hanging open.

"Wow, Coach has game," one said to the other as they walked past Kenna to the door. They nodded to her, "Ma'am," and then they disappeared behind the old steel door.

Kenna's face flushed when she heard the cheers erupt from the room soon after and thought about running away when the door opened again. This time a man about her age stepped out with a grin on his face. He was an obvious participant in the ribbing Will was getting inside.

"You must be Paige's friend. And well, we all know you're Will's special friend after the clinic you both put on out here."

"Oh God," she groaned. "Let me guess, by tomorrow morning everyone will know I was caught making out with Will under the bleachers. I feel like I'm in high school again!"

The man laughed and held out his hand, "Cade Davies. It's nice to meet you. I've heard a lot about you from Paige and Will."

She shook hands with him and noticed the strong grip he had. His dirty blonde hair was a little longer than normal, with strands tucked behind his ears and tickling the top of his collar. His hazel eyes seemed to dance with his amusement of the locker room antics.

"So, are you Paige's oldest brother? She told me all about you guys, but I can't remember the order."

"Nope, not the oldest. I'm brother number three. Come on, I'll show you around the school and the field while Will's getting the guys ready for the game." He led her out of the field house and toward the massive school.

"Do you teach here or do you volunteer like Will?" she asked as he opened one of the metal doors leading into the school.

"I teach science, mostly biology and anatomy/physiology."

Kenna looked over at him and took in his six foot plus frame, heavily muscled arms, broad chest, and tapered waist. It was clear he either worked out with the boys or did something else because he didn't look like a teacher. "You don't look like any science nerd I know," she laughed.

"I just became a teacher. I served eight years in the Special Forces. Got out two years ago and finished my degree."

"What division were you? And, if you don't mind my asking, what prompted you to join?"

"Right after the World Trade Center bombings, Miles, Marshall, and I joined the Army Rangers. Up here is my classroom." It was an obvious change of subject, so Kenna let it go.

"What about your other brothers. Paige said you were all into farming."

"We all are. Miles had gotten his bachelor of science at Texas A&M, which is the leading school in agricultural studies. He then got his MBA in agricultural management from Purdue. Miles is the brains behind our farm. He worked during college and assigned my mom as his power of attorney. He'd keep in touch with real estate agents here. When land near our parents' farm would go up for sale, Miles would try to purchase it. Lots of times he would only be able to buy ten acres of landlocked property on the cheap. No one wanted it because you couldn't get to the property without trespassing over someone else's land. And you really can't do much on a large scale with ten acres. Well, he started buying even more when he was earning a paycheck in the Army. It was like a puzzle. He'd buy strategically landlocked pieces on the cheap and would spend a little money on the connector piece of property. After we got out of the Army, Miles bought a total of seven hundred acres that had a common boundary with my parents' five hundred acres. We all liked the idea, so over the past couple of years we've all done the same thing. However, our farms aren't nearly as large as Miles'."

"What do you grow on your farms?"

"Cy and I both run cattle on ours. It takes the least amount of work. Cy is the black sheep of the family. He likes to take off for weeks at a time. So we run our cattle together and basically treat our two farms as one. Since he's away so much, he lives with Marshall and me out on Marshall's farm. He bought a tract of land with this hundred year old farm house on it that he's fixed into a modern day bachelor's pad. Marsh has his own security company, and he also runs some cattle too. We also all rotate crops such as corn and soybeans on part of our property."

"What about Miles and your youngest brother?"

"Miles just completed a house in the middle of his tract of land. Takes forever to get out there. He's started his own anti-corporate company called Family Farms. Large, impersonal corporations are getting into farming and driving down the costs of production and turning farming into mass production. It's killing off the smaller family farms. In obtaining his MBA, Miles studied how they do it. Now he runs his company to achieve two goals: keeping the family farms alive and competing with the large corporations. He manages a co-op of family farms to mimic the corporate farms. He has the family farms working together to combine their efforts while reducing their costs. As I said, he's the brains behind the farming. My little brother Pierce is still in school. He's at the University of Kentucky getting his degree in agriculture with a focus on soil composition and will graduate in a couple of weeks. He's the opposite of Miles. He's old school. He'll take over running my parents' farm. He's the one who decides what crops should be planted, when they need to be rotated, soil compositions, and all sorts of other things."

They exited the school and headed back to the football field. Kenna saw that cars were already starting to fill up the parking lot. She followed Cade past the ticket takers and up a few rows to where Paige sat.

"Hey, bro. How's the team looking this year?" Paige stood up and hugged her brother. Cade picked her up in a bear hug and Kenna smiled at the obvious affection between them, that, and the sight of Paige's feet dangling off the ground.

"Pretty good. The only trouble is that we're pretty inexperienced in key areas. I better get down there and make sure Will survived the hazing. It was really nice meeting you, Kenna. Hope to see you around at the games in the fall." With a chuck to Paige's chin, he went down the steps of the bleachers and disappeared into the field house.

Will was right. Paige has a lot of pent-up aggression. Kenna was surprised the first time Paige jumped up and screamed at one of the players. But by the end of the scrimmage, she was used to it. Paige knew a lot more about football than Kenna did and enjoyed trying to teach Kenna about the sport. Kenna loved watching Will with the kids. There was mutual respect between them, and it was clear Will enjoyed teaching them the game just as it was clear the boys were entranced by having a coach like Will.

Kenna knew with her head and her heart that she loved Will.

When the stands cleared and parents were making their ways to their cars, she looked onto the field to see Will coaching a boy no older than fifteen how to put the perfect spiral on the ball. The boy was short, skinny as a toothpick, and lacking any muscles that would make him a high school player. Yet Will took the time to teach and praise the boy's efforts. She smiled as she watched Will place the boy's hands on the football and explain one more time how to throw it.

CHAPTER 12

Will and Kenna drove in companionable silence into Lexington. Along the way, she watched the rolling hills go by until they reached town. Will rested his hand on her knee, causing her heart to race. They pulled up at a historic house that the owners had converted into a restaurant. Marabella's was a two story, brick house with white columns out front and a circular drive in the front. A valet opened the door for her when Will stopped.

"Good evening, Mr. Ashton," the valet said as he opened Will's door next.

"Hey, Nick. How is Ella doing?" Will put a supportive hand on Nick's shoulder and Nick beamed.

"She's doing great, thanks to you. They are even talking about letting us bring her home this week."

Will's smile widened to equal the one appearing on Nick's face, "That is wonderful news. Absolutely wonderful news. Let me know if there is anything I can do for you."

After Will pulled out her chair and she sat down, her curiosity won out. "Who is Ella and what is she sick with?"

"She's Nick's infant daughter. She was born with a cleft palate. Their insurance covered the dental surgeon but not a cosmetic one. I had a friend who's a plastic surgeon assist on the surgery to sew the outside of Ella's mouth back together to minimize any scarring or deformities. Both surgeons think she'll be completely healed by the time she is one. No red marks, and the skin is growing normally. Everyone is optimistic for completely normal speech. But we're also prepared to help with a little speech therapy."

"That's amazing, Will." She knew if it were possible, she just fell in love with him again. So many of the athletes she worked with used charity works like this to help them get out of legal trouble or boost their image. Will did it so a little girl wouldn't grow up with a scar on her face or a speech impediment.

"You know, the Derby is just a little over a week away. It's an event everyone should go to at least once. The atmosphere is amazing. Over one hundred and fifty thousand people show up every year. The infield turns into party central, and it carries all the way up to Millionaire's Row. You should come this year." He reached over the table and took her hand in his. "It would be nice to have you there."

"That sounds great. Do I need anything special for it?"

Will laughed. "You looking for a reason to go shopping?"

Kenna just smiled, of course she was. What girl wouldn't want a reason to go shopping!

"Of course you are. And yes, you will need some really great hats. Paige can help you out with that. Also, a spring sundress type thingy. My family is hosting a Derby breakfast the day of the race."

"Oh, so this is a whole day event?"

"Actually, it's a whole week of events for me. I'll head out on Sunday and stay up there for most of the week while some of my horses are racing at Churchill Downs. I'll also help the team get Naked Boot Leg prepared for the Derby."

"I never asked, but what does Naked Boot Leg mean?"

"It's a quarterback trick play when you fake a running play, and the quarterback circles back across the backfield looking for the pass."

Kenna gave a smile and a nod as if she followed what he was saying completely.

"So, tell me about Derby Day. What kind of things will we do?"

"Well, we have a private box. When we get there, we'll walk a red carpet of sorts. Even retired athletes are still semi-celebrities and the fact that our farm owns last year's winner. It's not unheard of for farms to have back to back winners. Calumet Farm in Lexington did it once in the 1940's and again in the 1950's. But it's certainly newsworthy when the opportunity arises."

"Red carpet? Do I wear an evening gown?" she joked while she entwined her fingers with his.

"Not that time of day. It's more cocktail attire. The evening gown comes in play at the after-party the track hosts."

Will sat back in his chair as the empty dinner plates were taken away and replaced with crème brulee. Kenna took a bite and moaned.

"Hey, shouldn't you reserve those kind of sounds for when we're alone?" Will sat back, crossed his arms and gave a little pout.

"We never seem to be alone. It's like we're teenagers with chaperones at every turn."

"I used to be pretty clever finding alone time with a beautiful girl when I was a teenager."

"Then maybe you can put those skills to use tonight." She looked at Will and noticed that his spoon was paused halfway to his mouth, and she decided to give him a little wink.

Will's hand shot up in the air, "Check!"

"Shh. You don't want to wake Miss Lily," Kenna said as she approached her room. Will had parked the car on the street, and they had approached the house on foot. However, they were having a hard time not laughing.

Kenna opened her door and turned on the light. She watched Will gently close the door and turn the lock. She was having a hard time remembering to breathe. She saw Will take a deep breath and let it out and then turn around. Her eyes met his and the yearning she was feeling reflected in his.

"Come here." His voice sounded huskier than normal. She took a step forward and stopped in front of him. "You are so beautiful." His hand gently brushed along her cheek before his head dipped and he took her mouth in a passionate kiss. He nudged her lips apart as his tongue slid in, stroking the inside of her mouth. Her fingers laced through his hair and ran down his back. She pressed herself against his chest and felt his erection against her stomach.

He pushed her shawl off one shoulder and ran kisses along its path to her neck. He placed a gentle kiss on the hollow of her throat and then kissed the shawl off the other shoulder. "Did I mention how beautiful you are?" His finger moved to unbutton the strap of her dress.

"Mmm," Kenna moaned, her eyes closed as she reveled in the feel of his touch. She held her breath as her dress fell to the floor and felt the cold air caress her bare stomach. She opened her eyes when she felt Will pull back. She opened them to see him staring at her.

"How did I get so lucky?" he whispered.

She smiled as she saw the look of desire in his eyes at her dressed in her matching black lace bra and panties. She closed the distance and began to slowly unbutton his shirt, revealing a hard chest sprinkled with dark hair. She ran her fingertips over his chiseled abs and stopped at his belt. He grabbed her hands and hauled them back behind her as he possessed her mouth. She felt the gentle tug on her arms as he walked her backwards until the back of her knees hit the bed.

She reached for his belt buckle and slowly unhooked it while Will nibbled his way down her neck. His hands moved slowly from her back to her smooth stomach. Her breath hitched when she felt his thumb glide across her aroused nipple. With an unsteady hand, she unbuttoned his pants and watched them fall to the ground.

"Oh my. I guess that answers my question of boxers or briefs."

Kenna pulled her navy suit coat down and shoved her hands into the pockets of her pants. The red toe of her heeled shoe was tapping as she stared at opposing counsel. "Mr. Nichols, I don't care how they do it in the big city of Louisville. I'm not going to dismiss the charges against your client."

"Look here, little lady. You aren't from around these parts. You don't arrest the coach of a program such as this."

"First of all, I may not know a lot about college football, but I'm pretty sure Mr. Faulk has been retired for at least ten years. Second, I don't care if he's the President of the United States. He was driving drunk and could've killed someone. His five-year-old granddaughter was in the car with him. You're lucky I'm not tacking on wanton endangerment charges. But if you keep pushing me, I will." Kenna's foot stopped tapping as she stared at Mr. Nichols receding hairline and red-tipped nose.

"And if he pleads no contest?"

"He loses his license for thirty days, mandatory alcohol counseling, and a hundred hours of community service." She kept her eyes on his and knew she was pushing it.

"One hundred hours! Ms. Mason that is uncalled for. You are clearly prejudiced against my client."

Kenna rolled her eyes, "Mr. Nichols, your client coached when I was still in high school. You think I give a damn about that? I'm giving him community service, and I want that service to be performed with children to make up for having his granddaughter in the car with him. I'll move you to the afternoon docket so that you can confer with your client." Mr. Nichols nodded and stormed out of the room, fishing out his cell phone as he left.

"Very impressive, Miss Mason," a voice said from behind her.

Kenna spun around to find Judge Cooper leaning against the door frame. "Your Honor," Kenna placed her hand on her heart, "you startled me. I didn't know anyone was in here." She gestured around the attorney meeting room just outside of the courtroom.

Judge Cooper shrugged his shoulders, "I probably shouldn't have stopped by and eavesdropped, but it was too interesting a negation to ignore. You know, Mr. Nichols is the most sought after attorney in the state, and his client is one of the most loved figures in the state."

"Everyone likes to remind me that I'm not from around here. But I guess that is a plus for once," she said as she glanced at the clock. She had fallen behind and needed to get these attorney conferences over soon.

"You may just be right. I'll see you in the courtroom in ten minutes. We have a schedule to keep after all."

Kenna hurried through her next three attorney conferences and then through a long morning traffic docket. It seemed from today's lengthy docket that no one believed traffic violations were really breaking the law. She glanced at her watch and figured she had just enough time to run to the Blossom Cafe for a quick sandwich before the afternoon docket started. She pushed open the door and was caught by surprise when several microphones were shoved in her face.

"Miss Mason, Miss Mason, what is the status of Coach Faulk's case?"

She guessed this was big news, but she didn't see how. Maybe it was because politicians and pro athletes got pulled over in New York all the time. It only got a quick blurb on page six. It had to reach the levels of vehicular manslaughter or getting pulled over with a hooker in the car to garner television coverage.

"I'm sorry, but I do not comment on cases."

"Just a quick update, Miss Mason!"

"You can see for yourself this afternoon. It's a matter of public record and I can't stop you from entering the courtroom. But, I will not comment about a case now, nor in the future. Now, if you all would excuse me, I'd like to grab some lunch. Thank you." Kenna pushed her way through the crowd and came face to face with Mr. Nichols.

"Ma'am, I may have misjudged you. Can we conference over lunch?"

She took note that his nose was no longer red and he seemed much calmer. "And what has changed your mind?"

"I saw you make your way through the media. I thought you were making such a stand so that you could get the media attention."

"No, I'm taking such a stand because your client did something wrong. Now please, Mr. Nichols, I only have fifteen minutes before we have to be back in court. We can conference over lunch if you'd like." She pushed open the door to the cafe and went in. She noticed that he followed.

Miss Daisy was making her rounds when she saw Kenna come in. "I got a table right over there for you. The clerk was in earlier and said court was running long. I went ahead and made you up some lunch. I'll go get it, dear." Before turning to leave, Miss Daisy glanced at Mr. Nichols, "Will he be joining you as well?"

"Yes, ma'am. If you have time, I'll just take whatever I can get quickly." Miss Daisy harrumphed but went to get their lunch. It was clear Miss Daisy knew Mr. Nichols and didn't have a high opinion of him. She wasn't really surprised though. It seemed the Rose sisters knew everyone. Miss Daisy brought out olive nut sandwiches with a side of mixed fresh fruit for them as they discussed the coach's case and came to a settlement.

They walked out the door and back to the courthouse, surrounded by reporters asking questions about their lunch meeting. Kenna had to work at keeping her mouth shut when a reporter suggested the prosecutor was in bed with the defense. She managed to not hit anyone on the short trek across the street although, she did smile when the heel of her shoe came down hard on an overly aggressive reporter's toe, accidentally, of course.

Court that afternoon went by quickly. Only a couple of cases had to have full hearings, and she was relieved when Judge Cooper granted her sentencing suggestion for Coach Faulk. She decided to leave the media to Mr. Nichols and went down to the basement of the courthouse where she then snuck out the backdoor. It was easy to slip out the courthouse, down an alley about three feet in width, and behind the row of buildings lining Main Street. She came out in a courtyard belonging to the library and walked around the building back onto Main Street. She was now a good block past the reporters. She looked up the street to her office and saw it was clear to cross.

"Hey! You looked great on TV this afternoon!" Tammy said as soon as she walked in the door.

Kenna gave a small groan, "I was on TV?"

"Sure was. They only ran a clip of you saying, 'No comment' though."

"You don't think this will get much coverage, do you?" Kenna was starting to worry that Coach Faulk may be a more popular figurehead than she thought.

"Well, it'll get plenty of coverage in the state but probably not nationwide. Why?"

"No reason. Just don't like being on TV. I always think I sound strange." Kenna tried to wave it off but took note that Tammy was looking at her a little too closely now. "Well, work to do. I'll be in my office."

"Knock, Knock." Kenna looked up from her computer to find Mo leaning against the door frame. He looked amazing in a European cut black suit that she was sure had Tammy drooling at her desk.

"Hey, what are you doing here?" She cringed when she realized how that sounded but was relieved when Mo just laughed at her.

"I came to sweep you off your feet and take you to my house to wine and dine you." Kenna couldn't stop the giggle from escaping when she noticed Tammy stop dead in the hallway behind Mo, using a file in her hand to fan herself.

"Sorry, Mo, but I have dinner plans with Will tonight. We're going to go to this new restaurant in Versailles tonight."

"I know, that's actually why I am here. Will called me and asked me to look in on you. Last night someone attacked one of the night guards on patrol. Knocked him unconscious with a shovel. Will is staying with Naked Boot Leg tonight to make sure nothing happens to him before the Derby."

"That's horrible. When are they going to find out who's behind this and arrest them?"

"We have a lead that we turned it over to the sheriff and to Will. My men caught a license plate number off a car that was speeding away last night. All we were able to find out was that the car was reported stolen in Washington D.C. three weeks ago."

Kenna felt the blood drain from her face. She looked down and saw the file she was holding shaking. "But these attacks have been going on for longer than that."

"Yes, but the car was stolen from the long-term parking lot of the Washington Dulles International Airport. The owner told the police he'd been overseas working for the past six months. His roommate was supposed to pick up the car in the long-term lot when he got back from vacation a week later. But the car wasn't there, so the friend figured the owner had his mom pick it up and didn't bother to mention it to the owner. It could be the person responsible for these attacks. Unfortunately, the sheriff's department here doesn't have a lot of pull in D.C., and the airport isn't willing to review six months of archived video surveillance."

"Well, I'm glad there's some kind of lead to follow, at least." She looked down at her computer and at the motion in her hand. It was already five thirty and there was no way to file it so late. She finished the notice and printed it out. She sat it on her chair to remind herself to file it in the morning when the courts were open. "Okay, I'm ready to be wined and dined."

Dinner was amazing, as always. Mo's French cook had outdone himself with the pheasant for dinner and they finished it off with chocolate mousse.

"Don't you think it's about time you tell me some about New York?" Mo asked as he scraped his spoon one more time along the side of his empty glass.

Kenna blanched, "Um, like what?"

"You know, you can trust me. You and I both know you have been avoiding telling us all something that happened up there. I can help if you need me to." He must've noticed she was close to panic because he changed the subject. "For now though, why don't you tell me about what you would do for fun. I have been to New York many times to talk at the United Nations or to see a play on Broadway. My family has donated to the museums as well. It is a city full of activity and life."

Kenna managed a wobbly smile. "Danielle and I would regularly go to the museums. If you contributed to the Middle Eastern exhibit about a year ago at the Metropolitan Museum of Art, then we saw it!"

"My family did. Since I was already over in the States, I attended the opening. My family, along with several others in the area, loaned out some of our most precious historical artwork. It is definitely an area of art that does not get much attention, and we were pleased to help teach so many about our art history." Mo stood. "Why don't we go into the sitting room and relax?"

Kenna stood and followed him from the informal dining room, down the hall, and into his private sitting room. The room wasn't as large as the formal sitting room at the front of the house, but the room housed the biggest flat screen Kenna had ever seen. It was outfitted with the most comfortable furniture too. She kicked off her heels as she curled up on one end of a couch and sunk into the cushions. Mo took a seat at the other end of the couch and turned toward her. She noticed he didn't take off his shoes.

"You mentioned that you and Danielle attended the exhibit. Was Danielle a friend of yours?"

"Yes. She was... is, my best friend. She was my paralegal and took her day job almost as seriously as she took her job outside of work. After we worked together for about three months, Danielle came to me and told me she needed a raise. I asked her what for, and she responded by telling me she was taking a second job on my behalf. Confused, I asked her what she was talking about. She told me that I needed someone to show me how to have a good time."

Mo laughed. "Did she show you how to have a good time?"

"Yes," Kenna smiled, "she did. She talked me into using my connections to get past the waiting lines at the hottest clubs. We would spend the night dancing away. It was the first time I did anything like that. During school, I was too busy studying. We would have a blast. My sides would hurt the next day from laughing as much as we did. We'd also go to museum exhibits, plays, yoga, defense classes, movies, art showings, and so much more together. She has a way of making any occasion fun. She's beautiful, smart, and fun. She's just a good person too."

"She sounds amazing. I would love to meet her someday." His voice had a sad tone. "Being in my position, it is hard to meet someone like that. I would love to have someone make me go out and try new things. I have a tendency to stick to what I know."

"Well then, let's start now. I see you have a basketball goal over there." Kenna pointed to the mini goal hanging on the closet door. A small basketball lay on a desk nearby. "I challenge you to a game of basketball."

"Okay. What does the winner get?" Mo looked over at the goal. "I know. Winner gets one favor from the loser to be named at a future time."

Kenna narrowed her eyes, "That's kinda broad, isn't it? What kind of favor?"

"I may need some legal assistance or someone to attend a political gala with, as friends of course. If you win, you may want to borrow my jet, or you may want my cook to make a special dessert for you. Something along those lines."

"Okay, deal." Kenna held her hand out and Mo shook it. They stood up, took off their suit coats, and placed them on the couch. As Mo tossed the basketball to her, she got serious. "Each basket it one point. First to ten wins."

Kenna was up nine to eight after a tough battle. Her silk shirt was sticking to her and her hair was a mess. Mo didn't look any better. His shirt was untucked, and he'd ditched his slick shoes to play in his socks. His normally gelled back, longer hair was shoved behind his ear, and a trickle of sweat ran down his angular face.

She really wanted to win. She was having a hard time deciding what she wanted. She knew whatever it was, he'd give it to her anyway if she asked. But this was definitely more fun. She worked her way closer to the basket with Mo hand checking her. She faked to her right, and when Mo took a step that way, she turned to her left and shot. There was a satisfying swish as the ball went through the net.

"I hope we haven't interrupted such a childish game."

Kenna and Mo spun around to come face-to-face with a very imposing threesome, all dressed in traditional Middle Eastern clothes. The man who spoke stood out front, his outfit made of the most magnificent silk Kenna had ever seen. He was shorter than Mo, probably only five feet eight. His face was cold, his eyes narrow and his lips pinched. Behind him stood the most regal woman Kenna had ever been in the presence of. She was dressed in beautiful, rose-colored silk trimmed with gold ribbon. She too was middle aged. After one look at her kind face, Kenna knew she was Mo's mother. Behind her was a young woman who looked like a model, regal in her bearing, but not as confident as Mo's mother. Kenna guessed that she was another bachelorette.

Ahmed's head popped around the corner, and his eyes went wide as he took in Kenna and Mo's disheveled appearance. Mo turned away from the group and took a deep breath. He tucked in his shirt, slipped on his shoes, and donned his coat before turning around. Kenna had to stifle a gasp as she saw Mo's eyes go blank and his lips pinched the same way as his father's. She looked at his mother and caught the look of sadness cross her eyes before she could hide it.

"Father, Mother, what a pleasant surprise." The tightness in Mo's voice told Kenna it wasn't as pleasant as he said.

"Son, I see you still have not learned the proper deportment that fits your station." Mo's father's eyes never left his son's.

Kenna walked over to the couch and grabbed her suitcoat and purse. "I'll let you welcome your family. I'm sure you'll want to show them all the amazing things you've done with the farm. Thanks for dinner and the game, Mo." Kenna kissed his cheek and gave his hand a supportive squeeze.

"Mo!" his father erupted. "I forbade you to use that name. You are royalty and royalty does not go by such a common name."

With her back to his father, she rolled her eyes and got some satisfaction when she saw Mo's lips twitch.

Ahmed pushed into the room, "I will escort Miss Mason home, sir." he said, bowing to Mo.

"There is no need for that, Ahmed. My son could better use your services showing Kalila to her new chamber. I will show Miss Mason to the door where our driver can escort her home," Mo's mother stated quietly.

Her quiet words invoked immediate action though. Bachelorette Kalila immediately turned around and followed Ahmed out the door.

Kenna couldn't stop the smile when she heard Ahmed muttering, "Not another one." Kenna turned, waved bye to Mo, and sent him a smile as she followed his mother out the door.

They had only taken a couple of steps before she turned to Kenna. "As you can guess, I am Mohtadi's mother, Fatima Ali Rahman. We've arrived here to bring a bride for my son. I am sure you can imagine our surprise on encountering him with another woman. It is therefore necessary for me to ask you a very personal question, Miss Mason." She waited until Kenna nodded before continuing, "What exactly is your relationship with my son?"

"I'm his friend and he is my very good friend." Kenna stopped walking and waited for Mo's mother to face her. "He should be allowed to have friends. He needs them. He needs fun, and he needs to be able to find the person he wants to marry. Parading all these women in front of him is just making him more hostile to the idea of marriage. I'd hate to see him marry the wrong person just to get back at his father and to satisfy this stupid deal the two of them made." Kenna kept her eyes on Fatima's, and knew she had swan dived over the bounds of propriety.

Mo's mother surprised her by smiling. "I believe we may get along very well, Miss Mason. Although my husband would not agree, I have made my case to him along those same lines. He believes he's right and there's nothing that can change his mind. It is comforting to know Mohtadi has a friend such as you."

"You can call me McKenna, or Kenna for short. I'm glad he has your support. He's such a wonderful and caring person. I hope he may find a person who appreciates those qualities more than his station."

"McKenna, you may call me Fatima. If I may ask, why are you not that woman?"

Kenna smiled "I'm involved with someone else. He's actually Mohtadi's neighbor, Will Ashton." She opened the front door when they reached it.

"That is too bad. I too wish for him to find love. All of Mohtadi's other siblings have married whom their father picked out for them. Most are unhappy but not all. Some of the matches have evolved into love, but it's very hard for Mohtadi to be the last one unmarried. It focuses all of his father's pressure onto him alone." The two women approached the front door. "It was a pleasure to meet you, McKenna. I do hope I will see you at the Derby festivities."

Fatima closed the door on her as she made her way down the steps. Kenna was relieved to see Ahmed pull the Mercedes behind the limo and open the door for her. It had been too long of a day and she was ready for the quiet of her bedroom. She turned to the formal sitting parlor. As she figured, Mo had moved his family to that room and gave Kenna a nod good-bye through the window before she got into the car. He was a good friend, and as such, she needed to find him a good woman.

CHAPTER 13

Kenna took a deep breath before speaking into the phone again, "Ma'am, I don't think you understand the situation."

"Sure I do. You just want to screw me. My ex-boyfriend got you all to take my baby away from me so that he can hang it over my head. I just don't understand what legal grounds you have to take my baby away from me."

"Ma'am, you were arrested on possession of marijuana charges. You were smoking pot while driving your baby to a meth house which happens to be *your* house."

"That's not illegal! It was just pot. And you can't prove that house was mine. I know the law and you can't prove squat."

Kenna tried not to bang her head against the desk as she reminded herself she loved her job. "Smoking pot is illegal, and we can prove the meth house was yours. You led the police on a chase to the house. You left all kinds of prints there. Your clothes and your baby's clothes were there. Further, your little son tested positive for meth and is still in the hospital where his father is taking care of him. That's enough evidence to keep you in jail for a long time. I suggest you contact your public defender if you need anything else. It is unadvisable for you to speak to me since our office will handle your prosecution. Good-bye."

Kenna hung up the phone and shook her head. She'd been getting these types of phone calls all day. It started bright and early with a woman who wanted to sue her landlord because she put in a request for her front door to be painted on Saturday. On Sunday, a worker knocked on her door to start the work, and the woman assumed he was there to rape her. Kenna had asked why she thought that his intention was to rape her.

The woman's only response was "What kind of man shows up on a Sunday to work when he should be in church?"

Needing to stretch her legs, Kenna stood up and walked out front to where Tammy was on the phone. "No, sir, I'm sorry. We don't defend those types of cases. Uh-huh, that's right. Sorry, good-bye."

"So, you're getting crazy calls today, too?" Kenna asked as she leaned against Tammy's desk.

"Full moon."

"Ah, that explains it. I need a calendar that shows the moon cycles to warn me." Kenna stood up and walked back to her office when Tammy's phone rang again. It was well known in the legal world, as well as with most other public service industries, that the full moon brought the crazies out of hiding. She didn't have court today and was glad for it. She grabbed her purse and went to meet Paige for a late lunch at the cafe.

Paige sat down just after Kenna's drink arrived at the table. "Ready for some shopping? I got Cindie to cover the shop for the rest of the day. Thought we could hit the stores in Lexington to find you the perfect Derby weekend wear. There's this fab little store downtown that carries some of the bigger names in fashion. Then we can go to my store and find the perfect hat for your outfits. Do you know how many you'll need?"

"Well, Will said there would be a Derby breakfast at his house. Then there will be the Derby and then the after-party."

"Okay, you'll need a nice suit or sundress for the breakfast. You'll need a cocktail dress for the Derby and then a gown for the after-party," Paige said as she made a mental list of the items.

"Well, I already have the breakfast covered. I have a beautiful sage green, scalloped dress with matching wedges."

"Okay, I can work with that. Before we go to my shop, let's stop and pick up your dress so I can match the colors." They paid their bills and walked to the bed and breakfast to get Kenna's car. She ran upstairs and brought the dress and shoes down.

"OOHH, look at this Dior. Tell me this wouldn't be perfect for the Derby," Paige said as she lifted up a navy blue, silk crepe, belted dress. Kenna tried it on. It fell to right above the knee and was fitted enough to show off her curves but not so fitted it was tight. It appeared to be sleeveless until Kenna started to button up the front of the bodice. She discovered silk ties that were intended to be tied in bows on her arms.

"Paige, this one is perfect." Kenna stepped out of the dressing room to model the outfit. Like any good dress it made her appear taller, took off ten pounds, and made her look utterly feminine.

"That is perfect. Do you have any red heels? Because I have a gorgeous hat that would go with it. The hat is bright red, so I'd like to tie it to the shoes if possible."

"I have the perfect heels. My feet won't thank me, but they do make my legs look great. I also have a red clutch I could carry."

"Perfect! One dress down, one to go. I think I found one, but it may be too wild. What do you think?" Paige handed her a black lace Valentino.

It had one shoulder and an empire waist. The wild part was its length. It was much shorter than your typical ball gown. It stopped inches above the knee, but when Kenna tried it on, she couldn't say no.

"You wear that with some black spiked heels and Will could go into cardiac arrest."

The dress enhanced her already ample cleavage and somehow

made her wide hips seem sexy. The dress emphasized femininity, and the laced edging around the hem showed off her legs.

"It's great and so different. But, I also love that royal blue silk dress, the one with the thin straps and draping." It was more traditional since it skimmed the floor. She loved the way the bodice was draped silk that seemed to float down to the floor.

"Why don't you get them both? Whichever you don't wear, you can just bring back after the Derby."

"Sounds good to me. Now let's go pick out some hats!"

PAIGE PICKED OUT A RED, wide-brimmed hat with a simple red organza ribbon that was tied into an elegant, multi-layered bow in the back to wear for Derby Day. Paige also found a hat with sage that matched Kenna's spring dress for the breakfast at Will's farm. It was a tan colored straw hat with a normal sized brim with a sage and tan stripped ribbon that went around the hat and trailed off the back of it. They were so perfect that Kenna couldn't wait to show Will.

"Thanks so much, Paige. I'm going to run out to the farm and show Will. He's on duty tonight, so I think I'll bring him some dinner too."

"Okay, have fun. Remember to check your hair for straw before you go to work tomorrow. It would take a whole new meaning to casual Friday if you didn't!"

KENNA PARKED her car in the circular drive and looked up at Will's parents' house. It was U-shaped and made of brick, which was painted a pristine white. The door and shutters were painted black and made the whole house look elegant.

The front door opened after she knocked on it and Betsy appeared. Totally put together as always, Betsy welcomed Kenna. "Hello, my dear. I didn't know you were coming over."

"Hi, Mrs. Ashton. I went Derby shopping and brought some

things over to show Will. I also brought him some dinner since I know he'll be out at the barn all night."

"You simply must call me Betsy. Will has already gone down to the barn to sit with Spires Landing and Naked Boot Leg." Betsy shook her head, "I hate that name. William named Spires Landing and I loved it. But, William told Will that Boots wouldn't become a race horse and he could name it whatever he wanted. The horse William chose, who was supposed to be the Derby contender, was named Spires Edge. Will took exception to the fact we didn't pick the same horse. One night, he and some of his old teammates who were visiting got carried away and picked this name for him. I call him Boots, but I'll let you know that while I smile and cheer for him, I cringe every time I hear his name called."

"I can understand that. Will tried to explain what the name meant, but I just did the smile and nod thing."

"Go on down to the barn, and I'll see you next week for the party." Betsy pointed down to the road beside the house that led to the stallion barn.

Kenna walked to her car and was putting the covered dish in the back seat when she heard the front door open again.

"Kenna!"

Kenna raised her head and smiled at William. "Hi, Mr. Ashton."

"It's William, and I wanted to tell you to honk your horn when you're approaching the barn. Normally, we don't want to disturb the horses, but since it's dark out, we started this so Will knows it's someone friendly coming towards him. I wouldn't want him to accidentally shoot you."

"Shoot me?"

"Yes, Will is sitting down there with a loaded rifle so make sure you announce yourself."

"Is the rifle really necessary?"

"Well, Spires Landing is insured for over thirty million dollars and Boots has the same potential. Wouldn't you use a gun to guard a barn with the combined worth of sixty million dollars?"

"I didn't think about it that way. I guess I would."

"Just be careful and make sure you honk. Good night, hon."

"Good night, William." Kenna got into the driver's seat and started down the small paved road. She passed some barns and followed the arrows pointing to the stallion barn. When it finally came into view, she honked her horn and saw the barn door open. Will stood there with a rifle leaning against the open door.

She smiled and waved, though she knew Will would have a hard time seeing the smile in the dim light. She looked around for a place to park and saw Will's truck in a small parking lot on the far side of the circled driveway.

She parked and reached around to retrieve Will's dinner when she heard him open her door. "This is a pleasant surprise. You're right in time. I was just starting to tell the horses about you."

"Good thing I decided to come see you then." She handed him the covered dish that had a big BLT sandwich and chips on it. "I thought you might want a snack."

"Thank you." He put the dish on top of the car and pulled her toward him for a searing kiss. "Come on, I'll show you around the barn and introduce you to the boys." He put his arm around her waist and led her to the barn.

She got to meet Spires Landing first and was shocked by how large he was. He seemed so imposing. But as Will had mentioned, he seemed only interested in the sugar cube she had in her hand. He nuzzled her with approval when she opened her palm to him.

Boots was just the opposite. He was smaller and more compact. He wasn't won over by the sugar cube. It took an apple to get him over on her side. "They're amazing. I can't believe how much personality they have."

"Yeah, they're something alright. Boots has a sense of humor and likes to play with his jockey before the race. Boots refuses to allow him to mount until the jockey scratches him behind the ears. As soon as he does, Boots lets him up. If he doesn't, Boots dances around and will try to buck him off. Spires, on the other hand, is nothing but a sweetheart. He'd be perfectly happy just letting people feed and pet him."

She went back to the hay bales set up as a table to snack on some of the chips. "What is this floor made out of? It kinda bounces."

"It's made from old tires. The rubber is easy on the horses and also very easy to clean."

Kenna sat down and grabbed a chip. "You want some?"

"If you're offering."

She was about to reach for another chip when she noticed he wasn't going for the plate, but was leaning down toward her. She lifted her face to his and melted into his kiss. With his lips never leaving hers, he laid her back on a bale of hay. She wrapped her legs around his waist and pulled him closer to her. She was rewarded when she felt his groan vibrate through his chest and felt his erection through his jeans. He ran one hand up and down her side, gently caressing the side of her breast. She arched forward and moved his hand to cover her breast. She sucked in a breath as she felt her breasts swell with anticipation. He cupped her breast and traced his thumb around her nipple until it was a rigid peak.

"As much as I'd like to continue, I'm expecting Jose to stay with me tonight. He should be here in the next couple of minutes, and I'm not too partial to the thought of anyone seeing you naked but me," he groaned into her neck before pushing away. "Besides, I have to get all this hay out of your hair."

Kenna bolted up, "Oh, I forgot! I wanted to show you these amazing works of art that Paige created for me to wear to the Derby. I left them in the car. I'll be right back." Kenna stood up and brushed some of the hay off of her pants and tried to take a couple of pieces out from her hair before giving up. She figured it would be easier to brush them out when she got her purse from the car.

She heard Will take a bite of his sandwich as she walked toward the open barn door. The sandwich had been a good idea. She was halfway to her car when she heard the first rumble in the night. She listened and decided it was definitely from a truck. She started walking toward her car again and smiled. It was a good thing she and Will stopped when they did or Jose would've driven up at a very inopportune time.

She took another couple of steps before she saw the truck lights break the hilltop just a little ways from her. Nothing seemed strange until the high beams were thrown. Blinded, she heard the engine gun. The truck rocketed forward, and it took her only a minute to process that this wasn't Jose.

"Shit!" Kenna turned back toward the barn and took off at a dead run as fast as she could. But she was too far away from the barn. The truck was going to be able to cut her off. She looked up at the truck and decided to try something new. She turned sharply away from the barn and ran parallel to it a short distance to a four plank fence. She couldn't make out any animals in the pasture through the darkness and scrambled over the fence. With a bone-jarring thud, her feet hit the ground. "Oh, this is going to hurt in the morning," she said to herself through gritted teeth as she pushed off again into a run.

"Kenna!" she heard Will yell before the first gunshot rang out. She wasn't sure if it came from the truck or if it came from Will. Since the truck was still coming on fast, she wasn't going to take the time to turn around to find out.

She heard tires skidding and another gunshot ring out. This time it was followed by the sound of breaking glass, and she was pretty sure Will had hit the truck. She was in the dark now, stumbling over the uneven ground. She decided to risk a quick peek. Turning her head, she saw the truck fishtail and then break through the four plank fence. Boards went flying and a horse cried out in front of her. She turned her head around right before running into a horse. The headlights from the truck were creeping towards her, and she could see there were at least five horses running away from the truck as it sped toward her.

Her lungs were starting to burn and her legs were going numb. She was taking deep, gulping breaths. She couldn't outrun a truck, but she could make tighter turns. She immediately turned at a ninety degree angle and continued to do so multiple times. She slowly worked her way back toward Will. The truck had to slow down to keep up with her constant changes in direction. She was only a couple hundred yards away when she tried to make the last push towards Will. But that was when the truck circled around and cut off her path.

Blinded by the light, Kenna tried to make a sharp turn. The truck was gaining fast. She saw Will rest the rifle on the fence and take aim. She turned and ran as fast as she could. She could feel the rumbling of the engine in the ground when her feet pounded the earth as fast and hard as they could. The truck was almost on top of her. She saw the bright lights become more focused and finally the truck drew even with her. She tried to look in the window, but the uneven ground made it hard to get a good view. Shots rang out and pinged off the metal of the truck until she heard a hiss of air. She prepared herself for another ninety degree turn, when in her peripheral vision, she saw the truck fishtail out of control. She gathered all her energy and jumped away from the truck a second before the tail of the truck whipped around at her.

She felt nothing but air for a second before she landed. Pain ripped through her hip as she landed, and her head snapped upwards before slamming against the ground. She heard Will call her name as blackness started to close in.

"Kenna! Kenna! Answer me, are you okay? Kenna?" She felt Will touch her head but the blackness was closing in.

Oh God, was she dying? She couldn't die without Will knowing how much he had come to mean to her. Pushing back the darkness, she tried to focus on the blurry image of Will leaning over her. "I love you, Will." And then her world went black.

CHAPTER 14

KENNA WAS WITH HER PARENTS. She was sitting on their favorite bench in Central Park smiling and laughing. "I've missed you so much." Her heart felt swollen with grief and happiness all at the same time.

She felt her mother squeeze her hand. "Come back to us, dear. Come on now, it's time to come back to us." Kenna shook her head. That wasn't her mother's voice.

"Kenna, I know you can hear me. Open your eyes. Come on, honey, you can do it."

That was Will's voice. What was he doing with her parents in New York? But as she tried to reach for her mother, the image was torn apart by a bright white light.

"That's right, dear. Open those eyes."

Miss Lily? Was that Miss Lily? Kenna struggled to pry open her eyes. She shut them instantly against the harsh light. She let out a groan when she saw stars behind her eyelids.

"Turn down the overhead light a little," she heard Will order to someone. Instantly, the bright light dimmed and the throbbing lessened. She opened one eye and then the other.

"Oh thank God!" She turned toward the prayer and saw the Rose sisters at her side. Miss Lily held on to her hand for dear life.

"Hi ladies," she coughed. It felt like she had swallowed half the pasture. Miss Violet turned and poured her some water.

"Thank you."

"Nonsense. Just drink up."

Kenna took the cup and gulped it down. She turned to the other side of her hospital bed and saw Will standing there looking pale and worn out.

"It's okay, Will. I'm all right. I just hurt a lot. Nothing some Rose Family Sweet Tea won't take care of," she tried to joke.

She heard a snort and looked at the foot of the bed and saw Paige and Mo. Behind them were Betsy and William.

"Hi everyone." She saw some smiles and knew the worst was over. "Can someone fill me in on what happened after I was apparently knocked out?"

Will sat on the side of her bed and took her hand in his. "I managed to shoot a tire and it exploded. They were forced to drive off. My parents heard the gun fire and called 9-1-1. You were unconscious for almost four hours."

Kenna looked around the room, "Where's Ahmed?"

Mo stepped forward a bit. "He's looking into some things with Agent Parker. They should be here soon."

"Who's Agent Parker?" she asked, looking around at the group.

"He's an FBI agent from the Lexington branch that we've called in to help us out. Red was more than happy to have his assistance when he saw that the problem was escalating," Will explained to her.

Betsy stood up and William followed. "It's late and we should let Kenna get some rest. They'll discharge you tomorrow so long as all your scans come back clear." Betsy approached the bed and bent down to give Kenna a motherly kiss on the forehead. "We're so happy you're okay. You let us know if you want to stay with us or if you need anything, okay?"

"Thanks, Betsy. I will."

William followed suit and gave her a kiss on the forehead and a pat on the hand before turning and leaving. The Rose sisters were next, leaving just Will, Mo and Paige with her.

"I want you to know I'm using all of my resources to find out what is going on. It is one thing to break down some fences but quite another to injure my friend," Mo gently squeezed her hand.

"Ah, don't take too much time away from your lovely bride," Kenna joked.

"Bride?" Will and Paige said at the same time.

Kenna tried to laugh, but it hurt too much.

"See what rumors you've started. There's no bride, unless Kenna changes her mind and decides to marry me." Mo winked at her and the tension in the room finally fell away.

All four of them stopped laughing when the door to the room opened. Mo and Will moved protectively in front of Kenna but then relaxed and moved back to her side when Ahmed and Agent Parker entered the room.

She noticed that Agent Parker took in the whole room and everyone in it in a matter of seconds. He seemed quiet but confident. He looked more like a boxer than an FBI Agent. He was tall, had a tiny waist, massive shoulders, and nose that looked like it have been broken a time or two. He was just a bit shorter than Will's six feet two, probably closer to six feet even. His hair was raven black. But it was his eyes that drew attention. From where she lay, she couldn't tell if they were silver or such a pale blue that they appeared silver from a distance. Whatever they were, they were intriguing. Apparently, she wasn't the only one who thought so. She tried to hide a giggle as she watched a flush creep up Paige's cheeks.

"Ma'am, I'm Agent Cole Parker with the FBI. Mr. Rahman," he said, glancing at Mo, "made a call to Washington about an incident near his property. The Director of the FBI contacted me just a few hours ago to request I investigate this matter."

Kenna had to cover her mouth with her hand and pretend to cough when Paige fanned herself behind Agent Parker's back. Kenna wanted to, too. His voice had a slight gravel in it over his amazing southern accent. The combination was enough to make any woman swoon.

Kenna glanced at Mo. She couldn't believe he would contact the

Director of the FBI over the incident. She couldn't tell if Agent Parker was annoyed by the situation or if he was just stating facts. His face was unreadable.

"It's nice to meet you, Agent Parker," Kenna said politely. "What can I do for you?"

"If you're feeling up to it, I'd like to talk to you privately. Then, if it's all right with you," he said turning to Will, "I would like you to take me to your farm and show me where the incidents have taken place. I've read the sheriff's report, and he too requested assistance from the Louisville Field Office. But the paperwork hadn't filtered through the channels to get to me yet."

Both Kenna and Will nodded their approval and Mo squeezed her hand.

"If you need me, you know how to reach me. Ahmed will stay here with you and drive you home when they discharge you tomorrow. As you know, there are certain things I am dealing with, so I must leave. If I don't see you before you are discharged, I will try to stop by your place." He leaned down and placed a friendly kiss on her cheek.

"Thank you, Mo. For everything. But you don't have to leave, Ahmed...."

Mo cut her off by narrowing his eyes and staring her down.

"Okay, he can stay. Thank you both," she said to Mo and Ahmed as they left the room. She heard a chair being pulled up and figured Ahmed was settling in for the night.

"I better get going, too. I'll update the Roses and see you tomorrow," Paige said as she came over and gave Kenna a soft hug. Kenna couldn't be sure, but thought she saw a slight tightening of Agent Parker's jaw when he watched Paige bend over. Too bad it seemed Paige wanted nothing more than to get out of there. She spared Agent Parker not a single glance as she left.

Will leaned over the bed and placed a gentle, yet territorial, kiss on her lips. "Agent Parker, I'll wait for you outside."

"How are you feeling, Ms. Mason?"

"Pretty stiff. Every now and then I get dizzy. Thank you for asking."

"Can you tell me your relationship to the Rahman family?" He pulled out a small notebook from the back pocket of his jeans and a pen from inside his navy FBI windbreaker before taking a seat next to her.

"We're friends, why?"

"I'm trying to get a feel for the situation. What about the Ashton family?"

"As you could probably tell, Will and I are dating."

"What about the parents?"

Kenna clenched her fist, "Don't even suggest they had anything to do with this. Betsy and William are wonderful. They are kind and loving people who are centerpieces in this community."

"What about your family, Ms. Mason?" Agent Parker brought his head up from his notes to look her in the eye. She knew he saw her hesitation and wondered what he thought about it.

"I don't have any. My parents were killed in an automobile accident."

He lowered his head and began to scribble some notes. "What brought you to Keeneston, Ms. Mason?"

"My job."

"You were an attorney from New York. How did that bring you to Kentucky?"

Ah, so he had already researched her. She was hopeful that no red flags had gone up to alert the boys back home to her location. But she had a sinking feeling it did. "I wanted out of litigation and wanted to be a prosecutor. I searched many states, and this was the first offer I got."

"To help me get all the facts straight, I'm going to ask you to walk me through the incident."

Kenna spent the next hour going over the incident time and time again. She was starting to get frustrated since it seemed like Agent Parker was trying to pick out every detail. But she told herself that he was just doing his job.

Finally, he sat back in his chair and put away his notepad. "I've asked around about you. It seems that most of the town holds a good opinion of you. That leads me to believe the driver of the truck didn't show up with the intent of killing you, specifically. I'm sure I'll learn more when I tour the farm and talk to Mr. Ashton, but it appears that the incident you suffered tonight was the result of the continued attacks on the Ashton farm. You just got caught in the wrong place at the wrong time."

"I must admit, I'm glad you're on the case, Agent Parker. The situation has taken a toll on the Ashtons and the Rahmans. I know most FBI agents get assigned locations, so are you familiar with this area and the politics of it? I know, as an outsider, that it's done a little differently down here. Horses worth millions of dollars and deals based on handshakes are not the norm."

"Yes, ma'am. I understand it all very well. I'm from a town outside of Nashville, Tennessee, called Murfreesboro. I graduated with a B.A. in government studies from Centre College in the small town of Danville, Kentucky. I obtained my Masters in Criminal Justice from Eastern Kentucky University in Richmond, Kentucky. I was first assigned to the D.C. office. When the position here became available two years ago, I put in for the transfer. Between the years I spent at Centre and EKU, I'm very familiar with the workings of small towns and the horse industry. But, I'm not sure the attacks are actually because of the horses." With that mysterious announcement, he stood up and zipped up his jacket.

"Just one more thing. I can provide you a detail for one night if you'd prefer it to Mr. Rahman's man. I don't want to alarm you, but Ahmed does have a certain reputation in the law enforcement world as a very dangerous man. If you'd feel safer, I can provide one of my men for the night."

Kenna thought Ahmed would be proud of his reputation and then finally understood the disbelief Mo showed when Ahmed admitted her success in interrogating him. "Ahmed has been very kind to me and I consider him a friend. I'd actually feel more comfortable with him here than with one of your men. But, if you don't mind my asking, what is he known for? Does he have a last name? I don't think I've heard anyone use it."

"No last name that we know of. He travels on diplomatic papers. Even though the government has asked for it, we haven't been provided it. He has a reputation among our overseas operatives as a man with no conscience when it comes to interrogation. It's a good thing you're a friend."

She smiled at Agent Parker and pulled up the blanket to her chest as he left. Before she could think further about the conversation, she felt her eyelids fall and was asleep before the door closed behind Agent Parker.

"AHMED, DON'T YOU DO IT." Kenna swatted at his arm, "I'm perfectly capable of getting out of the car myself and walking to my room. There's nothing wrong with my legs. I'm just a little bruised."

Ahmed's eyes narrowed, "You will not climb up those stairs and that is the end of it." He reached again for her but she shoved his hand away. She twirled around in her seat, opened the opposite door and got out of the car.

"There. See, I'm perfectly fine." She walked toward Ahmed, but when things got a little blurry, she had to place her hand on the trunk to steady herself. Before she could hide the wobble, Ahmed was around the car and she was lifted up into his arms. She gave him a light punch when she saw the 'I told you so' look on his face though.

Miss Lily hurried to open the front door and led Ahmed upstairs. "You just settle down right here and I'll get you something to eat. I bet you're starving."

Ahmed laid her in bed as she heard Paige shout from downstairs that she was here. Ahmed said his good-byes and handed off care duties to Paige and Lily. Paige took out a pair of soft cotton pajamas and fuzzy socks from her store. Miss Lily came upstairs with some corn chowder, crackers and a roast beef sandwich. Kenna took a sip of the cold pink lemonade and decided being pampered for one more day wouldn't be too horrible.

TWO HOURS LATER, Kenna decided being pampered was horrible. She wanted to be left alone, but people where constantly stopping by. They brought pies, casseroles, flowers, three copies of the weekly gossip rag they called a newspaper, and four copies of the latest *Southern Living*. Though she really did enjoy the newspaper, one copy would've been enough.

"Okay, everyone. Our patient needs her rest. Shoo, shoo. I'll see you all tomorrow at Church and give you an update." Miss Lily ushered people out the door, thanking them for the gifts they had brought. Kenna reached for a snicker doodle and realized the room was finally quiet. Paige went back to check on her shop and finish a custom order Derby hat. Miss Lily was still talking to people downstairs. It was glorious.

She stretched her legs and raised her arms over her head. The dizziness was better, and she decided to risk getting up to get her computer. She was happy when no blackness came and everything stayed in focus. Logging into her email, she was feeling pretty optimistic. For a while, she had to admit to herself that she had thought the mad trucker was someone hired to kill her.

The dizziness and blackness came back when she saw her email account. She didn't even have to open the email from Danielle to know it was bad news. There was no subject line, and when she opened the email it read,

HE'S COMING.

KENNA CLOSED the laptop and lay down. She stared up at the ceiling. Did it mean the men had found Danielle or that they were coming after her? Even with her mind in turmoil, she felt her eyelids fall and sleep took over once more.

Kenna's sleep was dreamless and she woke refreshed the next morning. She stood up and was happy to see all traces of dizziness were gone. She only had a slight headache remaining. She couldn't believe she had slept for so long, but her body was definitely thankful. She undressed and took a long, hot bath, further soothing her bruised body. She explored the massive bruising that ran down her right side, the worst of it being on her hip. The bruise on her shoulder was already turning yellow, but the bruise on her hip was still an angry purple.

She had just finished getting dressed when she heard a soft knock on the door a second before it opened.

"Hey, sweetheart, how are you feeling today? You look much better." Will came across the room and gave her an easy kiss on the lips.

"I do feel better. Just a little stiff, but that's all. How are things at the farm? Did something happen? Is that why you weren't here yesterday?"

"I was here yesterday. I was here all through dinner and left a little after nine at night. You were sound asleep and I didn't think I should wake you. Miss Lily even let me up to your room by myself. Of course, I had to leave the door open." He ran a finger over her cheek. "I've never been so afraid in all my life than when I saw you being chased by that truck. I was so scared I was going to lose you."

Kenna placed her hand on his chest and stepped into his open arms, laying her head over his heart and snuggling in. Will ran his hand gently up and down her back and rested his cheek on top of her head. "I need to ask you something, Kenna."

"Sure, what is it?"

"Right before you passed out, you told me you loved me. Did you mean it?"

She heard Will's heart speed up and felt the hitch in his breathing. She leaned her head back and looked at him, "Yes. I meant it. I love you, Will."

Will brought his lips to hers and a gentle kiss turned desperate. Both of them were desperate to show how much their love meant. "You were the first girl I ever loved and I love you so very much." His voice became husky and his eyes darkened before he took her mouth again in another passionate kiss. Kenna could feel warmth spreading across her body as a certain peace and excitement settled into her that only love could bring.

"Come on, let's get you some lunch and some fresh air. You feel up to eating on the porch, or do you want me to bring a tray up here?" Will asked as he brushed a strand of hair back from her forehead and placed it behind her ear.

"Let's go outside."

Will took her hand and helped her down the stairs. The more she moved, the better she felt. Miss Lily brought a tray outside and scurried back to the kitchen. It was Sunday, and she still had a couple guests coming in that afternoon, set to stay through the Derby.

They ate lunch in silence, and Kenna took the time to debate telling Will the whole truth. She knew this was the time. They loved each other and she wanted a life with him. The only way she could honestly have that was to tell him what really brought her to Kentucky.

"Will, there's something we need to talk about." She took a deep breath and had trouble meeting his gaze when he looked up from his sandwich. When she finally dragged her eyes to his face, she realized he wasn't looking at her but rather at the street. Kenna turned her head and followed his gaze to a massive limo pulling to a stop in front of the bed and breakfast.

"I wonder who that is?" Will mumbled.

The door was opened and out stepped Mo's mother. "Oh, that's Fatima, Mo's mom." Kenna and Will rose to greet her.

"I heard of your accident. I am so sorry. I hope you are recovering," Fatima said as she gave Kenna a quick kiss on the cheek.

"Thank you, I am. I'd like to introduce you to Will Ashton. Will, this is Fatima Ali Rahman."

Will bowed his head briefly, "Ma'am, it's a pleasure to meet you."

"Thank you. I've brought this for you both," she said as she handed Kenna a gold encrusted envelope.

"What is it?" Kenna broke the red wax seal and opened the envelope.

"It is an invitation to our Derby Ball on Friday evening. I hope you both can attend."

"Thank you, Fatima. It was so nice of you to think of us. Will, does our schedule allow for us to go?"

"We'll be honored to be there, Queen Fatima," Will said as he wrapped his arm around Kenna's waist.

"Wonderful. I'm sure Mohtadi will be pleased as well. I will let you get some rest." With that Fatima walked back to her limo.

"This should be a lot of fun. Last year, their party boasted many foreign dignitaries and was a who's who of the international rich and powerful." Will moved back and let Kenna sit back down on the swing.

"I guess it's a good thing I went ahead and bought a formal gown." Kenna paused, "Will, as I was saying before, there is something I need to tell you. You see, when I was in New York...."

"What the hell?" Will cut her off and stood up. She, too, had heard the sirens but didn't realize until now they were heading toward her. In New York, you tuned out sirens. Here, people looked out windows and came outside to see what happened.

Noodle came to a screeching halt in front of Miss Lily's and jumped out. "Will, there's been another incident. Someone put a copperhead into Boots' stall."

"Is he injured?" Will was already running to his car.

"I don't know. I got a report that a groom heard Boots cry and managed to kill it with a pitchfork, but I don't know anything else." Noodle jumped back into his car and started to turn around.

"I'm sorry, Kenna. I have to deal with this. I'll meet you at the cafe for dinner at six, okay?" Before Kenna had a chance to respond, Will was already driving off with Noodle's sirens leading the way.

"Miss Lily, what's a copperhead?" Kenna didn't even bother turning around to see if she was standing there. She knew at the first wail of the siren Miss Lily would be at the door to see what happened.

"It's a poisonous snake. It's a copper color so it would blend real easy in all that hay. I hope that horse is okay. It would crush Will if something happened to him," Miss Lily tisked.

BY DINNER TIME, Kenna couldn't sit still. She had been so close to getting this weight off of her by telling Will all about New York. Both times, she'd been interrupted. Then, another boulder set itself down on her when Will hadn't called to tell her the status at the farm. She paced her room, waiting for some news but none came.

Luckily, Paige had shown up with an array of locally made jewelry and distracted her by helping to pick out pieces to wear to all of the week's events.

Kenna looked down at her new watch, "Oh, it's almost six. Will wanted me to meet him at the cafe, but I haven't heard from him to know if I should still go."

"I'm starving. I'll go down with you. If he doesn't show up, you can be my date for the evening," Paige said as she began to pack up her jewelry boxes.

She and Paige walked into the cafe and found a table in the back. They tried to avoid the mob of well wishers and those who wanted Kenna to tell the story over and over again.

"I need to go." Paige turned to grab her purse, and Kenna looked over her shoulder to see what had freaked her friend out.

"Why, it's just Will and Agent Parker?" Kenna paused, "Oh, I get it. You have the hots for Mr. FBI and don't like that he makes you feel, how should I say it... flushed." Kenna grinned at her friend's obvious discomfort. "I thought with all those brothers, Parker would be putty in your hands. I also didn't take you for a coward." Kenna sat back against the booth and let her smile show. She knew she got Paige with that one.

Paige put her purse down when Will and Agent Parker approached. She scooted as close to the wall as she could get. Both men said hello as Will sat next to Kenna. Agent Parker sat next to Paige. Kenna smothered her laughter and had to fight pounding on the table in hysterics as she watched Paige cling to the wall. Likewise, Agent Parker sat so far on the edge of the seat, he was about to fall out of the booth. It just reminded her of the second grade when boys and girls thought each other had cooties. The side glances they gave each other was enough to confirm that these two were hot for each other.

"Well, Boots is okay and so is the groom who killed the snake," Will told the table. "I'm going to leave tomorrow morning with Boots and go to Louisville. Hopefully, the increased security there will help prevent any further attacks on him." Will turned to Kenna, "I'll be back Friday to take you to Mo's ball. The next morning, at ten, is the Derby Breakfast at my farm. Then we'll drive up for the Derby."

Kenna nodded her agreement to the plan.

"I'll be meeting you up there as well. Some of my men will be on the grounds dressed as farm hands," Agent Parker added. "I'll also need a list of all the events you're going to so that my team can be there, just in case this is personal and they try to make a move at one of these shindigs."

Will nodded and the two men continued to discuss the case while dinner was eaten. As soon as he was able, Agent Parker excused himself and Paige left soon after.

"What was up with those two?" Will asked.

"I think there's some major chemistry there, and they don't know what to do with it," Kenna laughed.

"Well, I know what to do with our chemistry. Come on, let me take you home."

CHAPTER 15

"IT SHOULD BE DOWN."

"No, it should be up."

"What about swept back?"

Kenna closed her eyes for a second and asked for patience. Paige and Lily were about to come to blows over the way she should style her hair for Mo's ball that night. Daisy was trying to find middle ground. Violet had conceded and had gone in search of a snack to prepare for the room filled with women.

"If I may interrupt for a second," Kenna put down her eyeliner, "I'd like to wear my hair down for the Ashton event and the Derby. Makes it easier to go from one event to the other. It's such a formal event tonight that I think I'd look strange if my hair was down. Besides, the back of the dress is really neat. I'd like to make sure everyone has a good view of it. The trouble is, I have no idea how to do anything other than a ponytail or a French twist."

"I guess that makes sense wearing it up for tonight. I can help you put it up," Paige said as she plugged in the curling iron. "I know exactly what I want to do."

"Here we go!" Violet opened the door and brought in a tray of fruit and cheese.

Kenna grabbed a piece of cheese before Paige started attacking her hair with lots of hairspray and the curling iron.

Daisy pulled out the royal blue silk dress. "Which shoes do you want for this?"

"The strappy bronze sandals in the trunk." She heard Daisy open the truck and gasp.

"This whole thing is filled with shoes! I didn't know one person could own so many shoes. You might have to be more specific, dear. How will I know which shoes I'm looking for?" Daisy asked as she started pulling shoe after shoe out of the trunk.

"They have a four inch heel and an ankle strap." She heard more grunting and saw more shoes being dropped onto the ground before she heard Daisy mumble something.

"What did you say?"

"I said, I think these are the ones. You have a couple of pairs that look similar." She saw Daisy walk toward her and hold out the pair of shoes she wanted to wear.

"That's them! Thanks for finding them. How are you doing, Paige?"

"Pretty good. Almost done."

"My head feels like it weighs ten pounds. What's going on back there?"

"It's the bobby pins. You have to use a ton of them to pin the wavy pieces down," Paige mumbled, yanked and then stabbed another bobby pin into Kenna's head. "There. I think I got it."

Kenna heard the accented murmurs and turned to the mirror. "Oh, I love it! Thank you Paige!" Kenna turned her head back and forth and hardly recognized herself. Her normally straight hair had a gentle curl and was swept back to the nape of her neck. Tiny strands were then curled and pinned in a chignon, forming a whimsical look to the classic up style.

"Oh my gosh, look at the time! Will is set to arrive any minute," Lily said as she looked at her watch. "Come on, girls, we'll go down and wait for him while Paige helps Kenna finish up."

Paige helped Kenna step into the gown and zip it up. The royal blue silk slinked over her skin, gently caressing it as she moved.

"This dress feels so good!" Kenna said as she twirled in front of the mirror. The silk hugged her silhouette while the draping emphasized her bust and then fell to the ground. In the back the draping fell away to form a short train that would be only slightly noticeable once she put on her heels. Sliding her feet into her strapped sandals, she heard Will pull up. Paige and Kenna rushed to finish getting the shoes on and applying the final round of lipstick before heading downstairs.

Will stood outside on the porch in a custom-made tuxedo, looking every bit the star athlete he was. There was something about men in tuxes that sent Kenna's heart pounding. But something about this man in a tux was enough to make her thank the Lord every day and twice on Sundays as Miss Lily would say.

He was talking to the Roses and didn't look up until she opened the screen door. She smiled when he looked up. It made her feel like the most beautiful woman in the world when he let his face show pleasure in her appearance.

"You look amazing. Now I'm going to have to spend the night fighting off the men in the room." She took his arm when he offered it to lead her to a limousine he had rented for the weekend. "Ladies." He tipped his head to Paige and the Roses. "Don't wait up," he winked as he opened the door for Kenna.

Kenna turned and waved good-bye to her friends. As they got into the limo, Kenna turned to him. "This is great, Will." She slid next to him and ran her hand up his thigh. She couldn't stop herself. The tux was calling to her and it was saying 'touch me'.

"There's more." Will leaned over and brushed his hand across her breasts as he reached for a little refrigerator door. He pulled out a bottle of champagne. "I thought we could sip some champagne as we drive out to the farm. Then we'll have to wait in a long line to get to the door. Whatever will we do to fill the time?" He popped the cork and poured two glasses.

"To the woman I love," he said, as he raised his glass and tapped it to hers.

"To the man I love," she said before taking a sip. "Hmm, so good." She looked over at Will when she realized he hadn't taken a sip and that he was staring at her hand. She, too, looked at her hand and realized it had started its own love affair with the tux. She was rubbing his leg up and down, up and down, and her hand was gradually working its way to his growing erection. "Oh! I'm sorry! It's the tux," she flushed.

"I hope that's not all it is," he said before he grabbed her into a passionate kiss. She should thank her runaway hand if this was the kind of kisses she got when it went wandering.

Will leaned back from the kiss and took his glass. He raised it, "To the tux," and then downed the rest of the drink.

Raising her glass she said, "Definitely to your tux," and followed suit, downing her drink. The second she finished the champagne, Will's hands were on her.

"I should've toasted this dress," he said before sliding his hand under the hem and working his way up her thigh. He bent his head and ran a series of kisses over the swells of her breasts before pushing it down and pulling out a taut nipple into his mouth. Kenna's head fell back as the sensations of Will's mouth, hand, and the silk sliding over her skin took over.

All too soon, he pulled back and a sound of displeasure escaped from her. "Don't stop, please," she moaned.

"I'd love nothing more than to continue, but we're here. We probably have five minutes before our limo makes it to the front door. Though I'd love nothing more than for you to step out looking like a satisfied woman, I figured you might want to freshen up. Also, I need to run through all my football stats for a minute."

"Football stats? Why?"

Will looked down at his pants.

Without a word from Will, Kenna came to understand. "Oh. You need a distraction." She couldn't seem to take her gaze away from his erection tenting out in his pants.

"Kenna, that doesn't help," he said through gritted teeth.

She pulled her gaze away and opened the small purse, looking for her lipstick and a small mirror. She straightened her hair and reapplied her lipstick. The door was opened and Will got out first, offering her his hand.

As she got out of the car, he leaned over and whispered in her ear, "I never did get to find out if you have anything on under that dress."

She gasped but then laughed when he winked at her.

He escorted her through security and into the ballroom of Mo's house. The party was huge. She was pretty sure she'd seen the governor, a music mogul, and maybe even the Vice President of the United States. There were members of royal families there from all over the world, mostly the younger sets. One of the princes of England was there with some royal from Sweden.

"Come on, I see some people I know." He placed her hand on his arm, covering it with his other hand and led her through the crowd. She met the owner of the NFL team Will had played for, along with some other horse people. One was actually an ambassador to one of the small countries in Eastern Europe.

They had made it halfway across the ballroom when a new dance started. Will pulled her onto the dance floor and swept her easily into the dance. They talked and laughed as they moved around the dance floor.

"Look, Will. There's Mo with Bachelorette Number Two. Or is that a new one?" she asked, using her chin to indicate where Mo was dancing with a beautiful woman in formal dress.

"Bachelorette Number Two?" Will's brows drew together.

"That's what I call them, the women his father keeps sending to his doorstep, hoping Mo will marry. He can't escape this one since his father is here. Normally, he just sends them back home. This one just happens to be the second one I've met. I'm pretty sure she's more like Bachelorette Number Fourteen or so," she laughed as Mo managed to catch her eye. "It looks like he needs us to rescue him. Come on, handsome, lead the way over to him."

Will steered her closer to Mo. By the time the dance ended, they were side by side.

"Will, Kenna, so good to see you again. Will, I must speak to you about a horse if you don't mind." Mo turned to Number Two, "If you will excuse me, madam, I have business to discuss with these two. Please, do not wait for me as this may take a while. Go and mingle. Maybe you will find someone you have a lot in common with." Number Two bowed her head and walked off into the crowd.

"Very nice, Mo. Could you be more dismissive?" Kenna chided.

"She's a mute. She's clung to my arm the whole night and has not said a single word. Thankfully, you two came along and can rescue me. My father has promised me a choice of eligible women tonight. Apparently he's invited upwards of ten women and their families here. If I wasn't hosting this party at my house, I would run and hide until they all left."

Kenna couldn't help it as a giggle escaped. Apparently Will was having as much trouble as she was not laughing, because as soon as her giggle escaped, so did a bark of laughter from him.

"If only I had won that stupid basketball game, then I could have made you come as my date. Maybe that would have kept the wolves at bay," Mo muttered.

"What are you talking about?" Will asked Mo. Kenna laughed again and tried to smother it with her hand over her mouth.

"Kenna and I played a basketball game the other night. The winner got to name a favor from the loser. I was the loser. If I had won the favor, I would have called for her to escort me to the ball tonight and help me keep those women away from me," Mo explained.

"So, what favor did Kenna win?"

"I haven't claimed it yet. I'll know it when I see it," she laughed, laying her hand on Will's arm and loving the feel of him enveloping it with his own hand. Mo and Will started talking about the horses competing against Boots when Kenna let her attention be drawn away from the conversation, and she started to people watch.

She felt it first. Will's arm muscles tightened beneath her hand.

"Shit. What the hell is she doing here?" Kenna followed Will's gaze as Mo turned to see what it was.

"Dammit, my parents were forced into inviting her father Senator Bruce. He sits on a committee that we need the support of to start raising the amount of oil we export into the country. I didn't think he'd bring his daughter as his escort. I'm sorry," Mo said in hushed tones as they watched Whitney sashay her way towards them in a dress that more resembled lingerie than a ball gown.

"Your Highness," Whitney said as she attempted a curtsey but only managed a clumsy bend that threatened to spill her breasts out of her dress. "Thank you so much for thinking about my family. We're having a wonderful time." She placed her hand on Mo's arm and managed to rub her breast against him.

"I'm so very glad," Mo said stiffly and with a sneer of disgust as he removed her hand from his arm and stepped away from her.

Pretending not to notice the snub, she turned to Will and tried to kiss his lips. Instead, she hit his cheek when he turned his head. "Hello, my love. Are you having a good time?"

"Until just recently." He pulled Kenna closer to his side as if trying to protect her, or maybe using her as a shield.

"Oh, Kenna, darling. I have such a surprise for you!" Whitney squealed, the sound sending shivers up Kenna's back. "You're just going to die! Look!" Whitney pointed over Kenna shoulder.

Kenna, Will and Mo all turned to see what, or rather who, the surprise was. Her reaction was instantaneous. She felt all the blood leave her head so fast that she thought she'd faint. She started shaking, and she gripped Will's arm with bone-crushing strength.

Chad Taylor, with a fitted tux, bleached teeth, and hair gelled perfectly in place, sauntered up to her. "Hello, sweetheart. Happy to see me?"

Will moved to place his arm around her waist and pulled her against him. Out of the corner of her blurring vision, she saw Mo move next to her on her other side.

Not to be left out of the center of attention, Whitney moved over to Chad and placed her hand on his arm. "Last week I was on the Hill with Daddy for lunch, and he had Chad with him. I was talking about how fortunate I was to speak with you about my legal matters and how I wanted you to be my lawyer from now on. I told him, 'Miss Mason is the wonderful new attorney everyone is talking about', and how you're the only woman in town taking on all these stuffy old men."

No, this couldn't be happening. Shivers overtook her body. She knew by using her own name it would only be a matter of time before they found her. She was lucky to have made it this long. But she still found that she was unprepared for this encounter.

"And then Chad asked me, 'Mason? Not McKenna Mason?' and I was like, 'Oh my God, you know McKenna?' What a surprise it turned out to be to find your boyfriend from D.C." Turning to Will she asked, "Did you know Kenna had a boyfriend slaving away in D.C.?"

Chad hadn't taken his eyes off of her yet. The cold, calculating sneer he was trying to pass off as a smile was only turning more predatory as he ran his eyes up and down her body, pausing at her breasts for a moment before traveling on. "It seems that these past couple of months have done wonders for you, sweetheart."

Kenna managed to drag in a breath and then remembered, *He's coming.* Danielle tried to warn her, but she was in such a state of denial she had thought someone was coming after Danielle.

She felt Mo shift next to her. She watched as he pulled himself up to his full height and a mask of impenetrable royal snobbery was placed on his face. "I don't believe we've met. I am Prince Rahman and this is my place." With a flick of his wrist he indicated the house around him. "Well, one of my places." The elitist tone froze the almost feral smile on Chad's face and finally made him break eye contact with her.

"Chad Taylor, I lobby for special interest groups in Washington. I believe we have...."

"Excuse me, I see someone more important I need to talk to." Without looking at anyone in the group, Mo walked away and into the crowd. Kenna watched where he was headed and almost felt a little relief when she saw he was headed straight to Ahmed.

Will patted her hand, "Royalty, you never know what they are going to do. I do believe this is our waltz, my love." With a territorial stare at Chad, Will turned to her, "Shall we?"

He was offering her a lifeline, a means of escape, and she took it. He escorted her to the dance floor and swept her elegantly into the waltz. As Will spun her around the dance floor, she saw Whitney and Chad move to the edge of one side of the dance floor. On the other side, she saw Mo and Ahmed with their heads together. She caught a small gesture Mo made in Whitney and Chad's direction.

"So, are you going to tell me what's going on? With that reaction of yours, I don't believe he's your boyfriend. Don't think for one minute I'm upset about that. However, I am upset you were keeping something from me that obviously upsets you. I'm here to share your problems, Kenna. I love you. All of you, even your problems."

Kenna couldn't stop the nervous laughter that bubbled up, "Then I hope you love me a lot because this is a whopper."

"Kenna, I'm here for you. I love you and nothing will change that. Trust me."

"Okay, the quick version is after my birthday in February, my best friend Danielle and I went back to my office late at night to get some papers. The senior partners hold a poker night once a month that local and national VIP's, such as judges and senators, attended. Chad had been with me at the party but said he had to meet a senator in D.C. and left early. Danielle and I drove back to the office. While she was changing her shoes and looking for her keys, I went to my office. I heard a lot of noise from the poker night but just ignored it till I heard a scream. I snuck down the hall and hid in a cubicle to look into the conference room. There was a stripper on our table, and I thought everything was fine. I was about to leave when she screamed again. I looked in and saw Chad knock her onto the table and rip off her top. She was crying and screaming. No one was doing anything. Chad then said he won at poker, so he was going first, and the rest could have her when he was done with her. He was going to rape her, Will. But the worst was standing there knowing the girl was about to be raped by some of the most prominent men in the state and country, and I couldn't stop it."

She felt Will's arms tighten around her. "What happened next?"

"I called 9-1-1 and reported the crime in progress. Then I grabbed a stapler, marched into the room and hit Chad on the head with it."

"That's my girl," Will chuckled.

"My boss lost it. He told Chad he'd deal with the girl, but Chad had to deal with me. He then attacked me. He pinned me against the cubicle, ripped my clothes, and hit me some. He was saying things such as how he was going to teach me how to behave like a proper girlfriend. Of course, I broke it off during this and told him I hoped he met a nice man in jail to become his new bitch. He forced my skirt up and that's when Danielle shouted for me to hurry up." She took a deep breath to calm herself.

Will stopped dancing, "Did he, um, did he manage...."

"No."

Will started dancing again although much more stiffly.

"When Danielle yelled out for me, it surprised him. I had tried to knee him before, but my skirt was too tight. When he lifted my skirt, he actually allowed me to fight back. When he leaned over me and told me he had always wanted a threesome with Dani and me, I went wild. I kicked him in the balls and punched him in the head. Then I ran like hell."

"Thank God you got away." He leaned down and kissed her forehead. "How did you come to Kentucky?" But before the story could continue, a bit of commotion caught his eye. "Hey, look over there. What is Ahmed doing with them?"

He spun her around so she could see Ahmed smiling at Chad and Whitney, handing them glasses of champagne. He toasted them and then hailed a waiter over with new glasses of champagne as soon as the first were empty.

"I don't know, but I'm sure it's not accidental. Um, I actually ended up here because of the job. That and I remembered you. I was hoping you'd be here to help me get this job. I wanted a town that was small but close to a bigger city so I could easily escape if found."

"You don't have to look for escape routes anymore. You're staying right here with me. But, I do think we should talk to Agent Parker about this."

"I don't think so, Will. Dani wrote me and told me there were arrest warrants out for us. There were powerful people in that room, Will. They could destroy me. They could frame me and put me in jail."

"Okay, how about we tell Mo and Ahmed first. See what they can find out." The dance ended and they look around for Chad and Whitney. They didn't see them but did see Mo being forced together with what appeared to be another bachelorette.

"Is everything all right, Kenna?" Ahmed had quietly appeared beside her.

"Actually, we were looking for you and Mo to seek your advice." She looked around again. "Where did Chad and Whitney go?"

"They had too much champagne and were driven home," he winked. "I'll go rescue Mo and meet you at his private parlor.

KENNA AND WILL STOOD BACK as Mo unlocked the door to his private parlor a short while later. Will and Kenna took a seat on the love seat as Mo picked up the basketball and tossed it from hand to hand.

"Okay, you going to tell us what's going on?" Mo asked.

"I am. And I guess I'm also going to call in that favor you owe me unless you want to go two out of three?" she said jokingly, trying to break the tense feeling in the room.

"You have unlimited favors. Now please, how can we help?"

Kenna told them what she had just told Will. Ahmed interrupted, asking specific questions now and then, but they generally sat and listened.

"And your friend, Danielle, do you know if she's safe? Do you have enough money?"

"I don't know about Danielle. She stayed in New York and

followed the people who were tracking her. She's the one who found out about the warrants, and she's the one who warned me that they had found me. I just didn't realize it at the time. And yes, I have enough money. I pulled it all out right before I left."

"The question is: What do we do now? I told Kenna she couldn't run and hide, that I'd protect her. I wanted to go to Agent Parker, but she's worried about the warrant. What do you two think?" Will put a supportive hand on her knee and gave it a quick squeeze.

"I'm sorry to interrupt. Kenna, you said your friend was following men. Did she describe them?" Ahmed asked.

Kenna nodded, "Yes. She called them the Men in Black, like the movie. She thought they worked for a senator because they kept referring to him. She couldn't find out which one though. Apparently they looked very governmental."

"Then we have an issue. Two men fitting that description stopped by the hospital the night I stayed with you. I heard them asking for you at the nurse's station. They flashed a badge and were directed to your room. When they saw me, they walked past without much of a look and left. I assumed they were FBI checking up on you per Agent Parker's request."

The room grew quiet. Kenna knew what that meant. It meant that if Ahmed hadn't been there, she'd be dead now. Will pulled her against him and rested his head on top of hers.

"Ahmed, go find Agent Parker. Don't tell him anything, only that I need to speak with him," Mo said. It amazed Kenna how fast the friendly Mo could disappear and be replaced by Prince Rahman.

Mo moved to his desk, pulled out his computer and began typing. She leaned against Will and snuggled into him. As horrible as seeing Chad had been and knowing everything was coming to a head, she had a sense of relief to know she wasn't fighting everything on her own now.

"You do realize that one of the senators in that room that night was probably Senator Bruce, don't you, McKenna?" Mo said quietly from behind his desk.

She nodded and was about to reply when the door was opened for Agent Parker.

"Mr. Rahman, I don't appreciate being treated like one of your personal security guards. I'm a member of the FBI. It's best you remember that before your man here interrupts me again while I'm doing my job of helping the secret service protect the dignitaries at your party." Agent Parker stopped in front of the desk and placed his hands on his hips. "I understand your concern over your friend, but no one is after her. I told you that the investigation led us to rule her out as the target."

Mo didn't bother to get up. Instead his eyes narrowed, and it seemed to Kenna that the room temperature had fallen twenty degrees. She needed to learn how to do that.

"First of all, you are a mister. I am royalty and you shall address me as such. Second, there is more going on than you know, Agent Parker. If you don't want a career-making case handed to you, then get out and I'll find someone else to bring down a couple of senators, sitting judges, and senior partners of the largest law firm in New York."

"Okay, you have my attention now." Parker took out his notepad and looked at Mo. A silent showdown occurred between the two, and it seemed they came to some understanding since Mo continued.

"Put that away. Nothing gets written down because I am going to tell you a fairytale first to see what kind of ending it needs." Mo didn't offer Parker a seat and Agent Parker didn't seem to mind. He stood still, with his hands behind his back, and listened as Mo told her story.

"That's an interesting story you have there. I assume one of the two princesses is Kenna. Who is the other one and where is she?"

"Sorry, Agent, it doesn't work like that. If you were writing this story, what kind of ending would it have? What would the knight do to help the princesses?"

"I don't know. The problem is I can't get rid of a warrant issued by the New York City Police Department. Technically, if I know of the location of a person with a warrant on her, I should notify NYPD. But if the storyline is true, it would be dangerous to send the princess back to New York. So I would advise the princess to not reveal herself to the knight yet. You get my meaning?" Agent Parker looked directly at her.

"Yes. So, the moral of the story is the knight doesn't rescue the princesses and is pretty worthless," Kenna shot back to him.

"No, the moral of the story isn't clear yet. There are some steps the knight must take to avoid mandatory reporting back to the king. Kenna, if you could describe the maiden, what would she look like?"

"Why?"

Dropping the pretense of the fairytale, Agent Parker answered, "I want to run a missing persons report to see if anyone fits her description. I'll also run a Jane Doe search on bodies that were found since you left. I must admit, I'm having a hard time believing any of this. But, if it is true, then that means the truck that tried to run you over may have actually been meant for you."

"There's something else, agent," Ahmed said. "The night Kenna was in the hospital, did you send team of men to do a walk by and make sure she was all right?"

Agent Parker's brows came together, and he narrowed his eyes as if sensing something important, "No, why?"

"Because around one in the morning, two men approached the nurse's station and flashed a badge. They asked after Kenna and then walked toward her room. When they saw me, they walked right on by. At the time, I thought you had sent them to make sure I was still there. But now that I know everything, I think they belonged to Senator Bruce."

"Senator Bruce? How did you come to that conclusion?"

"Without naming names, my friend stayed in New York and was being followed. She was able to turn the table on the men, the same two men that match Ahmed's description. She followed them and heard them talking about their boss, the senator," Kenna told him. "Then tonight, when Whitney was rubbing in the fact she had brought Chad here, she mentioned that she had told him about me while on the Hill. She was having lunch with her dad and her dad brought Chad with him."

Agent Parker closed his eyes, and she watched his lips move as he was working his way through things. "Okay, I see where you figured one of the senators was Bruce. I also agree with you that the men trying to find your friend, and who stopped by the hospital, are probably the private security employed by Bruce. Ahmed, would you recognize them if you saw them again?"

"Of course."

"Are they here tonight? Bruce is, and don't you think he would've brought his security? It's like a status symbol at these things." Parker turned to Ahmed.

"I'm sure he did. But the question is how to get them all together again?" And then, Ahmed just smiled. "Never mind, I know the answer. Go back to the party and just follow the flow." Ahmed walked out the door whistling as all three of them stared at him.

"Uh-oh. It's never good when he's happy, especially when he's whistling," Mo said as he stood up from his desk. "Come on, let's get back to the ball and see if we can get the senator in our sights.

The ball was in full swing and the dance floor was packed. They made their way around the room, slowly nodding and waving to the people they knew. Agent Parker was introduced as a friend of Will's from college when anyone asked. They were only about a quarter of the way through the room when Parker spotted him.

"He's over there in the corner with a young lady. I'm guessing the girl to be at most eighteen. The way he's touching her is almost enough for me to arrest him for statutory rape."

Kenna, Will, and Mo casually looked around and spotted one obvious security detail. Before Kenna could ask what Ahmed was going to do, she saw him walk in.

"Look, there's Ahmed." She watched him walk over to the band director and talk to him a minute. The band director nodded and went to the microphone as the dance ended. Ahmed made his way over to the group.

"Ladies and gentlemen, our host has asked that specific patriotic songs be played for the countries represented here tonight. For our first selection, we'll be playing a part of Tchaikovsky's 1812 Overture, which includes a Russian folk dance. The next piece will be a selection from Antonin Dvorak's Slavonic Dances. Please, enjoy." Polite clapping broke out among the guests as the orchestra started the Tchaikovsky piece.

The group stared at Ahmed, and he rocked back on his heels, whistling along with the ebb and flow of the music. Kenna looked at Will and he shrugged in return. No one had ever seen Ahmed so relaxed.

"Let us slowly make our way over to the senator. We have a little less than four minutes until we see all of his security team," Ahmed said as he turned and started slowly making his way over to the senator.

Mo arched an eyebrow but followed as the group moved to within hearing distance of the senator.

"Why don't we just become part of his group? Then we would hear everything and be up close and personal with his security," Will asked, looking around the group for their confirmation.

"We can't just walk up to a senator and become part of his group," Parker said.

"Sure we can," Will and Mo said at the same time. Mo and Will took the lead and Parker offered Kenna his arm.

"Senator, good to see you again, sir. Have you met our host, Sheik Rahman?" Will gestured to Mo. "Sheik, this is Senator Bruce. He is a powerful man in Congress and I'm sure just the person you would want to talk with." Will noticed that the senator had pulled his hand out from under the woman's skirt. Will could see his ego expanding as he heaped on the praise.

"Senator, it is nice to make your acquaintance. We should talk after the Derby about a deal I want to make with the U.S. to help lower your oil prices. If Will recommends you, I'm sure you are just the man who is powerful enough to bring such economic relief to your people." Mo bowed his head respectfully.

"Sheik, it just an honor for you to come to me with such a

proposal. I would love to hear it. Will is right, I'm the chairman of the..." His words were cut off by the boom of the bass drum simulating cannon fire.

By the fourth boom of the bass drum, Kenna saw three men hurriedly making their way toward the senator. Ahmed had come to stand next to her so he could speak more easily to Agent Parker. The three took a small step closer to the senator to hear what the security men were whispering to him.

"Is there a problem, Senator?" Mo had reverted to his royal voice, but the senator didn't seem to have heard him.

"What do you mean explode?" She noticed his voice cracked and leaned in closer to hear the answer.

"Yes, sir. There appeared to have been a small gas tank leak. When someone flicked a finished cigarette, um, well, the fumes caught and then the gas caught. The car, um, it exploded." The security guard's eyes were glued to his shoes.

"That is unfortunate, Senator. I have more people to see to, as I'm sure you understand. Let me leave you with Ahmed, my head of security. Ahmed!" Mo snapped his fingers and Ahmed stepped to his side. "See that my personal limousine is at the senator's disposal and make sure you take him wherever he wishes to go tonight."

"Sheik, I am honored. Thank you."

Mo nodded and walked off.

Kenna grabbed Parker's arm and followed Mo and Will as they made their way around the room. The orchestra started Dvorak's Slovakian Dances. Kenna tapped her foot and found herself swaying to the music as the men talked football with the prime minister of Bulgaria, who was surprisingly fond of the American sport. She closed her eyes and took it in. The piece was a fast-paced dance music that slowed to beautiful, almost playful movements before picking her back up and twirling her around.

She opened her eyes and found Will standing in front of her. "Mo has everything under control. Let's dance." He wrapped his arm around Kenna's waist as they went flying around the dance floor. His strong frame led her around and around, faster and faster. As he whipped her around the floor to the contagious music of Dvorak, the stresses and fears flew off little by little with every spin she made until all that was left were her Will and her. She looked up at him and saw his face was flushed, his dimples shining as the music built to a fevered pace. They flew around the floor, twirling, stepping and spinning. Her laughter rang out as her feet barely touched the ground. The song came to a dramatic end that left the people on the dance floor breathless and the crowd clapping.

The orchestra took a bow before starting a slow and beautiful violin piece. "May I have this dance?" Will took an elegant bow, making her laugh again. She offered him her hand and he led her in a traditional waltz by Strauss. "I know this has been a stressful night, but these are moments I will treasure forever. The feel of you in my arms, dancing and toasting with champagne... nothing has ever felt so right."

She smiled and stepped closer to him, her breasts brushing against his chest as the couple took another wide turn. His leg slid between hers.

"I know it sounds strange, but all I feel now is relief. I should've told you and Mo earlier. Will, this night has been magical. I'm curious as to how a football player is such a good dancer."

"It's kind of embarrassing, but in college my coach made me take ballroom and ballet classes to improve my footwork when I was scrambling."

"Well, make sure you thank him for me. This has been such a romantic night, excluding the exes, of course."

"Well, let me take you home and show you what other moves I have."

She laughed and shook her head. He couldn't be perfect after all. If cheesy lines were the worst of it, she was pretty lucky.

CHAPTER 16

KENNA SNUGGLED INTO HER PILLOW. Will definitely showed her moves she didn't know even existed. She drifted off to sleep with Will wrapped around her while strands of their waltz danced in her head.

She dreamt of her and Will alone on the dance floor. He pulled her close, so close there was no telling where her body ended and his started. As she reached up to look into his eyes, she found the leering face of Chad.

She opened her mouth to scream, but no sounds came out.

"Ready to be taught how to be a good girlfriend?"

She tried to pull away, but his hands gripped her tight enough to break her arm bones. As he leaned forward to kiss her, she jerked back as hard as she could. Kenna woke when she hit the floor. The impact jarred her and knocked the lamp from the nightstand. She took a deep breath to steady herself and rubbed her bottom as she stood up. She looked around embarrassed that Will might have seen her fall out of bed. But she didn't see him.

She went to the bathroom and found a note from Will attached to the mirror, telling her he was checking on the farm before breakfast. He asked her to call him when she was ready to be picked up. Not wanting to bother him, she called Paige and asked if she could pick her up on her way to the party.

Kenna took a quick shower and applied her makeup. She slipped into the sage colored sundress and tan wedges. She put on the matching Derby hat Paige had made and headed downstairs to wait for her. She only had to wait a minute before she saw Paige's car pull into the drive.

"Good morning. You look amazing!" Kenna told Paige as she got into the car. Paige was highlighting her light brown hair and hazel eyes with a warm, orange-colored sundress. Her hat's base was the same orange, but it was trimmed with a grass-colored green organza ribbon that was tied ornately in the back.

"Thanks, you too. I'm so glad that hat worked for you." Kenna noted that Paige looked a little nervous, well as nervous as someone as tough as Paige got.

"Is something wrong, Paige? You're acting a little shy and you're never shy."

"Actually, there is. I know we just met a couple of months ago, but how could you not tell me you had this boyfriend up in New York while you're chasing after Will? Does Will know about him?"

Kenna gasped and then cringed when she realized how bad it looked to Paige. "How did you find out?" she quietly asked.

"Your boyfriend stopped by my store looking for you this morning."

Suddenly scared, she couldn't quite stop her voice from shaking, "Did you tell him where to find me?"

Paige didn't say anything for a minute and then asked, "He's not your boyfriend, is he?"

"Not anymore. But, Paige, this is important. Did you tell him where I was staying?"

"No, I found it odd that your boyfriend wouldn't know where to find you. It was only after he asked that it hit me that something was off. He knew so many personal details about you that I didn't know what to think."

Kenna blew out a breath and sighed, "I had wanted to keep

everything quiet, but I see I'm not going to be able to do so. I had to tell Will and Mo last night when Whitney brought Chad to Mo's ball."

"Maybe you should just start from the beginning and I'll drive slowly," Paige said as she pulled out of the driveway.

Kenna started the story and told Paige all about Danielle, GTH, Chad, and the night she fled the city. As they neared the Ashton Farm, she told Paige about the previous night.

"Oh man, I wish I could've been there to see that," she laughed. "I know this is a serious situation, but come on! Blowing up a car? That's true friendship."

Kenna burst out laughing. "I hadn't thought of it like that before, but you're right. I'll make sure to give Ahmed a kiss although I'm sure Agent Parker will just lecture me again."

"Lecture you? Why?"

"Apparently Ahmed has quite the international reputation as a tough guy, something to do with how he interrogates people. I assume he doesn't care too much about the Geneva Convention laws on torture. Normally, I'd be freaked out. But he's just so sweet to me that I can't imagine any different side of him."

"Yeah, what's sweeter than blowing up a car surrounded by private security people?" Paige chuckled. But then she turned serious. "Just forget about Agent Parker. He's just so, so, controlling. That's it, controlling. Like, he thinks because he's in the FBI, he can just walk around being superior to everyone, telling them what to do and who to be friends with."

Kenna decided to keep her mouth shut on that one. She was pretty sure Paige was upset because it was Paige who normally controlled the relationship.

Paige stopped the car at the valet parking. They both got out and headed down the stone path toward the large white tent erected behind the house. Red roses were everywhere and soft music filtered up to them.

"Speak of the devil...." Kenna grinned as she spotted Agent Parker making his way toward them.

He stopped before them and tipped his black cowboy hat at them. The black hat went perfectly with his black suit. He definitely had the dark and brooding look down. "Ladies, you both look like spring itself."

"Thank you. You look quite handsome yourself. Is there any news from last night?" Kenna said for them both since Paige still hadn't picked her chin off the ground.

"I ran all the searches and didn't find anyone matching your description either reported missing or showing up as a Jane Doe. You're an attorney, so you know all the possibilities. Because we don't have evidence of a crime, we can't arrest Chad for assault at this time that is unless you decide to file charges. I have someone working to find the origin of the mystery warrant issued for you and your friend. I'll let you know what we find out."

"I was afraid of that. I did want to tell you that Chad stopped by Paige's shop this morning looking for me," she told Agent Parker as she waved at Will who was approaching them.

"Good morning, Cole. Glad you could make it out," Will said as he shook Agent Parker's hand.

"Cole?" Paige sputtered.

"That's me," Agent Parker gestured toward the tent. "How about we walk down to the tent and I'll get you a mimosa? You can tell me about your encounter with Chad."

"Okay, Agent Parker, lead the way."

"Cole, please, or Parker. Either work, but you all can drop the agent title. Today I'm just one of your group."

Kenna was pretty sure Cole had a death wish when he put his hand on the small of Paige's back and escorted her to the tent.

"Cole?" Kenna asked Will as she turned to receive his kiss.

"Yeah, who knew he had a personality? He stopped by the barn this morning when I was doing rounds and helped me feed the horses. He told me he has a friend doing him a favor and looking into things in New York. He realizes this isn't Mo pulling rank for nothing. The reports he's getting back from New York show deep shadows of corruption all through the FBI, the NYPD, the judicial system, and even Congress. He and one other person are trying to find something solid. They are in the delicate position of not knowing whom to trust and working on the case without permission from their higher ups."

"Wow! I guess there's more to Cole than I thought."

Will put his hand around her waist and pulled her in tight. "You look beautiful this morning. Getting out of your bed was the hardest thing I've ever done." He leaned down and gave her a quick but passionate kiss. "The rest will have to wait until the limo ride up to Louisville. Come on, let me introduce you to some of my friends."

Kenna spent the next hour being introduced to Will's old coaches from UK, coaches and teammates from the NFL, high school buddies, and even old teachers from grade school. In between meeting the special people from Will's life, she also met the Governor of Kentucky and a slew of Kentucky celebrities including Ashley Judd, Diane Sawyer, and William Shatner.

Kenna was whirling from all the names of the people she was meeting. She sighed in relief as she saw Mo and Ahmed approaching with Cole and Paige not far behind. She smiled from ear to ear as she watched Paige and Cole treat each other like two cats about to be thrown into a bag together.

"Well, we have some more news we thought we should share now that we have everyone together," Mo said. "Go ahead, Ahmed. Fill them in on what you found out."

"I took Chad's champagne glass from the party and ran his prints through my software. It triggered nineteen names. Chad has had a long history of identity theft and fraud in his life. Every time a warrant is issued under a name, he tosses it out and starts all over again. He has pulled jobs all over the world and is wanted by numerous countries, including England, France, Spain, and Russia. He's wanted for embezzlement, rape, suspicion of murder of a lovely young girl in France, and much more."

"Since I'm not acting in official capacity at the moment, I'm not even going to think about how many laws your software broke running criminal checks through all those countries' databases. I'm guessing they didn't give you permission." Cole pinched the bridge of his nose and closed his eyes.

"As you said, you're not going to ask. Now, the real question: What are we going to do to catch him?"

Cole filled Ahmed in on his activities off the record and agreed that Ahmed should keep digging to see what he could find on Chad and his patterns. "Now that we know Cole and Ahmed have a loosely based game plan, let's try to enjoy the rest of the day. Is everyone ready to head up to the Derby?"

"I guess that is my cue to head on home and crank up the TV. Smile and wave to me if you're on camera," Paige said as she hugged Kenna goodbye.

"You're not going?" Cole blurted. Everyone turned to stare at him. "What?"

Will cleared his throat and stared off in the distance. Mo and Ahmed stared at their feet as Paige flushed red.

"My dear, I would be honored if you allowed me to escort you. You look splendid. It would be a shame not to get you on TV as well." Mo gave an elegant bow that had Paige giggling.

"Really?! Here I design Derby hats and I've never even been before! Thanks, Mo!" Paige squealed as she jumped over and gave Mo a big smacking kiss on the cheek.

"Okay, we'll see you at the red carpet," Will said as he took Kenna's hand. They started to make their way to their limo.

"They were supposed to move my things into your limo when we got here. I hope they did." She opened the back door and leaned in, "Oh good! It's all here."

"What did you have moved into our car?" Will slid in behind her and started at the hat box, makeup case, shoe boxes, two hanging bags, and a duffle bag.

"You didn't think I was going to wear this same dress to the Derby and to the Derby Ball, did you?"

"Well, no. But...." He waved his arm at all the items.

"Stop complaining. Help me get out of this dress so I can change."

Will grinned ear to ear, his dimples coming out. "Now that is something I am happy to do."

"STOP IT," Kenna laughed as she smacked his hand away from the hemline of her dress. "We're about to get out of the car and I see photographers. I don't want a picture of you with your hand up my skirt."

"I can't help it. It's those sleeves that look like little bows on your arms. They make me think of you as a present. I just can't wait to unwrap you... again." He kissed her above the little bow on her arm, and she felt his lips lay seductive kisses along her clavicle.

She felt her eyes close and her head loll to one side, allowing him better access. He nibbled his way from the hollow point of her neck up to her ear.

"We're here." Then she felt him pull away suddenly and saw the door open. As the cameras flashed, Will stepped out and held out his hand for her with a huge smile on his face. That little... she'd get him back.

She placed her hand in his and stood up. She looked back and saw Mo's limo coming to a stop where theirs had just left. Will put her hand on his arm and angled her into the crowd of photographers lined up on both sides of the red carpet leading to Millionaires' Row.

With a smile, he leaned over and whispered in her ear, "Relax and just smile."

She took a deep breath and took in the feel of the place. Cheers went up from the end of a race, the crowds milled around looking at horses, and people tried to get their favorite celebrity's autographs. People were shouting to Will and he obliged every single person with an autograph. He even stopped for pictures with any kid who asked. They reached the television coverage line and started answering questions from the reporters.

"Will Ashton, Mr. Ashton! Over here," A young man shouted and waved. Will led her to the young man. "It's so cool to see you again.

Your tip earned me a ton of money last year. You think you can make it two for two?"

"I don't know, Justin, but I sure hope so."

"She's interviewing John Wall right now, but you'll be next." Justin turned and waved down another person walking the chute.

"Who are you doing the interview with and who's John Wall?" She tried to read the initials on the microphone, but could only see the back of a pretty lady's hat and a tall, athletic man.

"It's for Sports Network. They want me to do an interview since I'm a sports guy. John Wall also went to UK but played basketball. He's now in the NBA playing for Washington. Good kid," Will said and then put on a coy smile. "And, it's not just me. You're going in, too." Before she could refuse, he was pulling her toward the smiling lady.

"Will, it's so nice to see you again. How is retirement?" she asked as a make-up artist powdered her nose a little.

"Good, Stacy, thanks. Stacy, this is McKenna Mason. Kenna, this is Stacy Hartford."

"Nice to meet you. Will doesn't bring women around very often, you must be special. Okay, ready?" Not waiting for a response, she smiled into the camera. "We're here with Will Ashton, owner of last year's Derby winner, Spires Landing. You also know Will from his years as the starting quarterback for Washington. He retired to take over Ashton Farm just two years ago. I'm sure all football fans will be cheering on his horse in the Derby this year." She paused and turned toward them and smiled. "Do you think Naked Boot Leg can fool the field and come out in the lead at the end of the most exciting two minutes in sports?"

"I think so. He's nothing like Spires Landing but has a whole lot of heart and spunk. We'll see. It's a field of twenty great horses this year." She couldn't believe how calm he was. His hands weren't sweaty, and she couldn't feel any nervousness in the arm he had around her.

"Will, who is this lovely lady you have with you today?"

He smiled and tightened his grasp on her waist. She was pretty sure he thought she was going to bolt. "This is my beautiful and talented girlfriend, McKenna Mason."

"Girlfriend? My, my, you heard it first on Sports Nation," she said smiling into the camera. "Is it serious?"

"It sure is," Will said as he smiled down into Kenna's face.

Turning to Kenna now, Stacy continued, "That is an amazing hat. Who designed it?"

Kenna was expecting that question and relaxed, "Paige Davies, owner of Southern Charms, in Keeneston made it. She's the best designer I've ever seen. Actually, she's right behind me, being escorted by Prince Mohtadi Ali Rahman." She pointed out Paige. The information that Paige was being escorted by one of the world's most eligible bachelors drew all attention away from Kenna. Stacy practically knocked her over to get to Mo and Paige.

"That was cheating," Will whispered in her ear as they easily made their way down the rest of the red carpet.

They went through the open double doors and into a private elevator. An operating assistant pushed the top button, and they rode in silence to Millionaire's Row 6.

Will explained that Millionaire's Row was broken down into Row 4 and Row 6. Millionaire's Row took up two stories and was the calm amid the frenzy of Derby Day. The elevator doors swooshed open, and she stepped out onto thick, luxurious carpet.

She looked around and was almost blinded by the bright colors worn by celebrities of all sorts. Women were in bright dresses and brighter hats. Men dressed in pink, white, and blue shirts with outrageous bowties quietly mingled with each other.

"This isn't the real Derby. But, I needed to stop by to see some friends." Will remained calm and in control. "I'll take you downstairs to get the true feel of the day in a minute."

She nodded as he led her down the row, past the private betting stands and bars, past the tables where some people sat studying the racing program and others sat talking over drinks. People nodded politely in greeting instead of running for autographs. She saw actors, actresses, singers, models, and political celebrities ranging from royalty down to governors.

She looked out the wall of windows and past the balcony to see the track and a massive infield filled with tents and people. She slowed to look out the window as Will started waving to a friend nearby.

The elevator opened as Paige, Mo, Ahmed, and Cole stepped out. Lots of nods were sent Mo's way, and soon the gossip began as people put their heads together to figure out who Paige was. Then there were a couple of women licking their lips and blatantly inviting Cole to their table. Cole grinned and gave them a wink, causing Paige to narrow her eyes at him.

"Isn't this amazing? Do you know I was asked about my hats?" Paige said excitedly as she greeted Kenna with a hug. "This is so amazing!"

They made their way to the balcony to watch the third race of the day. The warm breeze greeted her as she took a spot at the rail. Paige had grabbed a program and scanned the horses when the trumpet called the horses to post.

"Who are you going to root for in this race?" Will asked as he slid his arm around her shoulders.

"I have no idea. How do you even pick one?"

"Well, there's the odds on favorite which is currently the number five horse Good Luck Girl. Or you can go with a favorite jockey, trainer, horse farm, color silks they wear, or lucky numbers. Some people try to guess based on the weather, speed of the horse, or breeding."

"Well, I like number three's name Special Kind of Justice."

"Okay, this is a one and one sixteenth mile race. They'll enter the gates way over there and cross the finish line here." Will pointed to a little straight lane where the horses were entering the gate off of the final turn.

"And they're set!" the announcer said. A bell rang, the gates flew open, and the field of ten horses shot out. The people started cheering and yelling for their favorite horses. Some called them by name and some by number. The hooves of the horses were pounding in the dirt as they flew past the grandstand. Kenna could feel the vibration in her feet, and the sound of forty hooves eating up the track resonated in her chest.

She gripped the rail and leaned forward. The sun hit her face, and the wind blew her hair back as she tried to see where her horse was. They were now on the far side of the track, and the cheers continued to get louder and louder as the horses pounded their way into the corner.

As the horses rounded the corner heading for home, the pounding of their hooves started off as a quiet rumble. The vibrations of over a hundred and fifty thousand people jumping up and down while yelling encouragement drowned it out. But as the horses neared the finish line, the stampede produced an overwhelming sound and feeling.

Kenna held her breath as ten half ton thoroughbreds pushed, wove, and barreled for the finish line. Neck and neck, the two horses in front were battling each other. A third was darting toward the front on the rail. "That's my horse! Oh Will, that's my horse. Go Justice!" She jumped up and down, screaming as Special Kind of Justice pushed closer to the front two horses.

The thundering of their hooves grew louder and louder as they reached the grandstand. The jockeys all rode low on their saddles, using every muscle in their bodies to push their horses faster and faster. The third horse started to fade, leaving Good Luck Girl and Special Kind of Justice battling it out as they approached the finish line.

The tension and excitement from the spectators rolled through the grandstand. Every muscle in Kenna tightened as she willed her horse to go just a little faster. And then suddenly, the horses crossed the finish line. Good Luck Girl had won by a head.

Kenna let a breath out that she didn't know she was holding. "Wow, that was so cool."

"Come on, let me show you around the grandstand before the

next race. Then, if you want, we can watch the rest of the races from my box, or we can come back up here."

"No, I want to see the grandstand."

"I'm going to stay up here a while before moving down to Mo's box," Paige said. "He has one near Will's, so we'll be able to cheer Boots on together. You two have fun!" Paige gave her a hug and went back to studying the racing program.

"NOW, THIS IS THE DERBY!" Will said as he was shoved to the side in the massive crowd. He had led her down the elevator and into the standing room only section of the grandstand. Kenna had been stepped on, bumped, and shoved... but all done in the nicest way. People couldn't help it, it was just that crowded. Everyone was so jovial that they'd just shout out an apology and wish you luck on your next bet before being swept away in the crowd.

She had even been flashed. Well, not really her. As a group of infielders went into the tunnel, a girl saw Will and flashed him. Will bought Kenna a soft serve ice cream cone and stood as close as he could to the rail. "Come stand in front of me. If you thought it was exciting upstairs, wait until you see a race from the cheap seats."

The trumpet sounded and the horses lined up in the gate right in front of Kenna. She was so absorbed in the sounds of the horses and clicking of the gates being shut, she didn't notice Will had been busy taking photos and signing autographs.

The bell rang and the gates slammed open. The feel of the horses breaking free of the start was so exhilarating Kenna couldn't help but be awed.

"You enjoying it?" Will had to yell.

"This is amazing although I hate that I can't see them when they are on the backstretch! She turned to watch the jumbo screen of the horses racing down the backstretch. She then peered over to her left, waiting for them to make the corner to the final quarter mile. Being in the crowd, as opposed to above it, gave her a whole new experience. The noise was deafening as cheers welcomed the horses coming into sight.

She felt Will step up behind her. His arms rested on her shoulders as she cheered for every horse to win. They came thundering down upon her as they strove towards the finish line. Cheers went up from those who had won and sighs went up from those who had lost. The quiet that follows the end of a close race was so strange to Kenna.

"Come on, let's go up to the box." Will took her hand and led her toward the middle of the grandstand.

His hand was warm and secure around hers. She loved the feel of her soft skin against his calloused palms. She gave his hand a little squeeze and Will smiled back at her. It was the type of smile that made her heart swell. It was such an intimate communication between two people who loved one another. She smiled back, and they slowly made their way through the crowd to the elevators.

They rode to the third floor where they were greeted by security guards. After flashing their owners' badge, they made their way past a series of boxes filled with eight chairs each. On the outside rail of every box was the engraved name of various farms. They passed Desert Sun, Mo's farm, and went down a couple of stairs to a box on the first row. Kenna had a direct view of the start/finish line and was able to lean over the rail to see the mass of humanity they had just walked through.

"Kenna! Will! Oh, look at you two together!"

"June! It's so good to see you again." Kenna raced over to the box across from the Ashton Farm box. "I thought you weren't going to make it to the Derby this year."

June kissed both cheeks as Julius shook Will's hand.

"We didn't think we were, but a friend from Florida has a horse racing in the Derby and asked us to come with them. Of course we agreed! You look divine. I want to hear all about what's been going on while we were in Florida. Will you be going to the ball tonight?"

"Yes, we are planning to be there."

"Great! We'll talk there." June lowered her voice and with a grin said, "When we can have some girl talk."

"It's a date!"

WILL ESCORTED her down a step and across the aisle to the Ashton Farm box.

"This next race should be a good one. It's one of the biggest in turf." Will pointed to the infield. "See where the gate is?"

"It's in the grass. Why is it there?"

"It's for a turf race. The horses run on the grass. After every turf race, tons of workers go out there and put the divots back into place, just like in polo." Will rested his arm around the back of his chair as he continued to point out the people around them.

The owners of all the Derby contenders were close together. The other boxes were owned by prominent farms such as Mo's.

Throughout the races, people stopped by the box to chat. Some would sit down and talk football, horses, and anything else until the next race began.

The box cleared out right as another race was set to begin and Will leaned over to her. "Are you having fun?"

"This is just amazing." She looked below at the people hurrying to place their bets and the people mingling about the other owners' boxes. Smiles were as plentiful as hats.

"After this race, I need to go down to the barn and help get Boots ready for the race. It's a tradition we have. After I walk him out for the on-track warm up, I'll come back up here. If you'd like, you can come down with me, or you can stay up here and watch the next couple of races.

"No, I'd love to go down to the barn with you."

Will sat back and watched Kenna as she enjoyed the race. She sat at the edge of her seat, and her hand gripped the rail as she watched the horses start from the gate.

She felt Will's fingers dance along the side of her neck and trace the shell of her ear. She temporarily forgot about the race as he took a small strand of her hair and twirled it around his finger before pressing a gentle kiss behind her ear.

"Come on, let's go see Boots," he whispered.

"But the race...."

"It's over. The number four horse won." He stood up and held out his hand for her. She took it and stood staring at the emptying track. How did she not see or hear the end of the race?

CHAPTER 17

WILL LED her through a series of elevators and hallways until they exited the side of the grandstand at street level. They walked through security and past the paddocks where horses were being prepped. They worked their way through the crowds. Will took the time to sign autographs and answer the same question from twenty different reporters on what he thought his chances were of winning with Boots.

Finally, they made it to the barn where all the horses racing in the Derby were housed. Security was very tight, and Kenna thought she caught a glance of Noodle and Dinky walking around in suits.

When Boots saw Will, he tossed his head back and let out a whinny. Will dug into his pocket and pulled out a sugar cube for him. "Hey, big boy. How are you doing today?" Boots nuzzled his hand and then hit him with his head when he wouldn't give him any more snacks. "That's good, get mad and take it out on the other horses on the track."

"Hi, Mr. Ashton. He seems to be eating up this energy. Some horses get freaked out about it. Every time he sees a camera or hears his name being yelled, he puffs out like a macho man," a very short man said. He was wearing the royal blue and white colors of the

Ashton Farm, so it was pretty easy to guess he was the jockey riding Boots.

Boots looked over and saw Kenna. He stomped his feet and threw his head back. The jockey laughed, "I don't know who you are, but you better go over there and say hi to Boots before he kicks the stall."

"But, he's only met me once when I gave him an apple out at the farm."

"Rodrigo, this is Kenna Mason, my girlfriend. And Kenna, you gave him an apple once he'll now want one every time. He's a typical guy." Will and Rodrigo laughed as Will handed her another sugar cube.

Kenna approached Boots slowly. She was terrified of doing something to mess him up before his big race. She was still awed by the size of this 'small' horse that stood taller than she. His chestnut coat was shining. The white star between his eyes and the white on his nose seemed almost three dimensional against the rest of his coat. Boots grabbed the sugar cube from her hand and nuzzled her.

"Aren't you a sweet boy? And so handsome. You'll be the fastest horse out there today, won't you?" she cooed to him.

Will and Rodrigo stared in amazement as Boots nuzzled even more, asking Kenna to rub his nose. She continued to talk to him, whispering encouragements and even gave him a big kiss on the forehead for luck. "Oh no! I left a red lipstick stain on his forehead! Come here, Boots. Let me wash it off."

Boots backed up and refused to let her clean his forehead. Will came over and called to him and even offered him another sugar cube. But Boots refused to have the bright red lipstick mark wiped off. "Okay, we'll leave it on. You're trying to make all the others jealous, aren't you?"

Boots threw his head back again and came over to nuzzle Kenna.

"That's my boy," Kenna laughed. "But, I have to go and let you get ready for your big race. Now, if you run faster than all the other horses, then I'll give you lots more sugar cubes and even an apple or two." Kenna turned to find a third man staring at her.

"Kenna, this is Art Stringer. He's Boots' trainer. Art, this is my girlfriend McKenna Mason."

"Ma'am, I can't believe that's Boots. He's normally only nice to Will," Art said. Then he turned to the horse, "Are you ready to win for Miss Mason, Boots? It's time to get you warmed up." Art was dressed in a nice suit and a beautiful tie made to match the Ashford silks. He was bigger than Rodrigo but still not a tall man. The biggest difference with Art was the calm assurance that he radiated. He was confident in the way he handled Boots and the way he talked to him.

Will was helping, and Kenna knew she'd just be getting in the way. She looked down at the other stalls and saw similar activities taking place in all of them. "Hey, Will. I'm just going to go over to your barn and see some of the horses who ran yesterday."

"Okay. Can you see the barn from here?"

"Yes. It's just right over there." She pointed to a barn that sat about one hundred yards to the left and slightly behind the Derby barn.

"See you in a few. Love you."

"Love you, too. Don't worry, Boots, I'll be back to wish you luck before you go." Kenna blew him a kiss and took off for the other barn.

SHE SHOWED her badge to security and walked into the peaceful barn. It smelled of honey, oats, and hay. For a moment, she listened to the shifting of horses on the hay and snorts as they ate. It seemed a world apart from the boisterous party going on around the track. She found the tack room and grabbed a handful of sugar cubes for the horses.

"That's a good girl," she said as she gave a cube to one of the fillies that had finished third in the Oaks. The sound of high heels hitting the rubber walkway had her looking around. She hadn't seen the security guard since she had entered the barn, and his shoes definitely didn't make that sound.

"Paige? Is that you?" she raised her voice slightly and she heard the footsteps stop. She froze. Her hand rested right behind the horse's ear where she had been scratching. The filly whinnied, having felt the tension enter Kenna's body.

She paused to listen and heard the footsteps start again. The person coming was definitely a woman with heels. Kenna looked around the barn and realized that the tack room was at the furthest point away from the security of the open barn door. Her only way out was in the direction of the person approaching.

Kenna willed herself to think. She took a deep breath as she watched the shadow of the woman appear on the ground. She made her way closer to an empty stall.

"Going somewhere, Kenna? Am I really that repulsive?"

Kenna stopped halfway through the door and looked out to see Whitney standing at the entrance of the hallway. "Oh, I didn't know who it was. How are you doing, Whitney?" She let out a nervous laugh and placed her hand over her wildly beating heart.

Whitney was no threat. She was dressed to the nines in a cream colored, satin mini-dress with black heels and an exquisite black and cream hat that was a good three feet wide.

She saw Whitney's eyes narrow and felt the hatred pouring out of her. Kenna needed to revise that threat level, and fast. Whitney stomped up to her.

"You... you home-wrecking slut. You're nothing but a whore, and you ask me how I'm doing?" Kenna took another step back as Whitney swept down on her. "I was just fine until you came here and stole my husband away from me."

Kenna held up her hands, "Whitney, calm down. I didn't do anything to purposely hurt you. You and Will are divorced. I didn't break up your marriage," she said in a calm and level voice. The look in Whitney's eyes told her she wasn't of her right mind.

"That's where you have it wrong. I've been working at getting him back and I was so close. He was getting so worn down from all those accidents that he was ready to leave the farm and come back to Washington. I know he was contacted by Sports Network about taking a broadcasting job that would have him on TV every week. He would have been famous again, and I would be right by his side, the Belle of D.C... people would come to my house for parties. I'd have my own reality show to show the glamorous lifestyle of a football player's wife and a politician's daughter."

Whitney took another step closer and shoved Kenna. She felt Whitney's hands hit her shoulders and as she backed up, Kenna felt her heel slip between the rubber walkway and the stall entrance. She reached out, trying to grab for the stall door but only managed to grab a hold of Whitney's arm.

Whitney let out a scream as Kenna took her down. She felt the impact when she hit the floor and again when Whitney landed on her. "Get off me!" She tried to push Whitney off of her, but Whitney latched onto her hair.

"You bitch. I hate you. I hate you. I hate you." She felt Whitney rip off her hat and was about to crumple it when Kenna let go with a punch. Kenna wasn't able to pull back very far, but Whitney wasn't used to anyone hitting her and fell back instantly.

"Don't mess up my hat. Do you know how long that took Paige to make?" She got up and grabbed the hat from Whitney's hand as Whitney pressed her hand to her cheek.

Kenna made it a step from the door when she felt Whitney's cold hands wrap around her ankle and pull. Kenna went down hard on her stomach but managed to save the hat. "Whitney! Stop it! Why are you doing this?"

Whitney had her by the ankles and was pulling her back into the stall. "I told you. I had everything in place. I spent so much time planning it and so much money hiring people to execute my plan. It was going perfectly! He was getting so tired of sleeping in the barn. He was worried about his workers and his horses. If you had just left him alone, I'd be married to him again, and we'd be living back in our brownstone in D.C. I would be famous again!"

"You. You're the one that hired the people to damage Will's farm just so he'd leave Kentucky? Boy, are you stupid. Even after knowing Will for five minutes, I could tell you that wouldn't work. Is that why you tried to run me over in the truck? So I wouldn't be competition for you? Umph!" Kenna was flipped on her back and Whitney jumped on her. She felt Whitney's cold, tiny hand reach for her throat and panicked. She started to kick and flail.

"Ha! You're so stupid. That was Chad. He flew here right after our lunch in D.C. to see you for himself. I'm just sorry that he missed you. He was just having too much fun scaring you to just get the job done."

Kenna froze at Chad's name. Of course it had been him. The way he tormented her was just like what he had done in New York. For once, Whitney was right. He liked to scare you more first. He had toyed with the stripper. He had toyed with her, not once, but twice. If he hadn't gotten off on seeing her scared, she'd be dead twice over by now.

"This is what we're going to do. I'm going to hand you over to your boyfriend and let him take you back to New York where you belong. Chad will be so happy I managed to get you away from Will. Then, Will and I will live happily ever after."

Kenna bucked and Whitney fell on top of her. Kenna grabbed her perfectly dyed blonde hair and pulled for all she was worth. Whitney screeched and rolled off of her. Kenna rolled with her and was now on top.

Kenna grabbed handfuls of Whitney's hair and started banging her head against the ground. "Where is Chad? Where is that son of a bitch?"

Whitney's laugh sent chills running down her spine. "You'll never find him. But he will find you." Whitney laughed again.

Kenna lunged for her throat and started squeezing it. "You will tell me where he is."

But all Whitney did was laugh.

Kenna felt an arm come around her from behind and wrap around her waist. "Kenna, let go. We got this now," she heard Will's voice whisper to her through the haze of anger. "Come on, sweetheart. Let go. She's not going to get away."

"She knows where Chad is. He... he tried to kill me."

"I know, love. We'll find him. Just let go."

She had to will herself to unlatch her fingers from Whitney's throat, the maniacal laughter still sounding. Kenna looked behind her and saw Mo, Paige, Cole, Noodle, Dinky, and Ahmed all standing at the stall door.

"From what we heard, we have enough to put her away for a long time although, I think she may end up in a padded cell," Cole said as he approached her with his handcuffs out.

"Wait a minute, Agent Parker. I think I hear something outside. I believe everyone needs to check it out. Maybe it's Chad," Ahmed said, not moving from where he was leaning against the stall door.

"What? Why would we leave her here to go check out some noise?" Dinky asked as he put his hands on his hips.

Ahmed stared at Cole. "You know it's not over. You know we have to find Chad for it to be over and to bring down the whole circle of corruption."

Cole looked down at Whiney and back to Ahmed. His lips were pressed together so tightly they were turning white.

"Why would...Oh, I see." Kenna looked down at Whitney and frowned. She was clearly over the edge of madness. If she was turned over to Cole, she'd be sent to a minimum security mental resort for a couple of months to serve a sentence for hiring people to cause these accidents. Her father would make sure she talked to no one. She'd be out as soon as the scandal left the minds of the press.

If Ahmed took her, his diplomatic immunity would allow him more leeway in questioning her. He might be able to find out what she knew about her father's involvement with Chad, not to mention who else might be involved. She could be the key to unlock the whole thing.

"I hear it, too. Let's go boys. We need to check it out," Cole ordered as he ushered a sputtering Noodle and Dinky out of the barn. Cole stopped next to Ahmed, "Follow Geneva or we'll have a problem. Make sure she gets turned back to me when this is over. That's all I ask."

Ahmed gave a slight nod of his head, and Cole walked out with

Mo and Paige leading the way. Noodle and Dinky followed Cole as the puzzle pieces fell into place for everyone else.

"Let me know what you find out," Will said to Ahmed.

Kenna was pulled to her feet and Will wrapped his arm around her waist to pull her in tight. "How did you all find me? And, thank you. I'm sure I'd have been sorry if I had hurt her."

Ahmed gave a knowing smile. "The group came down because Paige wanted a picture of you two with Boots before the big race. When you didn't turn up, we headed over here. We heard Whitney scream and followed the noises of the fight. We got here right in time to hear her tell you she had planned the whole thing. We also heard that it was Chad who tried to kill you."

"Thanks for rescuing me." She looked over at Whitney when she noticed the laughter had stopped. She was staring at Will with the look of a star-crazed fan.

"Let's make a deal," Whitney said to him in a remarkably calm and superior voice. "You and I remarry, you do the reality show with me, and I'll tell you all about Chad... or Ethan, or Jonathan, or any of his many names."

Kenna turned and stared at her. It was all a big act. She couldn't believe it.

"How about this," Will countered, his voice deadly soft, "you tell us all about Chad and everyone involved in his circle, including the role you and your father play, and I'll turn you over to the FBI instead of to Ahmed."

"No deal. It's all or nothing William and I'm holding all the cards. You think my daddy will let some security guard harm me. I don't think so."

Ahmed stepped forward and took her by the arm. "You had your chance. Move."

"Take your hands off of me. You're nothing but a security guard. You have no power," Whitney sneered at him.

Ahmed didn't flinch. His expression never changed.

Kenna, safe in Will's arms, turned to him, "Come on, Will. I think I hear a noise outside."

She turned one last time at Whitney to pity her. "Whitney, let me offer you some free legal advice. You may want to talk fast because even the FBI is afraid of him. By the way, he has diplomatic immunity. So he can do pretty much whatever he wants to you, and no one is going to be able to do a thing about it. Under the Vienna Convention, the host country can ask for immunity to be waived for prosecution, but it's up to the leader of the diplomat's country to decide. So, Whitney, do you really think the prince will waive immunity? You saw him turn his back and walk out of here yourself."

"That's impossible. I'm a senator's daughter! My daddy is a very powerful man and you can't touch me," she all but pouted.

Kenna shrugged. Will took her hand and led her out of the stall. "God, Kenna. How am I supposed to make this up to you?"

She looked over at him, and it almost made her want to go back in there and pull some more of Whitney's hair. Will looked totally dejected. His head was hanging down and he was practically shuffling his feet. He had done nothing wrong, but his expression displayed nothing but guilt.

"Stop, Will. Today is your day. Boots will be racing any moment now. You didn't have anything to do with this plot. I'm also fairly sure my ex had significant involvement too. Ahmed will turn her over to Cole in a few days, and then the whole circle will be brought to justice."

"You still love me? Even after all this?" He paused, "This is yours. Here you go." He handed her the hat Paige had made for her.

"Of course I do. I love you more than ever, especially since you saved my hat." Kenna went up on her tiptoes and gave him a kiss on the cheek.

"Come on. Let's get you cleaned up. We have five minutes until it's time to walk Boots out, and there's no one I want beside me more than you. That, and Boots seems to have a crush on you. He may not race if you're not there."

They laughed and Kenna stopped as she left the barn to fix her hair. She ran her fingers through it, and Will pulled out pieces of hay from her hair and dress.

He leaned over and placed one large hand on her cheek. "I love you."

"I love you too."

"Mr. Ashton! Mr. Ashton! What do you think Boots' chances are of winning?" a man's voice boomed from behind her. She smothered a laugh at his pained groan upon hearing the question.

CHAPTER 18

"How are you?" Paige asked as soon as Kenna made it to Boots' stall.

"Somewhat relieved, actually. It's good to have some answers. I know there are so many more to discover, but I feel confident we'll figure it all out. Right now, I'm just basking in the feeling that I'm no longer hiding."

"Good, then let's get my picture. It'll be for my shop! Mo, darling, can you take a picture for us?" Paige yelled.

Cameras flashed from the media and Kenna could already see the headlines: "Sheik Jumps to do Bidding of Hat-maker Girlfriend."

"You're so bad."

"I know. It's fun though. Mo's getting a kick out it. Says it'll drive his father crazy. So we decided to go all out for it."

"Smile ladies!" Mo took the picture and shot a grin to them.

"Riders up!"

Kenna and Paige moved out of the way for Rodrigo as Will gave him a leg up into the saddle.

"That's our cue to meet you in the box. Good luck, Will. Hope you don't mind, but I didn't confirm or deny any story involving Desert Sun Farm and Ashton Farm, specifically a collaboration between

Boots and my Desert Girl," Mo winked. He really was having fun today.

Will held out his hand to shake Mo's, "How about this. I give you the first breeding free. If one of us likes the foal, we'll have first right of refusal. However, if we both like it, we become co-owners."

"That sounds like a deal to me," Mo said as he shook Will's hand.

Turning to Kenna, Will slipped his hand into hers and gave it a little squeeze. "Let's lead our boy to the track."

"BOOTS, no. I'm not doing it." Kenna tried to turn away, but her heels kept sinking into the soft track.

"Come on. Just once, for luck. You don't want to jinx us," Art pleaded.

She looked at Will who nodded in all seriousness and to Rodrigo who pleaded in Portuguese to her.

"Aw, come on, guys. The jumbo screen is on us," Kenna complained.

Boots grabbed her hat with his teeth and yanked it off her head.

"Boots!" said Kenna as she reached for her hat.

One hundred and fifty thousand people roared with laughter, and her face felt like it was on fire.

"Boots, give it back," she hissed.

Boots just whinnied and tossed his head in the air, all while her beautiful hat lay dangling from his lips.

"Fine. I'll do it."

"You hear that, bud? She'll do it," Rodrigo purred to him as he nudged Boots closer to Kenna.

Boots brought his head down and nuzzled into her so that she could place a bright red kiss on his nose. The lipstick stood out against the white surrounding his nose and perfectly matched the similar stain about a foot up on his forehead. The crowd cheered and Boots bucked. Apparently it was a good sign since both Will and Art let out a breath as if safe from all jinxes.

Art led the way to the box as the horses warmed up on the track. They passed Mo's box where Ahmed was absent and descended into their box seat. William and Betsy stood to give everyone handshakes and hugs.

"He looks good out there, son. Of course any man getting a kiss in front of millions of people puts a little extra kick to his step," William said as he shook Will's hand.

Kenna flushed red again and was now paranoid about her face appearing on the jumbo screen. But, as soon as the call to post sounded, she forgot all about the cameras.

That little guy had wormed his way into her heart and his owner's, too. She felt like it was her horse out there and wished him a safe journey to the finish line.

She gripped Will's hand when Boots was led into the starting gate. She feared she had broken his finger when the bell sounded and the horses charged out.

"Oh no, I jinxed him. Look at him, he's in the back," Kenna cried as she watched the horses pass the first quarter mile.

"No, it's okay. That's the best spot for him. Rodrigo is holding him back. It frustrates Boots. When he's finally given his head, he flies. It also wears out the leaders while Boots isn't being pushed."

She looked at the jumbo screen to see that Boots, the number fourteen horse, was in sixteenth place out of the twenty horse field. She had nearly admitted defeat as Boots stayed in position past the half mile marker. A little over one half mile and about a minute to go and the race would be over.

"And there he goes," Will said smugly.

Kenna looked up and saw Boots tearing down the field.

"And here comes Naked Boot Leg! He's coming on strong! He's in tenth, ninth, eighth, and gaining ground," the announcer screamed.

"Go Boots!" Betsy screamed and she grabbed Kenna's left hand. Kenna grabbed back and held onto Will with her right.

"Come on, Boots, come on. You can do it boy!" she shouted, hoping her cheers would be heard by him.

"As they reach the last quarter mile, it's still Devil's Own Fun out in front and All That Jazz gaining ground on the outside in second. But it's Naked Boot Leg flying up the rail in third," the announcer relayed. "Naked Boot Leg passes All That Jazz. Devil's Own Fun is still out front by a length, but Naked Boot Leg is closing the gap. Devil's Own Fun out front by a half, by a neck, by a nose. It's nose to nose! It's Devil's Own Fun and Naked Boot Leg racing side by side!"

"GO BOOTS! GO BOOTS!" Betsy and Kenna screamed as they clung to each other.

"Back and forth between Naked Boot Leg and Devil's Own Fun as they come down to the wire and it's...Naked Boot Leg by a nose!"

The screams from the crowd and celebration that erupted in the box drowned out the rest of the announcer's call. Will grabbed Kenna and kissed her hard and fast. He released her to grasp his dad in a fierce hug. Betsy turned to Kenna and hugged her, tears running down her face, before turning to embrace Art.

"I think you owe Boots a lot more kisses and even an apple after today!" Will laughed as he grabbed her hand and dragged her out of the box. "Come on. Let's get to the winner's circle!" They stopped by Mo's box to exchange more congratulations and hugs.

"I am looking forward to our new partnership. Very much!" Mo laughed as he shook Will's hand.

"I am, too. Between Desert Girl's spunk and Boots' drive, I feel sorry for Art!"

Will started forward again and William caught up to him at the elevator down at the track.

"What partnership, Will?" William inquired.

"Mo and I are going to co-own Boots' first breeding to Desert Girl," Will explained to his father.

"The filly that finished second at the Oaks yesterday?"

"That's the one." Kenna could feel Will's hand start to sweat in hers. If she didn't know better, she would've only seen the calm and confident persona Will projected. But she did know him better. He wanted his father's approval.

"Damn good breeding those two will make."

Kenna felt his hand relax in hers, and his body began to hum with excitement again. The elevator doors opened and the crowd's cheers for Boots fell on them. Kentucky State Troopers helped clear the way onto the track as Rodrigo finished his interview.

Boots saw Will and tossed his head. He put his head down and snorted against his coat pocket. Will fed him a sugar cube before the reporter descended upon him.

"Will Ashton, two for two! How does it feel?" The female reporter asked.

"Wonderful! I can't even describe it."

"Better than your Super Bowl appearance?

Will laughed. "Much better since I won this one!"

"The photo finish showed Naked Boot Leg winning by a nose. There has been some question about Boots was being pushed too hard to win the race as evidenced by the blood on his nose."

"The what?"

"In the photo finish picture, you can clearly see bright red blood on his nose."

Will paused. Kenna thought he was trying to remember every moment of the race to see if he noticed the nose bleed. Kenna, who stood with William and Betsy behind the camera man, waved her arms to get Will's attention. When Will looked up, she blew him a kiss. It took only a second for Will's worried look to fade and he burst out into laughter. The reporter who was clearly confused just stood there holding the microphone out towards Will's face.

"Come here, Kenna."

Kenna smiled shyly and walked into the frame. "This is my girlfriend, McKenna Mason. In the pre-race, she kissed Boots on the star of his forehead and then the nose."

Kenna's face turned red again and Will slipped his arm around her.

"Apparently the tradition works! Will you be going to the Preakness with Boots as well?"

"Yes, she will. We'll all be going, and you better believe Boots will be getting his pre-race kiss!" Will thanked the reporter and led the group to the winner's circle for the official picture.

THE WINNER'S circle is a strip of perfectly manicured grass surrounded by a horseshoe of red blooming roses. Boots was walked in, and Will reached up to shake Rodrigo's hand again as he patted Boots on the neck.

Kenna felt somewhat like an outsider among the Ashton family and all those who trained and made Boots a Derby winner. She tried to move to the back of the crowd. But Boots snickered and tossed his head back. Kenna stopped and looked over at Boots who was now stomping the ground with his front hooves.

Boots took a step toward her and Art yelled over to her, "You better get up there to see him or we'll never make it to the Preakness Stakes!"

Kenna stepped forward and stood next to Will at Boots' head. Boots gave her a shot with his red nose, and she scratched the white star between his eyes while the Kentucky National Guard appeared carrying a massive blanket of red roses.

The heavy blanket was placed over Rodrigo's lap, and everyone got ready for the picture. Kenna stood next to Boots who kept nuzzling her for another sugar cube. Will stood next to her with his arm around her waist. His parents completed the first row. Art and some of the other farm personnel stood in the second row.

"Boots, stop it. It's time for your picture," Kenna whispered to him. Boots responded with a snort.

"Okay, get ready and smile!" the photographer shouted.

She smiled and felt Boots stop nudging her hand a second before she felt her hat being yanked from her head. She saw the flash from the camera, and laughter filled the track as everyone watching on the jumbo screens saw the official Kentucky Derby win photo of Naked

Boot Leg standing tall and proud with his blanket of roses and a beautiful Derby hat hanging from his teeth.

KENNA HAD NEVER FELT sexier in her life. She stood to the side of the dance floor at the Derby Ball in her black lace, single-shouldered Valentino and watched Will talking to some owners of different farms.

He kept glancing over to her as if making sure she didn't disappear. The way his chocolate eyes turned almost black when he looked at her sent shivers down her back and straight to her core.

"How was your first Derby?" Mo asked as he came to stand next to her.

"All in all, it was pretty amazing. Do you have any news?"

"Yes, Ahmed got the location of where Chad was staying from Whitney within minutes. He took some of my men and tried to get him. They estimated they missed him by five minutes. He left in a hurry, though. He left some papers behind. Ahmed is reviewing them and will probably want to go over them with you."

"And Whitney?"

"Turned over to Agent Parker just an hour ago. She was telling everything she knew to Agent Parker about her father's involvement and also naming some other big names. Agent Parker should have some very good leads to follow now."

"How is Agent Parker going to explain having a senator's daughter in his custody?"

"Agent Parker? If it comes up, he's going to tell his commanding officer he was at the Derby with me, providing protection on his day off. Whitney came up to him to turn herself in. She knew he was an FBI agent from his investigation of the accidents on Will's farm. She just couldn't handle the guilt of what she had done to the person she loved." Mo rolled his eyes, but Kenna could see Whitney pulling it off.

"Thanks, Mo. You weren't obligated to help me in anyway. But I'm forever grateful you did." Kenna leaned over and gave him a hug.

"You're welcome. Now, I have a sleepy Paige in the limo waiting to be taken home. I'll fill her in before she falls asleep. She wanted to remind you about your lunch tomorrow at Blossom's."

Kenna softly laughed, "You know, having a girlfriend suits you. Why don't you join us tomorrow?"

"Would love to. But my father wants to parade some more women in front of me while we pretend to have a business meeting. Goodnight and tell Will congratulations for me," Mo said as he turned and waved to Will before exiting the room.

She spotted June across the room and waved. June looked fabulous as always in a red Carolina Herrera.

"Kenna, dear. Fill me in on everything that has been going on. I see you here with Will and just now talking to the prince." June gave a wink and Kenna laughed.

"We better have another drink because it's one heck of a story!" Kenna looped her hand through June's arm as they grabbed two more glasses of champagne.

She was embarrassed to admit it, but she didn't hear a word of what June said. She had filled June in on the ups and downs of her relationship with Will and the happenings in Keeneston when Will caught her eye and smiled.

He finished his conversation without ever taking his eyes off of hers. She couldn't help the appreciative glance she gave him when he walked across the room towards her in his tux.

"Excuse me, June, but I believe Kenna owes me a dance." He slid his hand into hers as he led her to the dance floor.

"Did I mention you look breathtaking tonight?"

"About ten times, but it never hurts," she smiled up at him.

"Come on, let's dance." He swept her up into the dance and held her close. She closed her eyes and laid her head on his shoulder. She should've heard the band playing Sinatra's "The Way You Look Tonight", but the sound of Will's whispers in her ear were far more magical.

KENNA LOOKED across the table at Paige and smiled. She lifted her fork and took a bite of the chocolate and peanut butter pie.

"See, you can't stop smiling! What happened last night?" Paige rolled her eyes and took a sip of sweet tea. "Miss Daisy, she won't tell me," she whined.

Taking an order across the room, Daisy shot her a look that threatened the oncoming interrogation.

"Thanks a lot, Paige. Now the whole town will know Will and I spent the night together in Louisville," she said in a low voice.

"We already know that, dear. What we want to know is all the other stuff. Like about Whitney's arrest and why Paige was being reported as Mo's girlfriend," Miss Daisy said as she turned the order slip over to Miss Violet.

"That's not what I wanted to know," Miss Violet mumbled as she headed back into the kitchen.

"Me neither," Paige pouted.

"Well, I can answer Miss Daisy's questions. It started three months ago in New York City...." Kenna told the story to Miss Daisy and the growing number of customers who scooted their chairs closer to listen. Even Miss Violet came out of the kitchen to listen.

"Oh, you poor dears," Miss Daisy said, putting her hand over her heart. "That man Chad was in here looking for you one day. I thought it was someone you prosecuted, so I didn't tell him anything. Well, he'll know better than to come back here again. Won't he Violet?"

"He sure will. I'll go clean Clint now," Miss Violet turned and disappeared into the kitchen.

"Clint?" she and Paige asked at the same time.

"That's her Smith & Wesson .44 Magnum. Just like Clint Eastwood carried in *Dirty Harry*," Daisy answered. "But what I want to know is what happened to Danielle? Do you know where she is?"

Kenna watched Miss Daisy twist her apron out of concern for someone she had never even met, and she was touched. "No, I don't know. We email each other, but I never know how long it'll take her to check her mail."

"I'll put her name on the list at church and we'll all pray for her safety." Miss Daisy nodded, as well as several others. "Now that Whitney is in jail and singing like a canary and Chad is on the run, why don't you have Danielle come here?"

"Here?" Kenna couldn't seem to process the thought of Danielle in Keeneston. They had been hiding for three months. Just seeing Danielle again was hard to imagine.

"It seems like the smart thing to do. You have Mo and his security looking out for Chad. And you have Will and Agent Parker, not counting all of us now," Miss Daisy said, pointing to the room of around thirty people, all of whom were nodding in agreement. "We look out for our own, you know. She'll be far safer here with you and the whole town than trying to run on her own. That poor girl, all alone in that city...." Miss Daisy clucked.

WALKING BACK to her room at Miss Lily's, Kenna couldn't get the thought out of her head. She opened her laptop and hoped for a message from her. She was disappointed when she got no new mail.

DANI-

SO MUCH HAS HAPPENED. *It would take too long to explain in an email. I've been found, but I'm safe. I think we should face this together. I'm in Keeneston, Kentucky. I'm usually at the courthouse. Trust me, you can't miss it. Or at Ashton Farm with Will Ashton. It's time to end this.*

-K

. . .

KENNA HIT send and hoped she'd get to see her friend soon. She powered down the computer and got ready for bed. Will was pretaping numerous shows to air tomorrow morning, so he was going to be busy until later in the evening. She pulled out a book and walked downstairs to the front porch, curling one leg under her as she sat on the swing with one foot dangling to push herself as she fell into the story.

"HEY, SWEETHEART."

Kenna had been so engrossed in her book, she hadn't heard Will's truck pull up. The smile that came across her face could no more be stopped than the sun coming up every morning. "How was your afternoon?"

"It was good. Got a little crazy at the cafe, but they gave me an idea. Miss Daisy said to tell Danielle to come here. By now, the whole town is aware of my situation and will be on the lookout for Chad. Oh! Miss Daisy said he stopped by the cafe looking for me too."

"I think it's a great idea to have her here. You know Cole is still looking into it, and I'm sure it would be easier on him to have you both here so he can come to you with any questions or evidence that he digs up." Will sat down on the swing and placed her foot in his lap. He started to massage it and Kenna closed her eyes in utter joy.

"Mmm. How were your interviews?"

Will chuckled as Kenna purred. "They were good. Mom said the phones have been ringing off the hook for people wanting to breed to Boots. Art is trying to get him ready for the Preakness in two weeks. He's even trying to kiss him. It seems only you hold that magic with him. I mean, if I were Boots and I could get kissed by Art or you, you'd be the winner every time."

"Well, why don't we just test that theory?" Kenna gave him a wink and laughed as Will scooped her up onto his lap.

Will rested his forehead against hers. "I love you so much." His lips closed the distance and locked onto hers in a passionate kiss. His tongue slipped past her lips and swept into her mouth. She felt his hand lift the hem of her Syracuse University t-shirt and move up. He rested his hand on her stomach, his thumb making small circles on the underside of her breast.

She plunged her tongue into his mouth and arched her back, offering him her breasts. His hand cupped her breast and gently kneaded it. He ran his rough thumb gently over her hardened nipple and trailed his fingers to her other breast. He gently caressed her breast and slowly rolled her nipple between his thumb and finger. Kenna moaned into his mouth and ran a hand down his back, stopping to squeeze his ass before running back up to run her fingers through his hair.

He pulled back and she reached for him. "Sorry, hon, but our chaperone is home."

She picked up her head to see Miss Daisy's old Buick turn into the driveway. She groaned and put her head onto his shoulder. It was really time for her to find her own place.

"You know, you're a Kentucky girl now," he said as he played with the hem of her shirt. "It's about time you got some UK gear."

"A Kentucky girl, huh?"

Will kissed her neck right below the ear and whispered, "That's right. Made up of sweet tea and everything nice."

CHAPTER 19

"Your Honor, I object." Kenna rolled her eyes. She couldn't help it. When she got done with the docket, it would be the weekend. She felt ready to curl up into bed and sleep for a week. On top of working, she still hadn't heard from Danielle. She had flown to Maryland for the Preakness and just this past weekend had gotten back from the Belmont. Boots had finished second in the Preakness after being pinned against the rail in the final quarter mile. However, he had surprised everyone by pulling out a win at the Belmont. He won again by a red-kissed nose.

"Sustained," Judge Copper sighed.

"What does that mean? You can't be talking all fancy like. It's not fair and I'm entitled to a fair trial. I know my rights," Mrs. Westerly shouted. She pointed her finger at Kenna and Kenna was tempted to break it off.

This trial had been going on for over thirty minutes and she was ready to scream. The thought crossed her mind more than once to grab Noodle's taser and shock herself just so the EMTs would be forced to take her out the courtroom.

Mrs. Westerly was twenty-five years old. She was five feet tall and probably one hundred and forty pounds, most of which were boobs.

She had her hair wrapped in a colorful scarf and wore large hoop earrings. She had a posse of kids with her, consisting of five kids within six and a half years of each other.

Mrs. Westerly, once she arrived home from shuttling kids to various summer camps, had found Mr. Westerly dingdong ringing her best friend's doorbell. She had promptly grabbed the nearest object, one of her children's baseball bats, and tested her swing out on Mr. Westerly and her ex-best friend.

Granted, no one could really blame her. Most everyone cheered when they heard that Mrs. Westerly had broken his arm, considering Mr. Westerly had a habit of sleeping his way through the married women in his wife's Mother Day Out program.

When caught, Mr. Westerly hadn't admitted to the affairs. Instead, he told young Mrs. Westerly that he wasn't cheating but offering a service to her friends. Mrs. Westerly paused mid-swing and asked what service he was providing. He told her it was educational. He was teaching the women how to perform certain sex acts so that they would be better wives to their husbands. And that was when Mrs. Westerly broke Mr. Westerly's other arm.

Mrs. Westerly was fighting the charge of battery that Mr. Westerly had brought against her. Kenna personally wanted to give her a high five and let her walk free but couldn't. However, she did pursue the lowest sentence possible, that is, if Mrs. Westerly would just shut up. She was currently alternating between enormous sobs and fits of anger. Her prevailing theory was he deserved it, and she shouldn't have to be found guilty for that.

"Mrs. Westerly," Kenna said when Mrs. Westerly took a breath, "Ma'am, did you enter the house with the intent of assaulting your husband?"

"I told you, it's not assault. Assault suggests I did something wrong. I know my rights!" she shouted.

Judge Cooper banged his gavel. "Ma'am, just answer yes or no."

"But, I have my rights. I'm entitled to a hearing."

"You're having one. Now answer yes or no to Miss Mason's question, or I'll throw you in jail for contempt of court."

"No, you can't take my babies from me! Who would look after them?" Mrs. Westerly wailed. Kenna thought she looked dangerously close to hurling herself to the ground and kicking her feet.

"Ma'am, please, just answer this question. Did you go into your house with the intent of hitting your husband?"

"No, but I...."

"Prosecution rests your honor," Kenna said, cutting off Mrs. Westerly. She knew Judge Cooper hated that, but she figured it was better than hearing about Mrs. Westerly's rights one more time.

Judge Cooper banged his gavel and Mrs. Westerly stopped her ranting. "Ma'am, I find you guilty of...."

Before Judge Cooper could finish announcing his verdict, Mrs. Westerly collapsed to the ground and flailed around while praying to be saved by Baby Jesus.

"Knock it off!" Judge Cooper yelled from the bench. Mrs. Westerly stopped her screaming and lay quietly on the ground. "If you had let me finished, then you would have heard that the charges are reduced from a felony to assault under extreme emotional disturbance which is punishable up to 90 days in jail."

Mrs. Westerly resumed her screaming prayers to Baby Jesus.

"But, I find that during that particular situation, a person's emotions rule them. By not contemplating any action, you simply acted out of emotion. Therefore, I sentence you to seven days of in-house confinement."

Mrs. Westerly stopped praying and sat up. "You're not going to send me to jail. I can still keep my babies?" she sniffed.

"That's right. Report to the police station Monday at nine a.m. so that a tracking bracelet can be attached. You'll stay in your house for seven days and then will serve one year of probation. You'll also complete an anger management course. That's all for the day." Judge Cooper banged his gavel one more time. "Court is dismissed."

Mr. Westerly, looking exactly as one thought a used car salesman should look, jumped up in a somewhat awkward fashion since both arms were encased in casts. "But your Honor, she should be in jail! She attacked me!"

"Mr. Westerly, consider yourself lucky. If it had been my wife, you would've seen the barrel of a shotgun. Maybe it will help you keep it in your pants. If you continue your ways, some husband will do something far worse than two hits with a bat. Have a good weekend, Miss Mason," Judge Cooper said as he walked into chambers.

Kenna walked out of the courthouse and went right to her car. All she wanted to do was relax with Will for a while, maybe go out to dinner. She drove to Will's house, and Betsy pointed her in the direction of the barn after they exchanged hellos.

She parked next to the barn and walked inside. She paused for a moment to let her eyes adjust and then paused a second more to enjoy the sight of Will shirtless. He was wearing heavy leather gloves and jeans that rode low on his hips. He reached over to grab a bale of hay and moved it into a stall. He took his arm and wiped his brow. Turning to reach for his water bottle, he saw Kenna standing by the door.

"Hey! How was court today?" he asked, taking a slug of water. He walked over to the tack room, grabbed a towel and used it wipe away the sweat and hay.

"It was pretty straight forward until the last case. I'll tell you all about it over dinner." She walked toward him, ran her hand down his chest and stopped at his stomach. Will put the towel down and put both hands on her cheeks. He slowly leaned down and kissed her with an aching gentleness that had her melting into him.

"Before we head out, there's something I want to show you. You mind going for a short ride?" He reached around her and grabbed a white button-up shirt and put it on.

"That's fine. Do I need to change?"

"Nope, you're perfect. Come on, my truck is out back."

He buttoned up his shirt and tucked it in. He rolled up his sleeves and then took Kenna's hand in his. She smiled as he opened the door to his truck for her to jump in. Four months of living in Kentucky, and she was a pro at hopping in and out of huge trucks while wearing heels and a straight skirt.

Will pulled the truck out of the barn's lot and went down a road beside the barn. The road led further away from the main house and was surrounded by pastures. Some were full of horses, some with only a single stallion. They passed a field used for growing their own hay to help with the cost of feeding such a large operation.

"Where are we going?"

"We're about a mile from the main road. See that over there." He pointed to a gate in the middle of a fence. "That's a path to Mo's property. We own this side of the fence. He owns that side."

They took a turn that curved away from the gate and went slightly uphill. They reached the top and Kenna looked down at a beautiful two story, white brick house with a one story glassed-in sun room to one side. The driveway straightened out and newly planted trees lined both sides of the drive leading up to the house. The drive emptied into a big yard with a little red truck sitting in the circular drive.

"Where are we?" Kenna asked as she got out of the truck.

The house was amazing. It was so quiet and the house was perfect. There was a little strip of land that looked like it was being tilled for a garden, and the little red truck seemed to just fit in to complete the picture of country bliss.

"Will, who lives here?" she asked again.

Will shuffled his feet and stuck his hands into his pockets. He looked up into her eyes then and smiled. "I live here. Actually, I was hoping we'd live here." Will went down onto one knee and pulled a purple velvet box out of his pocket. Inside sat the most amazing four carat, emerald-cut diamond Kenna had ever seen. "McKenna Mason, I love you so much. You bring such joy to my life and nothing would make me happier than if you agree to be my wife. Will you marry me?"

Kenna felt her mouth fall open to answer but she could only nod. Will took out the ring and slipped it onto her finger. She fell to her knees and kissed him with every ounce of love she had for him.

"So, do you think you could be happy here?" Will asked, gesturing to the house.

"It's so perfect. I love it! I thought you had been living at the main house?"

"I have been. This house was just completed a couple of weeks ago and the landscaping was finished yesterday. But, I also have one more surprise for you." He pointed to the little red truck. "I was hoping you'd say yes. As an engagement gift I got you a Ford F-150 to match your M6. Now you truly are a Kentucky girl!"

BETSY AND WILLIAM were standing on their back porch with their eyes trained down the road that Kenna and Will were driving up.

"I'm guessing by their eager expressions you told them you were going to ask me to marry you?"

Will laughed and fingered the ring on her left hand. "I did. I had to ask my Mom for the diamond. It was my grandmother's. I had it reset though."

"Oh Will, that is so sweet. If it wasn't for Alda and my grandmother, we'd never have met." Kenna couldn't help laugh at Betsy as she shoved William's hand off her shoulder and came running down the stairs to meet Kenna as she got out of the truck.

"Oh my, let me see it," Betsy nearly begged.

Kenna lifted her left hand and showed off her diamond while William clasped Will's shoulder and shook his hand.

"It's just beautiful on you. It's been so long, I almost forgot what it looked like. We've had it locked away in the safe since Alda left for the nursing home twenty-five years ago." Betsy grabbed her up into a hug and kissed her cheek.

"We couldn't be happier for you both," William said as he pried his wife off of Kenna so he could give her a hug. "Welcome to the family."

"Oh, we must have an engagement party! William, we must have an engagement party for them." Betsy didn't wait for her husband to respond instead just took Kenna's hand and continued, "What about over the Fourth of July? We could have a cookout and fireworks. Oh, it will be so much fun!"

Kenna couldn't help it. Her eyes started to tear up.

"You've overwhelming the poor girl, Betsy," William said gently as he pulled Betsy away.

"No, it's not that. It's just that I realized I have a family again." And with that, she burst into tears of joy.

They had decided to celebrate at the cafe. Kenna called Paige and told her the good news. She invited her to join her and the Ashtons. Just twenty minutes later, they arrived at the cafe to find the Rose sisters, Paige, Mo, Ahmed, Henry, Tammy, Tom, and many of the Ashton friends already there.

"The Keeneston grapevine," Kenna said, shaking her head. Paige gave her a fierce hug, and the rest of the night became a blur of toasts, hugs and good food.

CHAPTER 20

EVERY NIGHT since the engagement a week ago, Kenna had spent her time organizing the new house she shared with Will. She checked out of the bed and breakfast and found it surprisingly hard to leave.

She had picked out linens and towels and then had a field day in Paige's store finding picture frames and other decorative items. She was currently in the kitchen filling the cabinet with everyday dishes she had picked out. The doorbell rang and she almost dropped the plate.

"Dani!" she practically screamed. Hope burst through her like sunshine as she made a dash for the front door. She yanked it open and found a UPS delivery man.

"Miss Mason?"

"Yes?"

"Package for you. Sign here." He handed her the clipboard and then a package no bigger than a five by seven box.

"Thank you," she said. Disappointment filled her, and for the first time she was losing hope of seeing her friend.

She took the box to the kitchen and found the new pair of scissors to cut the tape. She pulled open the top and a picture slid out with a note taped over it. She lifted the note and her breathing stopped. She thought she might faint. Her vision became tunneled as she stared at a picture of her, Danielle, and Chad taken the night of her birthday. Chad stood in the middle of the two women with his arms slung around their shoulders. Dani and Kenna were laughing, but Chad had an arrogant, predatory smile that made her stomach turn. With shaky hands, she picked the note up from the counter and opened it.

CONGRATULATIONS ON THE ENGAGEMENT, *sweetheart. I'll never forget my two favorite girls.*

KENNA DROPPED the frame and card. She didn't even hear the shattering of the frame.

She didn't notice Will running into the room until he stopped in front of her and shook her.

"Kenna. Kenna. Answer me. Are you okay? What happened?"

All she could do was point to the shattered photo. She saw Will pick it up along with the note and then curse. He ran over to the phone and dialed a number. "Get over here now." He hung up and dialed another number. "Yeah, it's me. There's been a package sent. Yeah, come to the new house."

The rushing sound of blood started to recede, and she tore her gaze from the note lying on the floor. Will came over to her and crouched on the floor, pulling her into him. "It's okay... It's okay. We'll take care of it. He's too scared to come here himself so he had to send it."

Kenna jumped when the front door opened.

Will stood up, "We're in here."

"Who is it?" Kenna asked.

"It's Ahmed. Cole will be here in about twenty-five minutes."

Kenna put a shaky hand on the counter and was about to pull herself up when she felt Will's hand under her arm, supporting her as she stood.

"You okay?"

"No, but I will be." Kenna took a deep breath and managed a shaky smile when Ahmed entered the room.

"Come over here and sit down," Ahmed gestured to the kitchen table. "We'll take care of this, Kenna. I promise." He bent down to take a closer look of the photograph. "What is this photograph from? Take your time and tell me everything you remember about it."

Kenna took a deep breath. "It was from my twenty-ninth birthday. That was my last night in New York. We were at a club called The Zone. Danielle and I had just arrived. Chad wanted the picture. He had already ordered my favorite drink, a sparkling peach martini. But for the picture, all three of us took a shot of Grey Goose vodka. Chad handed his phone to the bartender and threw his arm around both of us. He pulled us in close and said, 'I want a photo with my girls'."

"What had you and Danielle laughing so hard?" Ahmed quietly asked.

Kenna couldn't take her eyes off the photograph. She felt as if she was still being oppressed by the hot sticky air of the club. She could feel the burn of the vodka shot she had taken. She could hear Danielle's laughter. And she heard Chad ask the bartender to take a picture.

"Wait." Kenna closed her eyes and brought herself back to the night. "He called the bartender by name. He said, 'Hey, David. Do me a favor and take a picture of me and my two girls.'" Kenna opened her eyes and looked back at the picture of their faces caught in a moment of unguarded laughter. "Danielle had said, 'If Chad knows that hot bartender so well, maybe he can introduce me. I'm always looking for a man willing to serve me a drink!' And then we laughed because we always laughed at the thought. She had men falling over her constantly but she refused almost all of them. It was an inside joke that no man could actually last long enough to bring her a drink," she explained after looking up and seeing that Will and Ahmed didn't seem to comprehend the irony of the joke.

"Okay good. Agent Parker will be here soon. Let him collect it properly for evidence. I'm just going to take a picture of it and the note to see what kind of hits I can get. Cole and I have been working on this the past couple of weeks and he should have an update for us today." Ahmed bent down and photographed the envelope, note, the UPS box, and the photograph.

Will sat down beside her and put his hand on her knee. "It's okay, honey. We're all here for you and we'll find him." He pulled her into his protective embrace and laid his cheek against the top of her head. Kenna took a couple of deep breaths and sank into him. His warmth chased away the coldness that had seeped into her bones the second she had looked in the box.

She heard the sound of a car door closing and boots on the sidewalk. She knew Cole had arrived. "Will, I know it needs to be done, but I feel so drained."

"Don't worry. I'll take care of it. Sit there while I let Cole in and make you a cup of hot chocolate. I'll answer as many of the questions as I can for you." Will gave her knee a little squeeze before standing up and going to let Cole in.

Cole came in and swept the photograph, envelope, and note for fingerprints before placing them into clear evidence bags. He asked questions that Will and Ahmed answered while Kenna sipped her hot chocolate and fought the exhaustion that was setting in after the adrenaline had worn off.

"I'm going to help Kenna upstairs. I'll be back in a moment. Come on, honey. You're about to crash. Let me help you upstairs."

"Wait. I want to hear Cole's report." She turned to Cole, "Please, I haven't heard anything for a month and am desperate for some news from someone."

"Well, I took all the evidence to a higher up in the bureau in D.C. He allowed me to select a private team of four other men to work on this case with me," Cole explained.

"I thought you said you didn't know whom to trust. How do you know someone isn't filtering this information to Chad? Someone has to be. How else did he know I was engaged?" Kenna grabbed her mug and put it in the sink. She grabbed the countertop to prevent herself from pacing.

"I served overseas with all the people I selected. I know them better than myself. My friend, who is the higher up, technically has the authority to run these types of elite off-the-books missions. That's why I went to him. Whatever evidence we now gather is official and can be used as evidence in court. We've tracked Chad to New York City just to lose him again. He's popped up in New York, Philadelphia, Boston and D.C. What seems to be different from his other frauds is that he doesn't want to give this one up. Normally, he would've assumed a new name and relocated to start a new game. But we have surveillance video of his meeting with several judges and a few congressmen."

"What about GTH?"

"Nothing. They aren't cooperating and we have no evidence linking him to the firm in recent months. However, we do have some interesting taped calls between one of the partners Bob Greendale and Senator Bruce. It's enough to warrant a continual tap on both of their phones. Basically, we're getting all these different puzzle pieces and eventually we'll be able to put them all together."

"Thanks, Cole. I know you have done so much to try to find him."

"Ahmed has been a big help too. He has a lot of resources we don't, and he's using them."

Kenna turned toward the stairs but stopped. "I've tried not to think about her, but what has happened to Whitney? I glanced at the headlines and I haven't seen anything with her name in it." She didn't bother to turn around, but just kept her eyes locked on the back staircase.

"She pled guilty to a whole slew of charges. She agreed to provide us with testimony and is now in a safe house until this whole thing comes to a head. She told her daddy that after Will's engagement, she needed some time in Europe. We'll let her call every couple of weeks. We have agents overseas sending trinkets to him and so on. So far, he believes her to be on some grand tour."

Will escorted her upstairs and to their bedroom.

"Will, I'm fine. I just want to lie down for a bit. I'm so worried about Dani. Did you hear Cole? Chad's been back to New York. They could've found her. Maybe that's why I haven't heard from her in these past six weeks."

"Think positively. You have a wedding to plan and the engagement party in just a couple of weeks. Think of all the things you and Danielle can do together when she finally gets here. And she will. Have faith."

Kenna closed her eyes but didn't fall asleep. Flashes of her relationship with Chad kept her awake. He had to have said something he didn't mean to share. They had talked so much when they first met. So, she closed her eyes and let her mind lead her.

"No, that can't be right."

"Yes, sir, it is. Congratulations."

"No! No, do it again."

"The test came back a 99.98% match. Trust me, Mr. Heller, you're going to be a father." Kenna watched the man in his early forties fall against the podium. The mother-to-be stood next to her gloating with her massively swollen belly.

"But you don't understand, my mother is going to kill me!"

"Your mother?" Kenna and Judge Cooper said at the same time.

Mr. Heller had stood up and was now pacing the courtroom. "It just can't be. My mom said I was circumcised. I can't have kids since I'm circumcised. So the test must be wrong."

Oh God, it must be a full moon. This was only the second case of the day and it wasn't setting a good tone. Kenna looked to Judge Cooper, "Nope, not touching this one."

"That's what my mother told me. I should've listened," Mr. Heller said.

Kenna choked on a laugh that threatened to erupt and turned to Mr. Heller. "Sir, I assure you that you can still have children. In fact you'll be having one in a couple of weeks by the looks of it."

Mr. Heller stopped pacing and his face lit up. "Really? You mean I did it? My swimmers made it! I'm going to be a daddy!" He ran over to

Mommy-to-be and kissed her. "We're going to have a baby! I'm so sorry I didn't believe you when you told me. Mom told me I had been snipped. I thought that meant I couldn't have kids. I thought you had cheated on me." Mr. Heller dropped to his knees, "Marry me, baby."

"Yes!" Mommy-to-be shouted and hurled herself, belly and all, into Mr. Heller.

Kenna, along with the rest of the courtroom staff, stood open-mouthed at the scene. Judge Cooper cleared his throat, "Well. I believe paternity has been established. Miss Lanstinger, I'm going to dismiss your paternity and custody action for now. If you end up not getting married before the baby is born, then file a motion to renew, and I'll set custody and child support then. Next case, Deputy."

AFTER SHE WRAPPED up her portion of the docket, Kenna put the case files into her briefcase and said good-bye to Noodle. She made the short walk to her office and spent an hour returning calls to her clients. She glanced at the clock on her desk and rubbed her neck. It had been a long day. She kicked off the slippers she kept under her desk and put her Manolos back on. She turned off her computer and slipped her red suit coat on. She was due home in twenty minutes for a romantic dinner, and she had no desire to be late.

Will greeted her with a kiss and surprised her with his attempt at a home cooked meal. They discussed Boots' first breeding that took place that day to Desert Girl and relaxed on the porch swing she insisted he install on the back porch. Soon, she was drifting off with her head against his shoulder. She felt him pick her up and carry her to their bedroom.

Kenna was having the most glorious dream. She was on a cloud, and Will was running his hand down her side. He pushed her hair back and placed his warm mouth at the base of her neck. She stretched into the kiss and felt his erection rub against her back. Her eyes popped open but quickly closed again when his hand found its way under her panties.

THE NEXT DAY, Kenna hurried to get dressed as Will showered. She was hopping on one foot, trying to pull up her panty hose when she heard the doorbell.

"Shit!" She slipped and fell against the bed. Muttering about stupid men and their invention of the pantyhose, she hopped downstairs, still trying to slip on her purple Pradas.

She opened the door and couldn't make a sound.

"Hey girl! Ready for work?" Danielle asked. "Hey! Didn't you promise me those shoes?"

Kenna dropped her hand from her heart and hugged her friend fiercely, tears rolling down her cheeks.

"So, where can a girl find a place to stay around here?"

Laughing, Kenna put her arm over Danielle's shoulder. "I know the perfect place."

Forever Devoted - coming January 2018

<u>Women of Power Series</u>

Chosen for Power

Built for Power

Fashioned for Power

Destined for Power

<u>*Web of Lies Series*</u>

Whispered Lies

Rogue Lies

Shattered Lies - coming October 19, 2017

ABOUT THE AUTHOR

Kathleen Brooks is a New York Times, Wall Street Journal, and USA Today bestselling author. Kathleen's stories are romantic suspense featuring strong female heroines, humor, and happily-ever-afters. Her Bluegrass Series and follow-up Bluegrass Brothers Series feature small town charm with quirky characters that have captured the hearts of readers around the world.

Kathleen is an animal lover who supports rescue organizations and other non-profit organizations such as Friends and Vets Helping Pets whose goals are to protect and save our four-legged family members.

Email Notice of New Releases
kathleen-brooks.com/new-release-notifications
Kathleen's Website
www.kathleen-brooks.com
Facebook Page
www.facebook.com/KathleenBrooksAuthor
Twitter
www.twitter.com/BluegrassBrooks
Goodreads
www.goodreads.com

Made in United States
Orlando, FL
13 June 2024